The BRICK-EATERS

A NOVEL BY

THE RESIDENTS

The Brickeaters
ISBN 9781934170724

fh

Feral House
1240 W. Sims Way
Suite 124
Port Townsend, WA 98368
10 9 8 7 6 5 4 3 2 1

Cover design by Jacob Covey
Interior design: designSimple

Dedicated to my father.

PART ONE
BLOOD
JET

Abandoned in a barren corner of nowhere, the old man's body was found on a blacktop road next to his oxygen bottle. Some would say the dead man's sorry fate was fixed, that his life was a series of arrows all pointing at this exact spot. After all, with fifty-seven convictions and thirty-six out of sixty-four years spent in prison, Wilmer Graves never aimed at nirvana—not that I knew his name back then.

I was falling asleep on my couch when the news came on. I never watch that crap. To be blunt, I loathe the sensationalism, negativity, and celebrity gossip that passes for journalism in our culture. If my wife hadn't left me, if I hadn't had too much bourbon and if I wasn't desperate for something... anything... to suck up my empty hours, I would've been trimming my toenails or eating a kale salad or... well, not stupid and staring at the dumbfuck tube.

But I was. And the thought of an old man dying on the side of a highway, in the middle of the winter, miles from nowhere, alone except for an oxygen bottle tethered to his unnamed nose, grabbed me. Oh yeah, he had a gun, too. A huge .44 magnum just like Dirty Harry's... and it was loaded. Who was he? How had he gotten there? Would anyone claim the body? There had to be a story—and I needed to tell it.

Needless to say, the mainstream media ignores shit like this. After all, it's not like Tom Cruise buttfucked the pope or Beyoncé gave birth to an albino rat. No, stories about dead nobodies on the side of the road are history in seconds; I needed more information, but nothing was showing up. All I had at that point was a small item noting the discovery of an unidentified body on a two-lane highway in Henry County, Missouri; an anonymous call had tipped the cops—and that was it.

I had to work fast. A Google search told me that Clinton, a town with a population of 10K, was the county seat; a second search yielded the phone number of the coroner's office. A call there informed me that the body had been neither claimed nor identified, but the man's fingerprints had been forwarded to the FBI and they figured to ID him soon.

But sometimes you get lucky. Yeah, sometimes that sack full of filthy lucre falls in your lap—and yeah, sometimes the sack is full of shit, but you gotta look inside. So what the hell, I booked a flight to Kansas City. I figured there were two strong possibilities: nobody claims the body which is then cremated and disposed of—end of story, especially if the body can't be ID'd. But another possibility was someone coming forward to collect it, giving me a lead into the dead man's life. The TV news claimed the old man wasn't homeless, so maybe the stiff had some relatives that would miss him. It was worth a shot.

It took a couple of days to wrap up a few loose ends, fly to KC, rent a car and drive over to Clinton. Being from L.A., the idea of Missouri in January was maybe more appealing than the Siberian tundra, but not much; and, as the wind whistled across the plains and the temperature dipped into the twenties, I began to wonder what the fuck I was doing here. Maybe I should have thought this out a little more. At that point, cruising along the two-lane highway, I noted nothing but endless mounds of snow littering a landscape shrouded in gray. Turning up the heater, an involuntary shiver accompanied a quick glance at my Armani leather jacket and silk sweater. JEEZ! We don't allow this frigid crap in Southern California.

An hour and a half later, I arrived in Clinton. It had been six days since the body was found and I figured there was a decent chance the FBI had ID'd the body by then, so I went straight to the sheriff's office. Occupying the dingy, one-room building were two desks, a filing cabinet, a table and a gun rack; an empty jail cell was out back. Inside the room were two women: a cute twenty-something blonde who was making coffee, and a mid-thirties stubby, chubby and perpetually pissed-off lesbo deputy, sitting behind a desk. I went for the young one.

"Excuse me, Miss. I'm trying to get some information on the body recently found on Highway 18, west of town."

"You need to talk to Deputy Bodie, Mister. Hey Bernie, this guy wants some info on the dead guy." Deputy Bodie, deeply engrossed in a Weight Watchers magazine, didn't flinch. I walked over to her desk.

"Excuse me, uh, Officer Bodie, but I understand you found a body out on Highway 18. I was wondering if the body had been ID'd yet? What can you tell me about him?"

Without looking up from her magazine, the deputy responded, "And you are?"

"My name is Franklin Blodgett. The *L.A. Times* picked up this story from the wire services and thinks there could be a Sunday feature in it, so they sent me to check it out." It was a lie of course, but I figured the dumb dyke would be so snowed by the *L.A. Times'* cred, she'd bust a gut spilling the story. I was wrong.

"You got an ID from the *L.A. Times*?"

"Uh, no. I'm a freelancer... uh, not on staff. They only give IDs to permanent staff."

"Yeah, sure. Look, the guy's name was Wilmer Graves, case number 2896. He was a petty criminal who spent most of his life in jail... which is where he belonged. Died of heart failure but given his M.O. and the sorry state of his health, it's a miracle he lived as long as he did. I don't think the, uh, *L.A. Times* will find much interest in a bum like Graves." She still hadn't looked up from her magazine.

"Okay, well, thanks Officer Bodie, but that's really up to my editor. Can you tell me anything else about Graves? I heard they found the body based on an anonymous phone tip. Did you take that call? Do you remember anything about the caller?"

"I didn't talk to nobody, I don't know nothing and I'm busy. Maybe you should come back later... when you have an ID from the *L.A. Times*."

"But this could be an important story... and of course I would quote you extensively regarding any information I can get."

Irritated, Officer Bodie glanced up, looking at me for the first time. Noting my lime-colored jeans, flip-flops, aviator shades and vintage Aerosmith T-shirt, she rolled her eyes and snickered. "Hey, Patty, did you catch the getup Scoop here is wearing?" Looking back at me she continued, "Yeah, well, I guess you're from L.A. all right," after which she shook her head and rolled her eyes again. "But hey, we're busy here, Franky. Come back when you're real." She nodded toward the door.

"No problem, thanks officer. I'll get my editor to fax a letter to this office confirming my relationship with the *Times*. I'll be back later. Thanks, again." Jesus, what a bitch.

Given the dead man's name, Wilmer Graves, I was able to get a little more info: Graves was a petty criminal of no account who was discharged from Leavenworth prison six months earlier. While his record had remained clean since his latest release, the career crook was suspected of involvement in a string of recent robberies, and, since no one stepped forward to claim the body, nobody really gave a shit.

And maybe that was it. Maybe it was just the story of a two-bit crook who wound up in the wrong place. Graves probably got what he deserved, and if he didn't, who cared? Nobody except for me, and I had nothing to go back to but an empty apartment in L.A. Louise had left me for a goddam insurance salesman. Okay, maybe I'm no Stephen Fucking King, but I've written a couple of books, had articles in the *L.A. Weekly*, the *Reader*, *L.A. Magazine*, *Hustler*, *Men's Health* and several more—and my *New Yorker* rejections were encouraging as hell. Really!

Enough whining already. There was a story here. I was convinced of it… maybe it was just a hunch, but I had to find a way to get inside. To let the story start talking to me. Then it hit me—DUH! If the sheriff was tipped by an anonymous call, there had to be a record of it. That phone number existed and the caller knew something. Okay, maybe he just saw the body laying on the side of the road and called the cops, but why didn't he give his name? Why didn't he stick around? Okay, maybe he didn't want to get involved, but it was worth a shot. Find the number, call the guy, see what he has to say.

The next morning I got up early in search of a local clothing shop, eventually settling on Bell's Barn. A graceless box, Bell's was typical of what they used to call "dry goods" stores, looking straight out of the 1950s. As evidenced by the handful of elderly women shuffling through its aisles, the future for places like this, in the era of Walmart and Amazon, was something less than nada. If anything I saw its continuing existence as a minor miracle, but perfect for my purposes.

Ignoring the dowdy housedresses, checkered tablecloths and doilies, I wandered over to an aisle featuring work clothes, picking out a pair of Wrangler jeans, a flannel shirt, a Ben Davis jacket and a cloddish pair of boots. It was be-yond-the-valley-of-drab garb, but, without much scrutiny, I just might pass for bumpkin. After my pathetic encounter with Deputy Dawg, the least I could do was *TRY* to look like a local. I paid for the clothes and headed toward the door, pausing to look around in time to catch a cute blonde checking me out. Looking closer, I realized it was Patty—at least I thought that was her name—the young chick in the sheriff's office. Without the uniform, I couldn't be sure, but this could be the break I needed; hopeful, I cruised over to the women's department.

"Excuse me, uh, Patty? It is Patty, right?"

"Huh? Oh yeah, you're the guy from the *L.A. Times*, right? Frank?"

"Yeah, well, Franklin actually, but you can call me Frank. Are you off duty today, Patty? If so I'd love to buy you a cup of coffee and ask you a couple of questions. Nothing heavy, but I'd like to get a little more info about the Graves case, if possible. Are you busy?"

"Well, sorry, Frank, I just stopped in here to pick up a nightgown for my mom. I'm on my way to see her in the hospital. She had an operation yesterday."

"Gosh, I'm sorry to hear that, Patty. I won't bother you, but gee, I hope she's gonna be okay."

"Yeah, me, too. It's not too serious. She has diverticulitis; she should be all right but it takes a couple of weeks to re-cover from the surgery."

"Yeah, okay, I'll leave you alone… but, hey, could I maybe get some flowers for your mom? I mean, she doesn't know me and all, but still, nothing brightens up a hospital room like flowers."

"That's nice of you, Frank, but you don't have to do that. It's very thoughtful, but my mom is…"

"No, no… It's no trouble at all. Look, I'm all alone and

don't know anybody in town. I'll probably only be in Clinton for few days and it would help me connect with the local community, you know, if only in a small way. I could maybe even drop by the hospital and say hi. Everybody likes visitors when they're in the hospital."

"Yeah, I guess that would be okay. You know, you're awfully nice. I thought reporters were supposed to be all mean and cynical."

"Well, you can't go by everything you see on television. I'd love to get some flowers for your mom. What does she like? Roses? Tulips? Chrysanthemums? Maybe we could meet somewhere after you go to the hospital and I could give you the flowers."

"But you see, my mom…"

"I don't want hear any more about it, Patty. Like I said, it's really not a problem. I'm sure your mom is a great person. And it's not like I'm super busy. It would be fun to meet and maybe cheer her up a little."

Patty paused, reflecting on something, then looked up, her eyes meeting mine. "Okay, sure, I've got a couple of minutes before I have to be at the hospital. What do you want to ask? What are you trying to find out?"

"Well, it's like this. I know an anonymous caller tipped you guys off. I figure the sheriff's department has to have a record of that call and that record would show the caller's number. Now maybe there's a story here and maybe not, but if I could get that number, there's a good chance I could find out what happened. I mean, somehow Graves' body got out there on that road and nobody seems to be too interested in finding out how. Do you think you could get that number for me, Patty? Could you help me out… please?"

"I don't know… I mean, those records are supposed to be confidential and all. I could get in a lot of trouble if anyone found out."

"Sure, sure, you're right… it's too much to ask. I can eventually get access to those records but I'd have to have a lawyer and get a subpoena and… but that would take several days, maybe a couple of weeks and the whole thing would be cold as the stiff's body by then… but you're right. There's no reason for you to take chances, no reason at all. Sorry I bothered you."

"Look… you're a nice guy. Let me see what I can do. Why don't we meet at Terry's Café later this afternoon, after I go to the hospital. Then I'll stop by the office and see what I can find out? Terry's is right on 2nd Street near the middle of town… you can't miss it."

"Great, perfect… I really appreciate it. What time do you want to meet?"

"How about 4:30? Maybe we can go by the hospital, then, too."

"Oh yeah, the hospital, of course. Great. I'll meet you at Terry's at 4:30. Thanks, Patty."

Bingo! Jackpot! Home run! It looked like I was finally getting somewhere… and sweet little Patty was kinda cute. Maybe this trip wasn't such a lame idea…

With little to do until my date with Patty, I decided to check out the spot where Graves' body was discovered. I had no idea what I might find but I wanted to get a feeling for the place, plus who knows what the Clinton dumb dicks might have overlooked. It took some searching but I finally pinpointed the exact spot where the body was discovered. It was nothing like the spray-painted outlines you see on TV, just a white "X" by the side of the road with the case number, "2896," written next to it. I drove ten miles in each direction from the bingo spot, but it was deadsville. Some sections of the countryside were wooded but it was mostly cleared farmland. Several houses were set back from the highway and a few roads disappeared into the thickly forested area, but otherwise, it was nada, zilch, zero. This was looking like a waste of time.

Finally, driving west, as I reached the end of my ten-mile radius, I came to the town of Adrian, and decided to stop at the illustriously named Tic-Tok, a small café and lounge. Otherwise bland, the Tic-Tok was nevertheless notable for its curious collection of, what else... clocks—cuckoo clocks, cat clocks, owl clocks, teapot clocks, flag clocks, clocks made out of frying pans and clocks shaped like guitars. The list was both lengthy and random, but they all had one thing in common—none of them worked. The odd assortment of utterly useless timepieces crowding the walls of a depilated diner struck me as the perfect setting for a *Twilight Zone* episode where everyone constantly resets their watch and no one never leaves.

It was almost lunchtime and, except for a couple of truck driver types, the place was empty. Looking for life, I sat down at the counter. "Whachur poison, mister? Coffee?" The waitress' name was Hazel, or so it said on the clock-shaped name tag. From the sound of her voice, Hazel harbored a couple of pounds of pea gravel in her larynx. Looking to be in her mid-fifties and well worn, she also displayed a pronounced dent at the base of her throat. No shit—you probably could've put a quarter in it. It was hard as hell to keep from staring.

"Sure, uh, Hazel... and throw me a burger on the griddle when you get a minute."

"...ain't got nothin' but minutes, mister. You ain't from around here, are you?"

So much for the yokel outfit. "No, Hazel, I'm from, uh, out of town. Just passing through." I figured the L.A. origin was probably uncool.

"How do you want your coffee, mister? Black?"

"Uh, no, cream and sugar, please, Hazel." Her frown screamed *WRONG ANSWER*. I hadn't been in the place more than two minutes and already had two strikes against me—one more and they'd be feeding me to the hogs. "So Hazel, isn't this kinda close to where they found that stiff a few days ago? Kind of weird if you ask me."

"Yeah, I think they found him up on Highway 18 about ten or twelve miles from here." As she brought my coffee, Hazel leaned over the counter, dropping her voice to a whisper. Slightly self-conscious, she continued, "Hey mister, don't tell nobody, but I think the guy was in here not long before he kicked off. I ain't sure but it musta been him."

"No way! How do you know?"

She looked over at the two truck drivers across the room idly watching the news on a grainy old TV fastened to the wall and went on, "Well, accordin' to the paper, the guy was found lyin' next to an oxygen tank, and sure as shit, the guy in here had a tank and a tube comin' out of his nose an' all. An' he was pretty much the same age as the dead dude. It had t'be him, doncha think?"

"Hmm... yeah, I guess so. Can't be too many people fitting that description. Do you remember anything else about him?"

"Hell, he was smokin' like Betty's Bar-B-Que, that's for sure... an' him bein' on oxygen the whole time. He musta gone through half a pack of cigarettes while he was in here."

I was a little shocked. I mean, it was a restaurant after all, even if it was Missouri. "Are people allowed to smoke in public places around here? I thought it was banned..."

"Aw, nobody pays any attention to that shit. Okay, you're

only *supposed* to smoke in the 'designated area' which is a couple of booths over there in the corner, but that's a crock o' crap an' everybody knows it. Well, of course, I don't smoke while I'm cookin' an' stuff. I always take a break and go outside..."

"Was he alone?"

Hazel turned back to the griddle, flipped the hamburger patty and eyed me over her shoulder. "So how come you're so interested in that guy, mister? Did you know him? Was he a friend of yours?"

"Uh, no, Hazel, it's just... well, you see, I'm a writer for the crime show *DOA*, and my producer thought there might be a story in it, so he sent me to check it out."

"No shit!" Excited, the waitress shouted across the room at the two truck drivers, "Hey Lester, Tom, this guy is a TV writer. He wants to know about the stiff they found out on Highway 18 last week." Unfazed, Lester and Tom remained transfixed on the grainy TV.

"So was he alone?"

"No, and that was kinda weird, too. There was another guy with him, and the other guy was a lot younger and at least six-and-a-half feet tall, maybe more. He was like a basketball player or something 'cept he was too wimpy. You know, kind of a baby-face, momma's boy type, but real tall. Damnedest thing, those two together." Nodding at a table by the window, Hazel continued, "They sat at that table right over there... had two hamburgers, and fries... the old guy wanted peanut butter on his burger. Weird! Your burger's done, mister... whaddaya want on it?"

"Huh? Yeah... everything but onions, I may have a date tonight. So Hazel, what else do you remember? Did they just hang out or what?"

"Well, that was strange, too. You see, while those guys were in here, this gold Cadillac Escalade drives up and parks in the lot. Then another car drives up right behind it and the Caddy driver gets in the second car and drives away. Just like that... left a brand new Cadillac in the parking lot. The other two guys, they were watchin' real close out the window. It was a Saturday night and we was pretty busy so I wud'n payin' much attention, but I noticed those two guys starin' out the window at that Cadillac. Then after about a half-hour or so they just got up, paid their bill, went out an' got in the Cadillac and drove away. It was the damnedest thing."

"They left in the Cadillac. That is weird. But how did they get here? They must have come in another car."

"Well, I didn't see what kinda car they came in, but when we closed up that night, there was this Toyota or Honda or some kinda little Jap car in the parking lot. I noticed it because the parking lot was empty 'cept for that one car. Then, when I came back the next mornin' it was gone. Now I can't say for sure that it was their car, but it was sure as hell gone the next day."

"Yeah, okay, thanks Hazel... and thanks for the burger. Oh, Hazel, did the sheriff ever come around and ask you about any of this?"

"Naw, nobody said nothin' to me. The sheriff's too busy playin' dominos. He don't get too excited about anything. So whaddaya think, mister? Will you be doin' a TV show about it?"

"I can't say, Hazel. It's really up to the producer. I'm just gathering information right now, but it's a good story... thanks. If the producer likes it, we'll be in touch. You know, we could even shoot a scene in here... maybe even interview you. I'll let you know."

"Hey! Great, mister. Thanks! Thanks! Hey mister?"

As I looked up from my burger, Hazel was pointing her forefinger and thumb at me in a pistol-like gesture. "Make my day, dude! Make my day!"

I smiled and nodded but quickly returned to eating my hamburger while mulling Hazel's story. What if the anonymous caller was the guy with Graves in the café? If it was, he obviously knew plenty... I really needed that phone number. So far kissing up to Patty was working big-time, but I had to keep the wheels greased, which meant finding some flowers back in Clinton. Besides, she was a cute number. Who knows, I might get lucky.

The drive back to Clinton took me back past the spot where Graves' body was found. My research said the old man had an accomplice on his recent crime spree, and just as the ex-con had not been positively ID'd, there was no clear description of the sidekick, but the old man apparently hadn't acted alone. Thinking about the stuff Hazel told me only led to more questions. Why would someone leave a brand new Cadillac in a parking lot in the middle of nowhere for a pair of weirdos like Graves and his young friend? Was the old man's dinner companion also his partner in crime? And what happened to the other car? And why would the young guy dump Graves' body out on the road? Did he kill him? And if he did, why tip off the cops? It didn't make much sense.

On the return trip, I was about three or four miles past the location of the body when I spotted an old farmer with his pickup pulled over at the side of the road. The hood was up so I figured the guy must be having problems. Stopping the car, I rolled down the window. It was freezing outside.

"Having trouble, old-timer? Can I help?

Barely looking my way, the old man snorted, "Hummph... Don't need no help. Need a new truck. But hey...

thanks for stopping... looks like a radiator hose. I guess I could use a ride into town, if you're goin' that way."

I pulled the car onto the shoulder and got out. Approaching the truck, I glanced in the back and was shocked to see a huge hog, covered with a grisly combination of caked mud and blood oozing from a series of cuts and lacerations covering its body. The pig was laying on its side and could barely raise its head.

I'm not a mechanic, but with steam rising from the engine and water spewing out onto the ground, it wasn't hard to spot a busted radiator hose. Standing next to the farmer, I said, "Sure, I'll give you a ride into town, mister, but what about your pig?"

"I'm afraid Bessie's not gonna make it." At that point he reached into the cab of the pickup, removed a rifle, walked around to the rear of the truck and shot the pig through the head. With blood suddenly spurting out into the open air, I recoiled in horror. Recognizing my shock, the old man said, "Sorry if I caught you off guard, son, but I just couldn't leave ol' Bessie out here to freeze to death. Even if I got her into town, there wud'n much chance the vet could save her, but a cold front's comin' through." The farmer opened the door of the pickup, pulled out a tarp and covered the still twitching body. The bright color of crimson immediately seeped up through the tarp. Increasingly uncomfortable, I looked at the old man who turned back to me, sighed and said, "She wud'n gonna last much longer out here. It's too damn bad... I really liked that pig."

A few minutes later we were speeding down the highway, headed back to Clinton. The image of the pig, both before and after the execution, was still vivid in my mind. "What happened to the pig, uh, Bessie, mister? I mean, she was pretty messed up before... uh, well, uh, you..." I didn't quite know how to finish my sentence... before you blew her brains out?

Sitting on the seat next to me, the old man was lost in thought. Staring out the window, he finally began to speak, "Damn strange what happened to ol' Bessie... she was a good pig... smart, stayed close to home... hell, she was damn good company, for a pig. Better'n a lot of humans for sure. It was just a few days ago when it happened. I was about to go to bed when I remembered somethin' I had to do in the barn. Ol' Bessie come out to greet me and all of a sudden there was this gigantic explosion—KAWHOOM! It was like a sonic boom or somethin' but a hunnerd times more... an' close by... an' jus' like that ol' Bessie bolted... took off like a bobcat was on her ass. Hell, she was gone in a flash... jus' disappeared into the woods. I didn't know what to think. I mean, that explosion kinda spooked me too, but I was tired an' figured Bessie would be back soon enough... but she didn't come back. When she wud'n home by noon the next day, I figured I better start lookin'. Damn if I didn't search for that pig for three days, b'fore I finally found her... all tangled up in some barbed wire in the woods about two miles from the house... still can't figure out how she got that far from home. That damn explosion musta really spooked her."

The old man paused, lost in thought again, then continued. "Anyway, it was good I got there when I did 'cause the goddam coyotes had found her, too, an' they was about to have a feast... it was a sight. There she was stuck in that barbed wire with the little bastards nippin' at her an' Bessie squealin' like a skint puppy. I shot three and the rest scattered, but I was in a fix. It was gettin' dark an' I couldn't leave... the coyotes would come back sure as shit, but Bessie was too big and crippled up to get her in the back of the pickup. So I called my son Jake and told him what happened. Jake said he could round up some guys and they'd come lift her up into the back of the truck, but then they didn't get here 'til this mornin'. I spent the night sleepin' in the cab of my truck next to that pig... luckily it wud'n too cold. Anyway, they showed up about an hour ago and we managed to pick her up and put her in the truck. Then I started in to the vet's office... she was in pretty bad shape, but I thought there was a chance she might make it 'til that goddam radiator hose went out. It's been a shitty week, I'll tell you that for sure." Still staring out the window, the old farmer grew quiet once again.

"That's a pretty weird story, old-timer. So what do you make of that explosion? Anything like that happen around here before?"

He turned and looked at me for the first time. "Son, I ain't got the faintest idea what happened, but somethin' got blown to hell... ain't no doubt about that. I mean, it's just quiet farmland around here. Ain't no terrorists or you-nee-bombers or any of that shit in Henry County. But whatever it was, it cost me my best pig... I'll tell you that."

The remainder of the trip back into Clinton was spent in silence. As soon as we reached town, the farmer directed me to a gas station with a mechanic and I dropped him off. I knew he needed a ride back to his truck, but I told him I had some business to take care of. Besides, the pig was dead. I couldn't see where there was any rush for him to get back. He thanked me and got out at the gas station and I went looking for flowers.

The floral business was not exactly thriving in Clinton. There was one shop, Bud's, which was about two blocks from the hospital. Not only did it appear to be at least two hundred years old, with an inventory primarily consisting of dried and plastic flowers, but a layer of thick dust created the impression that Bud's hadn't been stocked since the Nixon administration. There was even a photo of Tricky Dick on the wall behind the counter. A sleepy-looking teenager looked up as I walked in.

"What can I do you for, mister?" he asked cheerfully. I might have been his first customer in two weeks and the young man was eager to please.

"I need some flowers, kid. How about a bouquet of Bud's best buds?"

"Huh? What?"

The kid was not impressed with my urbane humor. "Flowers, sonny. I need some flowers. Preferably some grown during this decade, if you get my drift."

"Huh?" The kid paused for a moment, deep in thought. "Oh, you mean fresh flowers, right?"

"You got it, kid. How about some roses?" The teenager looked doubtful and shook his head. "Or maybe tulips? Daffodils? Gladiolas?" With the pitch of my voice rising, the back-and-forth movement of his head sped up. Soon, as I watched his shoulders slump, a palpable sense of gloom crept across his countenance. This was not working. Running out of time, I tried again, "What have you got?"

The teenager frowned. "Gosh, mister, we don't get any fresh flowers in until tomorrow morning." He paused as if thumbing through a mental inventory. "Well, we do have some corypanthas in pots in the back. How about that?"

This was no time to be picky. I needed that phone number, plus my hopes of action with the sweet young Patty were on the rise... I couldn't show up empty-handed. "Yeah, okay, kid, corypanthas it is... Just put a ribbon and some nice paper around them. And hurry, okay... I'm running kinda late."

The teenager hustled off to the back room. I heard him shuffling around, tearing paper and crinkling ribbon with abandon. After a few minutes, he returned beaming. Thrust out at arms' length was a medium-sized flower pot, immaculately wrapped in gold foil with peppermints, tinsel and red ribbon gaily surrounding the center of the container, but the focal point of the arrangement, where I expected to find a cluster of blossoms, buds and foliage, was a grapefruit-sized object covered with claws. It was a cactus.

"It's a cactus! Kid, this is a cactus!"

Dejected, the teenager slumped down onto a stool behind the counter. "But... but... you said you wanted a corypantha... and this is the nicest one we have. See, it has a brand new bloom about to open on top."

Sure enough, on close inspection, I saw a pink floral object about the size of a quarter crowning a thicket of sharp, curving thorns. It was a flower... sort of. I had to get out of there. "Yeah, okay... I'll take it. I'll take it. How much?"

"It's three-fifty, mister. And I'll throw in the wrapping for free!"

"Great, kid, great." I gave him four bucks and said he could keep the change. Rapt with ecstasy, the teenager was beaming like a lighthouse on the dark side of the moon. Once again I had made the day of another delighted Missourian.

I jumped in the car and aimed it in the direction of Terry's Café. And as I drove, the image of Patty, young and fresh, with an easy, open smile, unexpectedly sparkled in my mind. Okay, I didn't know her for shit and maybe my motives were more mercenary than benign but something about the kid had gotten to me... meanwhile, it was 4:45, I was late *AND* packing a cactus... this could be tricky. After deciding to leave the, uh, floral arrangement in the car, I parked and hurried in. Patty was sitting at a table by the window, drinking a cup of coffee. She looked a little anxious.

"Hi, Patty. Sorry I'm late. How's your mom?"

"Oh, hi Frank. It's okay. I haven't been here too long. Mom's all right, but not great. She was better this morning, but this afternoon she seemed kinda down. Recovery from the surgery takes several days... maybe a couple weeks. That's a long time to be in the hospital." She paused and gave me a funny look. Yeah, she was cute but I needed that goddam phone number... it was time to start tap dancing.

"Uh, well, I guess you're wondering about the flowers." She just looked at me. "Well, you know Clinton is not exactly the floral capital of, uh, Missouri. I tried to find some, but, well..."

"Where did you go... Walmart? I thought they always had fresh flowers there? It really doesn't matter... you see..."

"Gosh, Patty, I didn't think of the Walmart." WALMART! Jesus, how dumb could I be. Of course they would have flowers at the Walmart, along with camo diapers, XXXXL cargo shorts and fifty-pound bags of bacon. Attempting to avoid another collision with mid-American culture, I blurted out, "You see, we don't have Walmart in West Hollywood. But I did find a little florist shop over near the hospital."

"You mean Bud's?" She looked worried.

"Uh, yeah, I think that was the name on the sign. Yeah... so I went into Bud's and this young guy waited on me. He wasn't much help, though. To tell you the truth, I don't think his elevator went above the second floor... as a matter of fact, I'm pretty sure it was stuck in the basement. He said..."

"Elevator? What are you talking about... is that some kind of joke, Frank? That must've been Lonnie... a skinny kid with glasses and pimples? Lonnie is the kid brother of my best friend, Sissy Anne. I know him pretty well. Lonnie's real smart and he loves helping people."

Right. "Well, yeah, uh, sure, I guess I must have misjudged young Lonnie. See, I was kind of distracted. I really wanted to get those flowers for your mom. I mean, you know, it was pretty important to me and all they had at Bud's was dried flowers... and some plastic ones..."

"My mom loves dried flowers!"

FUCK! I wasn't hearing this.

"She's allergic to most of the real ones. I tried to tell you at the clothes store, but you weren't listening. Real flowers give her hay fever. She would've been sneezing like crazy, but once they're dried, flowers don't have as much pollen and they're okay. She would've loved some dried flowers, Frank."

Great... suddenly I was a guy who didn't listen, trashed her best friend's brother and nearly gave hay fever to the chick's sick mother. Fuck the phone number.

A few awkward moments passed in silence. With my poor brain desperately seeking a path to redemption, Patty stared out the window in this remote, distant way. Maybe she was a cat lover. If so, I could mention Ernie, my Persian, and show her a YouTube video of Ernie mangling a toy mouse, but the way things were going, she would say her favorite uncle died throwing up blood after being bitten by a rabid cat. Finally, Patty turned back to me and spoke, "I'm sorry, Frank, but I have to go back up to the hospital and see Mom."

"Okay, Patty, I understand. No problem." I had one last shot... I had to go for it. "Um, Patty... I know this is kind of weird, but I did get something for your mom over at Bud's. It's pretty strange. That's why I didn't bring it in. It's out in the car." She gave me a look like maybe I bought a bouquet of hemlock, poison ivy and wolfsbane and couldn't wait to give it to her mom.

"What is it, Frank?"

"Well... I know this is going to sound kind of bizarre, but they had this potted cactus at Bud's. I think the kid called it co... ry... pan... tha... or something like that. Okay, I know it's weird, but..."

"CORYPANTHA! Frank, my mom totally loves succulents! She will completely freak! We have to go take it to her right now!"

"But... but... I thought maybe we might..."

"How did you figure that out! You are totally cool, Frank. C'mon, let's get the corypantha and go over to the hospital."

Okay, now pay attention here. This is important because it's the way life really works. I'm sweating my balls off, completely failing to impress young Patty until KABOOM!, she's blown away by a goddam cactus that I bought by mistake. I mean JESUS! all of a sudden I was some kind of hero... whatever... I'll spare you the incredibly tedious boredom of the mom visit, but if you ever want an hour to feel like fifteen fucking years, just go visit some old bag *YOU DON'T EVEN KNOW* in the hospital. Patty's mom was so out of it, she barely recognized her daughter and she sure as shit didn't know who I was.

Anyway, a couple of hours later we were freezing our asses off in my rental car, sitting outside the hospital. We obviously couldn't sit there long... if I was going to make a move, this was the time, but first I had to get that phone number. I said, "Your mom seems like a really nice person, Patty, but... well, I don't want to be rude or anything, but it kinda felt like she was on another planet. I guess she must've been pretty drugged up." I paused for a moment, then waded in, "Oh, by the way, did you ever find out anything about that phone number? You know, the guy who called in the anonymous tip on the stiff."

"Oh, sorry... here it is." She handed me a scrap of paper. "Sorry, I meant to give it to you earlier, but I've been a little distracted."

Jackpot! I took the paper, looked at it long enough to see a phone number, then stuck it my shirt pocket. Hmmm... Maybe things were gonna work out after all.

"You know... I've been thinking about what a swell guy you are. I mean, I'm sure you've been pretty busy since you got here and the fact that you still found time to get that corypantha for my mom is really impressive, and gosh, you had to be bored silly sitting around that hospital room. I... I... I like you, Frank... I really do."

Man! I couldn't believe it! A few hours earlier, it felt like I was striking out big-time, but now this cute chick was practically falling into my arms. Shit, I guess sometimes you do get lucky. Her eyes were glassing over. I think she was even starting to breathe hard. I reached over and put my arm around her.

"You know what I like best about you, Frank?"

"No, what's that, Patty?"

"You really remind me a lot of my dad."

HUH? What? Whoa? Let's back up a little here. "What was that? What did you say?"

"My dad. You remind me of my dad. Oh, he's a little older than you but probably only a couple of years. He and my mom are divorced so I don't see him as much as I would like, but I've been thinking about him a lot lately. He... he's sick and..." Unable to continue, Patty starting choking up.

That open and clearly marked path to pussy was suddenly curving, cratered and filling with fog. "Um, what's wrong with him?"

Barely gaining her composure, Patty said, "They... they think he was exposed to sarin nerve gas in the first Gulf War.

29

He… he…" At this point she totally lost it and turned her face into my shoulder, sobbing uncontrollably.

What a weird fucking day! Starting with meeting the chick in the hick clothing store, seeing the spot where they found the stiff, followed by hole-in-the-throat Hazel, Farmer Brown, slayer of hogs, the cactus; visiting Patty's zombie mom in the hospital and now this. I'm thinking I'm about to get laid and discover I remind the babe of her fucked-up father with Gulf War syndrome. Man, I thought the Midwest was supposed to be boring. I decided it was time to head back to my motel room. Tomorrow is another day and all that crap.

"Gosh, Patty, I'm really sorry to hear about your dad. Uh, you know, it's getting pretty cold in here. I'll drop you off at your car and maybe we can talk about it some more tomorrow. What do you think?"

Calming down, she agreed, "It's been a long day. You're right… thanks. You're such a nice guy… you… you remind me so much of… my dad." She broke down again.

Jeez. "It's okay, Patty, everything will be all right." I reached around and gave her a little hug, then slowly removed her blubbering face from the shoulder of my Ben Davis coat. She was a sweet kid and all, but a guy can only take so much."

"Sure, Frank, sure. Thanks. I appreciate you being there for me."

I woke up the next morning with two things on my mind. I now had possession of the anonymous caller's number so I had to check that out, but I also had to be careful. If it was just somebody who happened to see the body on the side of road and called it in, well, that was it—a dead end.

But if it was Wilmer Graves' accomplice, I had to play it cozy and get as much info as I could before he figured out I was on to him. And, if he was involved with Graves, at some point I had to let the cops know. If this story turned out to be as big as I hoped it was, I couldn't afford to be seen as withholding evidence.

But the other thing that kept coming back to me was Farmer Brown's explosion. The fact that it happened right around the time that Graves' body was found couldn't be accidental. Okay, I guess it *could be* some kind of weird coincidence or maybe the old farmer was nuts, but I wasn't buying it. The two had to be connected, but what was that explosion... and where did it happen? And, assuming I found it, what would be left? No one else had mentioned a big boom, but judging from the farmer's reaction, something had happened... but what?

Most people don't know about it, but there's a website called ResMap.com that gives access to real-time satellite imagery. I didn't know exactly how it worked, but I figured a little time on the site would allow me to search the area surrounding the spot where Graves' body was found. If there was an explosion remotely like the farmer's description, then it had to leave some kind of crater or signs of destruction easily seen in satellite photos. It was worth investing a little time to learn the ResMap software.

Meanwhile, I had to find out what I could get on the anonymous caller. If he did turn out to be Graves' sidekick, I was off and running. I figured the guy was using a cell phone, so I used the number Patty gave me to check out some reverse number lookups, but they all looked like scams. Yeah, sure... I could risk ten or fifteen quankers, but no way was I going to give a credit card number to supercelsleuth.com.

Finally, in frustration I just typed the number into Google and BINGO!... there it was. The search engine told me

the guy's name was Theodore Hendricks and his phone was a landline in Blue Springs, Missouri, a suburb of Kansas City. If this was the guy, he apparently drove back to KC and called the tip in on his home phone. Are we talking major doofus here or what—either that or maybe this wasn't Graves' henchman after all. Maybe this guy just spotted the body, drove home and made the call. Maybe...

When in doubt—GOOGLE! I typed in "Theodore Hendricks" and "Blue Springs, MO" and there it was... BINGO! again. I was on a roll. The guy had a LinkedIn profile. Hendricks was listed as an "Internet Content Screener" working for Trusti-Tek, inc. Trusti-Tek was a provider of Data Purification Services, meaning that companies like YouTube, Facebook, Google, Vimeo, Twitter, Tumblr, etc., outsourced their censorship problems to Trusti-Tek and its competitors. In other words, if you collected all your girlfriend's turds for six months, made a video of yourself eating them slathered in maple syrup, posted it on YouTube and some asshole flagged it as "inappropriate," then Ted Hendricks or one of his colleagues would eventually wind up watching it... among other, less tasteful images and videos. It was not a pretty job.

I had a decision to make. I could just call the number and see what I could get out of Hendricks, or I could drive up to Kansas City and talk to him in person. If he was the accomplice and I screwed up the phone call, that was probably it—clamarama! But... I had his address. What the fuck... I took off for KC.

As I sat behind the wheel of my rented Chevy Sonic, the landscape blurred around the perimeter of my vision. It had begun to snow again and the swirling flakes smeared the air with fuzzy streaks like stranded hairs racing through the drab gray background, a backdrop reflecting my increasingly bleak mood.

The drive back up to Kansas City had given me time to think, not a good thing since the subject poised to invade this unguarded moment was Louise. With nothing immediately pressing against my consciousness, my mind became a yo-yo, rappelling back and forth between opposing poles of anger and depression. I really loved her and thought she loved me. Shit! I knew she loved me, still loves me, but she wanted something I couldn't give her. It was always about kids, at least as far as the fights went. She wanted them and I didn't... the age-old she-he cliché, but somehow it had to be more than that. And the guy... Ed... the fucking insurance salesman. I mean where does someone even meet an insurance salesman, much less get so involved they wind up hosing the asshole and leaving their life partner. The guy's a piece of putty. Who wants to fuck putty? You think you know somebody, you spend a couple of years with them, having great times and shitty times but real times, and then they go off and fuck putty. How can that be?

Even worse, when I wasn't torturing myself with thoughts of Louise moaning under the mass of Mister Mush, which was practically all the fucking time, I found myself thinking about Patty. No shit, Patty... with the cute smile and the drugged-out, post-op zombie mom. The one who said I REMINDED HER OF HER GODDAM FATHER! I mean, could there possibly be a bigger turnoff than to be reminded of a chick's father, a Gulf War burnout with post-traumatic stress disorder? But somehow, some inexplicable how, she and Louise were merging into the same person. It was like the Vulcan mind meld except the melding was them and the mind was mine, or whatever was left of it. But they were both these seemingly fragile little blondes, projecting the kind of vulnerability that gets me every time, but under the surface, they had this gritty, unyielding toughness. Like, man, you could jock them around and, yeah, they might break down and cry, and totally lose control, but don't you believe it because when the shit came down, they would take care of business. High-functioning. And ultimately that's what pissed me off about Louise, because underneath it all, she decided that I just wasn't that together. Not high-functioning. That I was just a guy to have fun with and fuck, but not there for the long run. Not like the Putty Man. The Doughboy. The Jello Joe. And it wasn't true! Goddammit! It wasn't true! I was just as good as that pile of pudding. I was... I was... I was...

And that's the way it went, around and around, back and forth, over and over in my mind until I finally arrived in Blue Springs.

That night I stayed at a Days Inn in Blue Springs formulating a plan to connect with Ted Hendricks. The Trusti-Tek offices were located in the Freight House district of Kansas City. I figured if I hung out near the entrance to the building around noon, it wouldn't be too hard to spot Hendricks leaving for lunch. I had seen a photo of him on LinkedIn, and Hazel, the waitress with the crater in her throat, said Graves' sidekick was a baby-faced white guy at least six-and-a-half feet tall. It should be a no-brainer. Of course, there was always the chance that this was a mondo dumbo wild goose chase and Ted Hendricks would turn out to be a transsexual midget, but I didn't think so.

The next morning I staked out a spot near the window in the Starbucks across the street from the Pendergast Building where Trusti-Tek had their offices. Sipping my double caramel macchiato, I went over my plan to engage Ted Hendricks in a conversation. The fact that he was employed as an "Internet content screener" was a real stroke of luck. It was an unpleasant but critical job established as a byproduct of user-created content in the digital age. The *New York Times* had done a major article on the mental health hazards of people with this particular job a few years ago. It was easy enough to tell Hendricks that I was doing a followup or a similar piece and see if I could get him talking.

When I still hadn't seen anyone answering Hendricks' description by 2:30, I decided to go over and check out the building. Upon entering, I couldn't miss an imposing African American guy sitting behind a security desk in the lobby. His name tag said "LEONARD" in all caps. With a voice rumbling like Barry White on steroids, Leonard was obviously no one to fuck with.

"Can I help you, sir?"

"Uh, I'm looking for a Theodore Hendricks. I understand he works for Trusti-Tek on the, uh…" I looked over at the building directory. "…fourth floor. I'll just go on up." As I started walking toward the elevator, Leonard stood up. Thinking better, I paused.

"Excuse me… do you have an appointment?"

"Uh, not exactly, but I'm sure he'll want to talk to me."

"You are no doubt correct, sir… but I'll call up to make sure. What did you say his name is?"

"Hendricks… Ted Hendricks."

"And you are…"

"Franklin Blodgett... with the *Wall Street Journal.*"

"Just a moment, Mr. Blood-Jet." He picked up a phone on his desk and dialed. "Yes, this is Leonard at security down in the lobby. We got a guy here named Franklin Blood-Jet... says he's from the *Wall Street Journal* and wants to talk to Ted Hendricks. Yeah, okay, I'll hold." Still wearing my Wranglers, Ben Davis coat and clodhoppers, I looked around the lobby as Leonard slowly sized me up. "I guess the *Wall Street Journal* doesn't pay so well these days."

"Huh?" I looked down at my bumpkin costume. "Oh yeah, I've, uh, been interviewing some people over in Clinton. I, uh, got these clothes..."

He held up his hand. "What's that?... he says he doesn't know anyone from the *Wall Street Journal?*... but he's coming down, anyway... okay, thanks." Looking up at me from his desk, the security guard casually remarked, "He'll be down in a minute. Why don't you wait over there." He nodded toward a couple of chairs across the lobby.

"Yeah, sure... thanks, Leonard." I sat down, waited and looked around. Kansas City was not exactly Paris or Milan, but it wasn't Clinton either and I was downtown... most guys had suits on. Oh yeah, there were hi-tech hipsters around, fashionably dressed down in their $300 "distressed jeans," '70s retro shirts and beanies, no doubt snickering at my Ben Davis hick gear... and I said I was from the *Wall Street Journal.* Oh well...

The elevator door opened and there he was. Shit, he was six-foot-ten if he was an inch... and looked like he was about thirteen. Momentarily taken aback, I managed to regain my composure as Hendricks' eyes darted up and down the lobby looking for someone who might be from the *Wall Street Journal.* With no one but yours truly and Big Leonard inhabiting the space, his gaze eventually settled on me. Hendricks' face was a beacon of insecurity.

I walked up, held out my hand and looked straight up. Man, was he tall. "Mr. Hendricks?"

"Uh, do I, uh, know you?" He said in a voice that was reedy, strained and at least an octave too high. In addition, Hendricks either ignored or was unaware of my outstretched hand. He also seemed to be oblivious to my bumpkin attire. It didn't take much to tell the young man was in distress.

"Uh, no, I don't think we've met, Mr. Hendricks. I'm Franklin Blodgett from the *Wall Street Journal*. I've come to ask you some…"

"The… the *Wall Street Journal*? What would the *Wall Street Journal* want with me? I don't understand." Hendricks was getting more nervous by the second. I had to figure out a way to calm him down.

"It's not really you, exactly, that we're interested in, Mr. Hendricks… may I call you Ted?" Hendricks ignored me again. "It's really your job that we want to know about. I understand you are an…"

"My job! My job! What about my job?" Glancing up from his magazine, a look of concern crossed Leonard's large face as Hendricks' voice began to rise. He was starting to lose it.

"It's okay, Mr. Hendricks… Ted. I understand you are an Internet content screener? Is that correct?"

"Yes, but there's nothing wrong with…"

"Please, just give me a minute… the *New York Times* did a major article on people in your profession a couple of years ago and now the *Journal* has asked me to do a followup. I won't take up much of your time. Please, just give me a few minutes…"

"Oh… well, I really need to get back to work, but…"

"Five minutes, Ted, just give me five to ten minutes. We can go over to Starbucks and I'll buy you a cup of coffee."

"Well… I guess so." Hendricks was obviously uncertain, but it seemed like answering a few questions might be the easiest way to get rid of me.

We walked back across the street with me marveling at how close Hendricks' head came to the top of each doorway, always ducking at the last possible moment, without ever actually hitting one. We found a table with lots of legroom, then I ordered another macchiato for myself and a tall regular coffee for Ted. The kid was incredibly nervous; something was bothering him.

"So, uh, how did you hear about me?" he asked as I sat down with the drinks. Hendricks mostly kept his head down, only looking up occasionally. Making eye contact was obviously difficult—most of the time he just stared at this coffee. "There are lots of people in the office doing the same job as me. I don't understand."

"Uh, it was your, uh, supervisor who recommended you, uh…"

"Charley… uh, Mr. Warren? You spoke to Mr. Warren?"

"Uh, no, my boss called him a few days ago and he mentioned you."

"Oh, but Mr. Warren has never said a word to…"

"Could you just tell me a little about your job, Ted? It must be fascinating."

"Huh? Fascinating!?!… fascinating…" Hendricks seemed to ponder the word like it was a tiny alien doing breaststrokes in his cup of coffee. After a pause of several puzzled moments, he blurted out, "Do you like worm soup? I mean, if you like watching videos of some guy filling up a blender with worms and turning it on high, then, yeah, I guess it's fascinating. That's what I was doing when Leonard called and said you were in the lobby… yeah, fascinating… Yesterday there were all these pictures of a guy having sex with a tied-up goat… the goat was struggling and it had like a bondage hood on but you could see its eyes were open and staring in this desperate, pitiful helpless kind of way… and it had a ball gag in its mouth… a ball gag in a goat's mouth… the… the guy must have taken fifty or sixty pictures with his cell phone while he was doing the goat... and he posted all of them... yeah, I guess it was fascinating... and then there was..."

"I get it, Ted, I get it. You see a lot of disgusting stuff." The kid was struggling to keep it together. I felt kind of sorry for him.

"Sometimes I can't get it out of my head. I'll be at home having dinner and I'm raising a spoonful of soup to my mouth and all of a sudden this dead mouse pops into my mind... this dead mouse, stuck to bottom of a hiking boot... and you can see how the mouse is all deformed... it's been squashed up in and around the knobby bumps on the sole of the shoe... and the photo was shot really close up so you can see every single mouse hair and its yellow rodent teeth and..."

"Lots of dead stuff, I'll bet... pictures of dead animals... and dead people... do you see a lot of pictures of dead people, Ted?"

"I see them all the time... all the time... too many dead people... dead people are all around me." Hendricks looked out the window as if he was thinking about something specific. "Sometimes I dream about them..."

The disturbed Internet screener was slipping further and further out. It seemed like this was the time to hit him with a high hard one and see how he reacted, so I went for it. "I recently heard about a dead guy that was found all alone, just laying on the side of a road not far here... it was over near Clinton. Did you hear about him, Ted?"

"Huh, what... what are you talking about?"

Hendricks' face quickly turned the same color as a baby's butt left in the sun all summer. He tried to soothe himself by taking a sip of coffee, but his hands were shaking so badly, he had to place the cup back onto the table.

"Wilmer Graves... I think that's what the guy's name was... Wilmer Graves. Did you hear about him, Ted?"

"What! Willy?..." Hendricks' eyes slowly rose from his coffee cup and met mine with an intense stare. He was catching on. With the wheels furiously turning in Ted Hendricks' brain, he paused briefly, then blurted out, "Who are you? What are you doing here? Why are you asking me about poor Willy? It's Beasley... it's Beasley you should be looking for!"

Suddenly realizing that he had said too much, Hendricks abruptly stood, bumping the table and knocking over his cup of coffee as he rose. Biting on his words, the Internet screener said, "I can't talk any more. I've got to back to work."

"But, Ted, wait..." I watched as Hendricks' exceedingly long legs quickly devoured the space between our table and the entrance, but this time he misjudged—or blindly ignored—the height of the doorway, banging his head into the metal as he crossed the threshold. Wiping blood away from his forehead, Ted Hendricks disappeared into the traffic.

I needed to get back to Clinton, but still wanted to see what I could dig up on the Hendricks kid. A little earlier I spotted the entrance to the Pendergast Building's parking garage and figured if I hung around, there was a good chance I could catch him leaving; it was worth taking some time to follow the kid home and see where he lived. Hendricks would no doubt freak if he knew I was following him, but the techie was so worked up, I'd probably have to set his face on fire before he noticed.

Sure enough, about an hour and a half later, a ten-year-old Honda appeared at the parking garage exit; the Honda was a perfect ID for the one hole-in-the-throat Hazel saw in the café parking lot back in Adrian. Practically sitting in the back seat, a familiar baby-faced driver sat behind the wheel, his head nervously darting back and forth, before pulling out into traffic.

Maintaining a discreet distance, I followed Hendricks for about a half an hour until he finally pulled into the driveway of a nondescript suburban house in Blue Springs. I drove past, then stopped about a block away. Getting out of my car, I casually walked back toward the kid's house, being careful not to attract any attention. It was starting to get dark so I figured I was pretty safe, but didn't want to take any chances that Hendricks might spot me.

Graves' accomplice had pulled the Honda up under an open carport, grabbed a backpack from the back seat and disappeared into the house. I waited a couple of minutes to let him settle in, then casually strolled up the driveway, ducking into the shadows under the carport. Curious as to what I might find in his car, I pulled out a small flashlight and peeked through the windows. Looking at the front seat, I was startled at the large accumulation of empty coffee cups, candy wrappers, potato chip bags and other assorted trash littering the car. There was even an old pair of sneakers on the floor of the shotgun seat.

I then turned my attention to the back which was just as messy, maybe worse. Clothes, a small suitcase, books, magazines, a pillow, fast food wrappers and more coffee cups turned the back seat into a pint-sized garbage dump. Ted Hendricks either kept an insanely chaotic car or something had been going on here and he hadn't slowed down long enough to clean up the mess.

I had seen enough to get the general picture and was about to move on when something odd caught my eye. It was a box, partially covered by magazines and old newspapers, with a bold and lurid message screaming from its only visible surface. Shining my light directly on the box, I read the words "eSPY - NO SECRET IS SAFE!"

Quietly opening the car door, I reached in and shoved the clutter aside, revealing the cheesy packaging of a decidedly third-rate surveillance kit. In tacky Day-Glo lettering the box proclaimed "eSPY - HI-TECH SPYING MADE EASY!," "eSPY - NO MORE SLEEPLESS NIGHTS - NOW YOU KNOW!," "eSPY - TRAVEL A LOT? - KNOW WHAT HAPPENS WHEN YOU'RE GONE!," and "CONTAINS 4 NIGHT VISION CAMERAS!!! - A 500-MEGABYTE GENUINE DIGITAL HARD DRIVE!!! - A HIGH RESOLUTION B&W MONITOR!!!" What a hunk of junk. Why would someone like Hendricks be carrying a piece of crap like that around in the back seat of his car? There was a lot of shit going on that didn't seem to add up.

At that moment, just as I got out of the car, I heard a hand on the doorknob leading from the house into the carport. Watching as it slowly opened, I froze in panic, then quickly ducked down behind the car. I was about to bolt into the darkness when Hendricks appeared, immediately followed by the incessant yipping of a tiny Chihuahua. Realizing it was too late to run, I fell to the ground and rolled under the car. Standing in the doorway, the kid's back was turned so he couldn't see me, but the fucking dog did. The barking rat ran straight at me, stopping two inches from my face. A cross between a giant insect and shrunken drill sergeant, the Chihuahua was utterly relentless. I was trapped! Not only was the little shit's shrill and incessant barking piercing my brain like a screaming spike, but he apparently had just eaten dinner so his breath smelled like rancid chicken liver. It was torture, but I didn't have any choice except to gut it out.

The kid was having an animated conversation with someone. I figured it was either a girlfriend or a roommate, but I couldn't hear anything over the runt dog shrieking at my face, so I concentrated, trying to follow the one-sided dialogue as best I could. The kid was still upset. He yelled, "I know it's almost dinner time, but you said you wanted me to take Archie for a walk!"

The dog was straining on the end of a leash. As Hendricks paused to listen to whoever was in the house, he stepped down from the doorway into the carport allowing just enough slack for my tormentor to lunge forward, biting me on the nose. Jerking my head back, I gritted my teeth and stifled a scream as my left nostril began squirting blood like a skewered chicken.

Still standing at the door, Hendricks yelled back into the house, "What did you say? I'm sorry, but Archie's barking so much I can hardly hear you." The kid paused again as I eyeballed the ferocious Archie preparing to hurl his taut body at my naked nose with renewed passion. Watching the blood as it flowed from my wounded nostril out onto the carport floor, I cringed in anticipation. The hairless rat was having the time of his life.

Hendricks yelled again, "SHUT UP, ARCHIE," and jerked on the leash, delaying the latest onslaught if only for a few seconds. Nevertheless, still squalling like a baby leaf blower, Archie was not about to let his guard down. "ARCHIE! DAMMIT! WHY ARE YOU BARKING SO MUCH? Is there something under there?" These were not the words I wanted to hear.

As I strained to look through the blood now seeping into my eyes, I saw Hendricks' shadowy silhouette moving downward as he squatted near the front of the car. It was not a good sign—as my jaw tightened, panic made its way from my stomach to the base of my throat. Hendricks was now on his hands and knees, allowing me to see the outline of his head as the dog's owner peeked under the car, searching the area near the end of the leash. "Margo, I think there's something under there! It might be a raccoon! Quick, bring the mace!"

MACE! SHIT FIRE! We were well past the point of discretion here. I had to get the fuck out... and fast. Scooting out from under the car, I sprung to my feet. It was dark in the carport. I ran hurdles in high school and still had a little speed, so I figured if I could catch him by surprise and get out fast enough, maybe the kid wouldn't recognize me. It was the only chance I had, so I grabbed it; quickly springing into action, I headed for the carport doorway and the open night air. With blood stinging my eyes and all but gluing them shut, I was one step from an all-out sprint when I crashed into a trash can, then tripped on a rake. A distinct "pop" echoed through space as my face connected with one of the brick pillars supporting the front of small house. Groaning in pain, my head then bounced off the concrete driveway as I rolled over on my back, reeling with the feeling that life is complicated. Oh yeah, my nose was broken, too.

Groggy with pain and shock, I struggled to get back to my feet, took a step or two, then stumbled and fell again. Laying in the middle of the driveway, I could hear Hendricks shouting through my mental haze, "Margo! Margo! I think it's a burglar! Call the cops! CALL THE COPS! ... uh, no, wait. Don't call the cops... uh, I think he may be hurt... stay back... STAY BACK! Let me look."

The jig was up. Not much to do now but face the music. Dazed, I looked back toward the house as a flashlight slowly creeped down the driveway, until... WHAM! The beam hit me in the face. His voice shrill with disbelief, Ted Hendricks stared and shouted, "MISTER BLOOD-JET! IS THAT YOU? What... what were you doing under my car?"

45

I was sitting at the table in the breakfast nook of Ted Hendricks' kitchen. Seeing my blood-covered face and coat, and sensing the pain numbing my eyes, the Internet screener graciously took pity, but this was not a joyous reunion. With his body language screaming *PISSED OFF*, Hendricks left and immediately returned with a washcloth, a roll of toilet paper and some tape. Closely observing the scene was Ted's girlfriend, Margo, who scowled, brought me a cup a coffee, then retreated a safe distance.

Ignoring his rage, Hendricks cleaned my bruised and battered face. After gingerly wiping most of the blood away, he unrolled several feet of toilet paper and taped a huge wad of it across the center of my face. Stepping back to admire his handiwork, the kid shrugged his shoulders, then looked me straight in the eyes and said, "Okay, so what's this all about? I want to know what are you doing here, Mr. Blood-Jet, if that's actually your name?"

My consciousness was slowly returning, but unfortunately, that only made the pain worse. It appeared that, while my nose was indeed broken, I didn't have a concussion. I guess some people would call that lucky. Personally, I call it careless and fucking stupid, but I suppose it could have been worse—Hendricks might have had a pet weasel that ripped my face off, but that only happens in the movies. Regardless, it was time to do some fast talking.

"It's Blodgett, Ted. Franklin Blodgett... please call me Frank. I am a writer but no, I don't work for the *Wall Street Journal*. I'm sorry I had to lie to you, but I'm trying to do a story on Wilmer Graves and I think you are somehow involved... and the more I find out, the stranger the story becomes..."

"Look, I can't tell you anything about Willy, okay? I probably said too much already, but that's it... understand?"

Margo, sizing everything up from across the room, was also upset, but her concerns were a little different than the kid's. Confused, she said, "What's this all about, Ted? Who's Wilmer Graves and what's he got to do with you?"

"I can't talk about it now, Margo. It... it's personal..."

"Personal! Ted, you disappear for nearly a week, show up with no explanation and I'm supposed to act like it's okay! Then you find this guy hiding under your car... what's he doing there? It's not okay, Ted... yeah, it's personal all right... it's personal for me if I can't trust the man I'm engaged to! Do you understand that?"

"Okay... okay... but let's talk about this later. It's not a good time for..."

"It's never a good time, Ted! You've been back from wherever the fuck you went for five days now and haven't said a thing! I can't deal with this... I'm sorry, but I'm going home!" With that she left, slamming the door behind her.

"Margo! Margo! Wait! Wait!"

The chick was not waiting, a fact confirmed by the sound of a car door, followed by an engine starting and driving away. In the silence that followed, Hendricks' mood was dull and dark, covering the kid like a concrete cloud. After a long and tense moment, he turned back to me—it was just the two of us, Ted Hendricks with his heavily bandaged forehead and me with half a roll of toilet paper taped to my nose. We looked like some kind of wounded war twins, except of course Hendricks was three feet taller than me. Okay, that's an exaggeration, but you get the picture. Leaning down from somewhere up above, Hendricks stuck his face in front of me and screamed, "Look what you've done!"

"Hey, yo, Ted... Okay, I shouldn't have been snooping around your car and I'm sorry I lied about the *Wall Street Journal*, but if you disappeared on your girlfriend while you were out sticking up gas stations and formal wear joints with Wilmer Graves, it's not my fault, dude. Meanwhile, your car looks like a rolling garbage can and you've got a junior G-Man spy kit in the back seat. So what the fuck is going on here?"

At that point the highly strung Hendricks finally reached the end of his rope, a rope that had somehow become twisted around the core of his being, gradually growing tighter and tighter over a period of weeks. His defenses shattered, the kid collapsed like a discarded rag doll, flopping his gangly form into a chair and sobbing like a baby.

"Look, kid, I realize you're pretty fucked up over all this. Maybe it would help if you talked it out."

Shaking and unable to speak beyond a babble of random blubbering, the kid was still able to violently shake his head back and forth. Finally, after a torturously long minute, he gained enough composure to stammer out, "N-N-N-NO! N-N-N-NO! I... I C-CAN'T T-T-TALK ABOUT IT! I CAN'T TALK ABOUT IT!"

"Okay, it's up to you... but whatever happened is probably gonna come out sooner or later."

Hendricks shook his head again. "N-NO! N-NO!"

Another tense silence, broken only by Ted Hendricks' erratic sobs, slowly filled the room. I didn't know what to do. I obviously needed to get to a doctor, but I hated to leave Hendricks alone in this condition. Through all of this insanity, two things were becoming fairly clear to me: there was little doubt about the kid having been Graves' accomplice, but it was equally obvious that Ted Hendricks was not a criminal. It just didn't make any sense.

Finally appearing to regain his composure, Hendricks raised his head and stared across the room. Suddenly snapping back to reality, the techie called out, "Margo's inhaler! She forgot her inhaler!" Jumping up from his chair, he crossed the room in two giant steps, reached over and grabbed the inhaler then turned back to me. "I'm sorry, Mr. Blood-Jet, but you have to go now. Margo left without her asthma inhaler. If she has an attack without it, I'll never forgive myself. You have to go." And with that, the kid put on his heavy coat, opened the back door, practically pushing me out of the house.

Standing in the driveway, oscillating back and forth between my throbbing nose and the freezing bite of a northern Missouri winter, I watched Ted Hendricks squeal out of his driveway and roar off into the night. Oh yeah, one more thing. Even though I only saw her for a few minutes, totally immersed in the murky fog of pain, Ted Hendricks' girlfriend Margo made an indelible imprint on my mind. She was absolutely the most stunning woman I had ever seen. Radiating a clean and uncluttered sexuality with every breath, every move, every iota of her being, the lovely Margo also left me with one clear and nagging question: what the fuck was she doing with a doofus like Ted Hendricks?

Despite the incessant pain pounding in my broken nose, the return trip to Clinton gave me more time and headspace to think. Hendricks' involvement with Wilmer Graves was obviously no longer in doubt. The kid's reaction to the mention of Graves' name, along with the suggestion of his involvement in the convict's crime spree, had caused him to completely lose it. Also, as I thought back to our earlier encounter in the coffee shop, I remembered something else he said: "Beasley." It was something like, "You should really be looking for Beasley." So who the fuck was Beasley and how did he fit into this strange and oddly expanding puzzle?

As the blurry outlines of a gloomy landscape floated past the windows of my rental car, I glanced out at the pitch-black sky. Not unlike the drive to Kansas City, the return trip to Clinton not only gave me time to consider the story slowly unfolding around me, but it also opened the space for more personal reflection, a door into a deep well of self-doubt and recrimination that always seemed to echo with a longing for Louise. But by now the well had become a little more crowded—not only was I in there, along with my nagging what-ifs and woulda-shouldas, but there, alongside Louise, were two more recent attachments: the perky and genuine Patty and the more than memorable Margo. And of course, the insanity of even vaguely considering Margo as an "attachment" was hardly lost on me. The tricks of the mind are unbounded, and no matter how much I played a mental game of Whack-A-Mole with images of Louise, Patty and Margo popping out of an endless series of black holes, another one always came bouncing back. WHACK! No more Louise! WHACK! No more Patty! WHACK! WHACK! WHACK!... no more Margo! WHACK! WHACK!... until finally only one was left... only one that I couldn't shake... only one that kept tapping me on the shoulder with one hand and grabbing my balls with the other, while looking, staring, searching into the depths of my soul.

And who was it?... Patty, of course. Oh, don't ask me why... these things have no rhyme or reason. They are what they are, as they say, and making sense is not what they're all about. I tried to Whack-A-Mole her away... she was too young... she lived in Clinton-buttfuck-Missouri... I reminded her of HER FATHER... she might even be a virgin, for chrissake! But nothing worked. I couldn't get her out of my head.

It was midnight when I finally pulled into the parking lot of the Roadside Inn where I was staying in Clinton. Totally exhausted, I dragged myself up the stairs, opened the door and collapsed on the bed. And of course the last thing I thought of before instantly drifting into the infinite, fuzzy and familiar shroud of sleep was Patty, and how badly I longed to see her smiling face across the table sipping a hot cup of coffee in the morning. It was crazy.

I woke up the next day feeling refreshed. A good night's sleep had done wonders for my mind, body and overall out-look on life. The Patty thing was still there, but I managed to mentally push it into a cave back behind some big rocks. It was silly... why would she be interested in me? And of course she was far too young for an experienced man of the world. It was absurd.

Feeling brave, I looked in the mirror and even that wasn't so bad. Okay, my face was a mess, but the nose could have been worse. A little swollen, but still straight—well, almost straight. And a Google search told me that there's nothing they can do about a broken nose; eventually it heals and it's good as new. And yeah, I probably needed a stitch or two where Ted's Tiny Terror sunk his razor-like canines into my tender flesh, but what the hell... a scar or two merely adds character to a real man's face.

So, that was it, enough brooding about that dumbfuck Louise, because that's all this craziness was. Pining about lost love... who needs it? There was nothing going on with Patty... no Margo... what a joke! Let Louise have the god-dam insurance salesman. Now it was SHOWTIME! Eat some breakfast, drink some coffee and crank it up!

Twenty minutes later I was sitting in Terry's Café staring at a plateful of fried eggs, bacon and hash browns. You know, some things just make the world right and this was it—a genuine greasy-spoon breakfast. Life doesn't get any better.

Okay, I'll admit I did scan the café for Patty and felt a slight, only minor, twinge when I realized she wasn't there, but it was okay. It was okay.

As I sipped my coffee, my mind flashed back a couple of days to just before I left Clinton. The episode with Farmer Brown and the story about the explosion spooking him and his pig came rushing back, and with it came the idea of Res-Map and the ability to view real-time satellite imagery. If a big explosion did occur, I should be able to find evidence of it on ResMap. It might take a while, but it should be there. As soon as I finished breakfast, I rushed back to my room and booted up my computer. My Dell Inspiron wasn't the fastest or hippest laptop around but I figured it would get the job done. I went to the ResWeb.com website and downloaded the software that would allow me to view live satellite images directly in Explorer. It took a few minutes to install the browser plug-in, but after a couple of minutes I was up and running.

The farmland and forest surrounding Clinton covered a huge area, but since I had seen the farmer and his broken-down pickup on Highway 18 a few miles west of Clinton, that seemed like a good place to start. It was also not far from the spot where Graves' body was found. Okay, the old farmer was out there—maybe the explosion only happened in his head. And if it was real, maybe it didn't have anything to do with Hendricks and Graves, but I had a feeling... a strong feeling.

I spent the whole morning on my laptop starting back at Adrian, MO, and slowly working my way back toward Clinton, searching every square mile of land around Highway 18. I was getting really tired of staring at a computer monitor and was just about to go out for lunch when BINGO!... there it was! A small circular, dirt-colored area that strongly suggested the presence of a crater. It wasn't a big crater, at least by Siberian or Crater Lake standards. I guess it was only about sixty to seventy-five feet in diameter, but big enough to indicate some serious damage. The dirt bowl was in a heavily forested area not far from where Graves' body was found and only a few hundred yards off the highway. A dirt road led from the main highway into the thicket, but the area was so secluded that you'd never find it accidentally.

Something had happened in that clump of woods. I had no idea what I was going to find when I got there, but I had to check it out.

Twenty minutes later I was on the outskirts of Clinton speeding down Highway 18. It wasn't far; I would be there in forty-five minutes, maybe less, but I couldn't keep from wondering what I would find. Nothing up to this point gave the slightest indication that either Graves or Hendricks would have the inclination, much less the knowledge, to create an explosive with this kind of power. But if not Willy Graves or his baby-faced sidekick, then who—and more importantly, why?

It was early afternoon and the road was completely deserted. As I cruised through the countryside, it occurred to me that there are certain details of driving down an open highway that are always the same: the telephone poles speeding along the side of the road, the birds perched upon the wires, the scenery moving slower and slower as it recedes into the distance, but this time it was different. No doubt the details were similar enough, but that's not where the difference originated. It was me. I had created a sense of anticipation completely unlike any I've ever known before. Sure, expectations are the core of any trip. You're going somewhere and something will happen when you get there. Maybe it's a family trip and there's a feeling of familiarity that accompanies the journey. Maybe it's a vacation and a sense of impending discovery defines and informs the sensation of moving from one place to another. But none of these feelings were valid for me at this particular moment, a moment that was brand new, unfolding in real time... and I embraced it.

As I approached the one-lane dirt road leading south off the main highway, I felt a sense of eerie foreboding. To begin with, I was looking out the car window at a life-sized landscape that only a couple of hours before had appeared in a God's-eye view on my computer screen. The juxtaposition of distance versus immediacy was unnerving, not unlike those moments when you're sitting in a Burger King biting into a Whopper and all-of-a-sudden-out-of-nowhere you think, "OMG! There's probably ten million people all around the world doing this exact same thing RIGHT NOW!" Of course, turning onto a dirt road in rural Missouri is not the same as sitting in a Burger King, but that's not the point. The idea is that reality is so much larger, deeper and more complicated than we pitiful humans can comprehend that when we do get tiny glimpses of it, we are immediately compelled to back away, bite into our burger, and go on about our business. So here I was experiencing an all but instantaneous transformation from being God to being an ant, an ant driving a car up a dirt road in Missouri. It was weird.

But not nearly as weird as what I found upon entering the area I had pinpointed on ResMap. Stopping the car, I got out and gaped at a scene of destruction and immediate mutation from one reality to another unlike anything else I had witnessed. Okay, I had seen pictures of tornado wreckage, images of rubble remaining after an earthquake, the ruins of bombed-out villages in news photos, but those were only pictures, facsimiles of life. This was real, and standing in the middle of nothing but dirt, rocks and a few fragments of grass all splayed out in a series of irregular concentric circles was more than weird—it was mind-boggling.

The center of the crater was about four or five feet below the surrounding area. The explosion had obviously taken everything that had previously existed at ground zero and dispersed it over a large circular area, with the remaining fragments growing larger and larger as they retreated from the center. Starting with dust and small splinters of rock at the center and ending with trees leaning back away from the crater, the scene was a huge and highly organized mandala of destruction. As I walked outward, I searched the ground for anything that might give me a clue as to what had happened. No one had created an explosion like this to blow up a few rocks and trees. Something had been here before the big bang and there had to be pieces of it laying around.

As I reached a point twenty-five or thirty feet from the center of the crater, something shiny caught my eye. I bent down and picked up a piece of metal about the size of a matchbook; one side of it was coated with a yellow-ish metallic paint while the other side was plain. Moving a little further away, I discovered another, slightly larger piece, and a few minutes later I found two more. Okay, I admit I'm not the smartest guy in the world, but somewhere in the shadowy recesses of my mind, an alarm was going off. My "Spidey-Sense" was going AAAUUUUGAAAAH! AAAUUUUGAAAAH! And then it hit me! THE CADILLAC! The gold Escalade that Graves and Hendricks had driven out of the café parking lot a couple of weeks earlier in Adrian. Someone had blown up the Cadillac not long after they drove away in it. But who? Once again it didn't seem likely that Willy and Ted would have driven a brand new car from the café parking lot out here to the middle of the woods and blasted the hell out of it. But then nothing about this whole deal made any sense.

Then WHAM!!! It hit me again! A car bomb! Somebody had tried to kill them. That had to be it. A bomb, a massive explosive device was hidden in the Cadillac and somehow Wilmer Graves and Ted Hendricks escaped the explosion. Graves' body was found not far from here; he must have died shortly after the two of them got away. After Willy died, Hendricks would have walked back to the café, got in his Honda and driven home. No wonder he wouldn't talk about it. Ted Hendricks knows that somebody out there tried to waste him and they might be coming back to finish the job.

WOW! My head was spinning like an ice skater on acid. It was going to take a little while to sort all this out, but one thing was clear. I had to report this to the cops and if Ted Hendricks thought he was in trouble before, he was about to find his mojo mired mondo deep in doo-doo.

I needed a plan of action and it seemed like the best place to start was Patty. First of all, she was the only person I knew in this crummy town and secondly, well, actually, there wasn't any other reason, so it was Patty. Regardless, unless I was planning on bailing on the whole cockeyed business and going back to an empty apartment in L.A.—DUH!—I had to bring the cops in, but as soon as I showed my face to the lesbo bitch from Bumpkinville, she'd be busting my balls with the *L.A. Times* crap again. I needed someone on the inside and that was Patty... end of story.

Of course, as usual there was a problem. I didn't have her phone number and didn't know where she lived. The only places I could expect to find Patty were her work, and I wasn't quite ready for the den of Deputy Dawg, and the hospital, where she went to visit her mom every day. So the hospital it was.

Meanwhile, I hadn't eaten any lunch yet and I was starving. I was getting kind of tired of the limited offerings at Terry's, where I'd been having breakfast every morning and decided to try something different. I'd spotted a little place on the edge of town; it was really just a small trailer with a sign proclaiming KATIE'S KATFISH SHACK. We do have food trucks in West Hollywood with Korean tacos, Indian crepes, Irish burgers, etc., but we don't exactly have "Katfish Shacks" so I opted for some local color. Katie's was really a take-out joint—seating was a couple of picnic tables—but the weather had gotten a little better so I decided to go for it.

The Katfish Shack was a one-person operation and it was a guy, probably in his early thirties. I swear to God his name tag said Bubba. It's not just reality TV shows about junk dealers and frog farmers. There actually ARE people back in the South and the Midwest named Bubba. Anyway, the place was deserted except for him and me, so I stepped up to the window to order.

Bubba was apparently texting on his cell phone, which he put aside. Turning to the window, he took a quick look at me, raised his eyebrows and said, "What does the other guy look like?"

"Huh? Oh... yeah." I had forgotten that it looked like someone had worked me over with a tire tool. "Uh, I had a little accident... bumped into something..."

"Yeah, I'd say so. What did he use, a piece of pipe, a black-jack, a weed-eater?" I noticed that Bubba had a slight twitch in his left eye.

"Funny... So how's the catfish in this place?"

"Mister, this is absolutely the best catfish you will ever eat." Bubba emphasized the word "eat" by slapping his open palm on the counter. "This catfish is guaran-fucking-teed or your money back." It wasn't a big deal, but the guy had an edgy quality that made me a little uncomfortable. What the hell... I was still curious about the catfish.

"Sold. Hit me with your best shot, Bubba. How about three pieces of fish, some fries and a beer?"

"You got it, mister."

Seemingly happy to have a customer, Bubba went to work, carefully coating the catfish fillets with cornmeal and slicing real potatoes, then dipping wire baskets containing the fish and fries into small basins filled with obscenely hot oil; meanwhile, I checked the place out. While Katie's was something less than a landmark structure, it was incredibly clean. As I looked around, I amused myself with the idea of a Katfish Shack showroom, a massive warehouse displaying different models—a chrome Katfish Shack with a fiber-optic Internet connection, one with marble counters and gold fixtures, another with a DJ station, lights and a small stage for a pole dancer... and right in the center of the building would be Katie's, the perfect example of the ideal Katfish Shack. Every pot and pan, every utensil, every spice jar, knife and cutting board were neatly distributed and arranged around the small, spotless interior. Nothing was out of place, no crumbs on the floor, not even a speck of dirt or grease on the immaculate white walls.

And overlooking this compact and pristine scene were half a dozen photographs of a middle-aged woman. One picture showed her face grinning next to the head of a Labrador retriever, another found her beaming over a plate full of hot catfish, in another she was standing at the top of a ski run, poised to dash downhill. I could only assume it was Katie and wondered where she was. Maybe it was her day off.

Finally, the catfish was ready. Obviously pleased with himself, Bubba plopped a styrofoam take-out carton in front of me along with a bottle of Bud. I grabbed a plastic fork, sat down at the nearest table, and dived into a generous serving of still steaming, golden fried catfish. It was incredible. Okay, I like fish. I eat a lot of salmon, halibut, tuna, trout, and I eat it grilled, smoked, roasted, blackened, broiled, but no fish ever tasted like this. I added just a touch of lemon and salt—OMG! It was magic in my mouth. I paused for just a moment and looked around. Stunned, I desperately needed some kind of reassurance but the truth was undeniable: I was feasting on an incredible culinary delight cooked in a fucking trailer in Clinton, Missouri. SHIT! Why weren't there thousands of people lined up behind me?

I had to compliment the chef. "Bubba, my God, this is fantastic. I've never tasted anything like it."

Delighted, he slapped the counter again. "Yeah, cool, man. Glad you like it, but I really can't take any credit. It's Katie's special cornmeal coating and frying technique that does it. I just follow her instructions." Bubba's eye was twitching like crazy.

"Where is Katie? I'd love to compliment her—this is totally amazing!"

The fry cook was cleaning up the counter, restoring the Katfish Shack to its previously gleaming and flawless condition. He paused, looked down and replied without ever directly addressing me. When he finally spoke, the words were slow and deliberate. "Katie's gone, mister. She... she passed away last year."

"Oh... I'm really sorry to hear that, Bubba. Were you close?" I was afraid I already knew the answer.

Once again, Bubba was slow to respond. "Katie... she... she was my mom. Well, actually my stepmother, but she raised me like her own son. She was a great... great lady." Overcome by melancholy, the fry cook stared at an invisible spot on the floor.

At this point I was a little uncertain how to proceed. I

had opened a can of worms and down in the dark interior, something ugly was peeking out. Regardless, I had gone this far... "So, uh, what happened, Bubba? You know... you really don't have to tell me if it makes you too uncomfortable." And I sure as shit hoped it did. I mean, he was a nice guy and all, but I really just wanted to finish my catfish and move on, but it wasn't going to be that easy.

Lost in his own twitchy world, Bubba continued, "Katie was a real outdoors type. She loved camping, fishing, hiking—anything that got her outside. After she broke up with my dad, Katie started spending a lot of time out hiking by herself. God knows everybody warned her, told her find a partner, but she wouldn't listen. As soon as the weather was nice for a couple of days, Katie would just shut down the Shack and take off. She had a spot that she loved in the Ozarks, just below the state line in Arkansas. She went there all the time. One day she was alone hiking and she must've fallen and broke her leg... no one was there so we had to kind of figure all this out later. Anyway, when she tripped or whatever, she fell on a fire ant mound... do you know anything about fire ants, Mister... do you... DO YOU!?!"

"Uh..." I was more than a little uncomfortable. Still not addressing me directly, Bubba was getting worked up.

"Fire ants! FIRE ANTS! I HATE THE LITTLE FUCKERS! They're aggressive as hell and as soon as one stings, they send out these weird kind of chemicals that make all of them want to sting at once! THE FUCKERS..." As Bubba paused to compose himself, I ate a little faster. This was not going to end well. "Katie... Katie... they said when she fell on the mound the ants all came charging out and started stinging her. Her fucking leg was broken... she couldn't get away... but they said it probably wouldn't have mattered. They think she was allergic to the fire ant venom and went into a kind of shock. I mean nobody knew she was allergic, not even Katie... she'd never been stung by one, but the allergy... the allergy made her throat swell up so much she couldn't breathe. They said she died of suffocation. On top of that, when we found her the next day her whole body was covered with blisters from the fucking fire ants. The fuckers! THE FUCKERS! I HATE THEM!!!! It... it was ugly, mister... ugly... ugly." At that point Bubba turned and looked at me. Tears were in his eyes. "And you know what else? YOU KNOW WHAT ELSE, MISTER?"

"Uh, no, uh, Bubba. Uh, what else?" Needless to say, I was quickly losing my appetite for catfish. I managed to get a couple of bites and a few french fries down and decided it was time to find Patty, but Bubba wasn't quite finished.

"You know why the fucking fire ants are here? You know why? Palm trees, that's why! PALM TREES! People want to fix up their fucking yards with palm trees and ferns and shit from South America and when they get them, they come with fire ants! Fire ants come in palm trees from South America! Who needs fucking palm trees! HUH? CAN YOU TELL ME THAT MISTER! CAN YOU? FUCK NO, YOU CAN'T! FUCK NO... fuck no..." At that Bubba flopped back down on the little stool that lived behind the counter and just sat there, sobbing.

I felt sorry for the guy, but Jesus, was everybody around here nuts? In thirty seconds I had gone from eating some of the most amazing food I ever put in my mouth to listening to a guy blubbering about his dead stepmother covered with blisters. I had to boogie. "Hey, Bubba, I'm, uh, really sorry to hear about Katie and the fire ants and the palm trees and all, but, uh, I've gotta go. Catch ya later, okay?" The fry cook never looked up as I got in my rental car and left.

I remembered Patty showing up at the hospital around 4:00 in the afternoon, so I hurried on over there and didn't have long to wait. As I watched, the young blonde pulled into the parking lot, got out of her ten-year-old Jeep, and walked toward the main entrance to the building. My irrational impulse to create some kind of romantic connection between us had mostly faded; nevertheless, It had been a couple of days since I had seen Patty and she was even more babistic than I remembered. And shit, it had been AT LEAST two weeks since I had gotten laid, but hey, I REALLY needed to focus on the "business" aspects of this trip and not the distractions. Totally. Absolutely.

Walking in her direction, I shouted, "Patty! Patty, it's Franklin... Frank... wait up."

She stopped, looked back in my direction and gave me a big smile. "Frank! It's good to see you. I was afraid you had gone back to L.A. What's going on? You look great!"

"Uh, yeah, it's nice to see you again. I've been checking out some leads on the Wilmer Graves story and some pretty interesting stuff has come up. I'd like to talk to you about it, uh, when you're free." Being around her again was making me a little nervous.

"Of course! I'd love to hear what you found out, but I have to go up and see my mom, right now. You can come along if you want."

I can't say I was thrilled with the idea of hanging out with Patty and her turnip mom, but I needed to talk to her and she was TOTALLY convincing about being happy to see me—hey, life is funny... who knows? So I opted to hang with her and the boring old biscuit bag in the hospital room, at least for a little while. I mean, it was either that or go back to the motel and stare at the tube.

We got in the elevator and headed up to the room. "So how is your mom, Patty? Is she recovering from her surgery okay?" I was feeling kind of stiff and awkward.

"She's a lot better... thanks. They said she might be going home in a few days. Oh yeah, Mom is definitely getting back to her old self. You'll see. So where did you go?"

"It's kind of a long story... I can't get into it right now, but I drove over to Kansas City. I'm not sure how much you know about the Graves situation, but they think he was involved in a string of robberies... mostly convenience stores and formal wear rental places. The cops are fairly certain it was him, but the thing is Graves had an accomplice for those stickups, a young guy who drove the car, and I'm pretty sure he's the one who phoned in the tip about Graves' body. I looked him up in KC and talked to him... I'm convinced he's the guy. But that's just the start, the story gets weirder and weirder. That's what I wanted to talk to you about."

The elevator door opened and we headed toward Patty's mom's room. "Wow! It sounds like you've done some great work, Frank. I'll bet you could even become a deputy if you wanted to. I really want to hear more, but I have to go in and see Mom now."

As Patty opened the door, I entered with her and checked out the scene. It was exactly the same as when I left two days earlier. As her daughter sat in a chair beside the bed, Patty's mom meat was as lifeless as a week-old Thanksgiving turkey. Exuberant as ever, the young woman greeted her mother, "Hi, Mom! You look great! The doctors say you should be going home any day now!" A small globule of drool, caught in a crevice at the corner of Mom's mouth, broke free and ran down her chin in response. Not missing a beat, Patty grabbed a kleenex and wiped it away. The kid was devoted, no doubt about it.

"This is Frank, Mom. You remember Frank, don't you? He's the one who brought you the nice corypantha." No reaction. To say she was corpse-like would be an insult to the dead, but maybe I'm being too negative. I had despised hospital rooms since I spent several nights sleeping in a chair next to my mom after her gallbladder surgery when I was a kid. Only she never recovered. The memory of my mother laying there with tubes running in and out of every opening in her body totally terrified me. Hospitals were places where people went to die. Okay, all right, I know I had a shitty attitude. Maybe it wasn't such a good idea that I came along. Feeling guilty, I pointed a weak smile in the direction of Patty's mother, politely excused myself and went to the bathroom.

Even going to the toilet in a hospital room is depressing. As I stood there pissing, I found myself fixated on a bedpan lying on the floor. You know what a bedpan means? It means you're so fucking weak and debilitated you can't even get into the goddam bathroom. It takes all your effort to somehow maneuver your carcass over a weird bowl-shaped thing in order to piss and shit. And then the feces and urine collector takes it away, and you wait... and wait... to die. Okay... all right... I told myself I needed to lighten up, if only because of Patty. Hey—no way she lets herself get hosed by a Gloomy Gus.

As I came back into the room, Patty was telling her mom about her little brother. She talked about how well he was doing in school and how much he loved being on the basketball team and how cute his girlfriend was and all that typical kind of mother-daughter family crap. Finally after about an hour that seemed like forty-two eternities with your dick in a George Foreman grill, Patty told her mom that we had to go. Propped up in her bed, with her eyes staring into the ultimate void, the old bag looked exactly the same as the moment we entered the room. Upbeat to a fault, the cute young blonde stood up, leaned over and kissed her mom on the cheek. "I love you... I love you, Mom... with all my heart and soul." It was really kind of touching. No shit—it was.

As we headed back to the elevator, I saw her wipe a tear away. Whatever else, the kid hung in there like a trooper. I tried to make some conversation... something, anything that would get Patty's mind off her pathetic and broken-down mother. I said, "I didn't know you had a brother. He sounds like he's doing okay."

"No, not really, Frank. I just didn't want Mom to worry. Tommy Joe just got suspended from school. They caught him smoking pot on campus, the little shit. I keep telling him, 'Smoke it at home! Smoke it at a friend's house if you have to, but don't smoke it at school!' It almost seemed like he wanted to be caught. He's running with the wrong crowd, Frank. I don't know what to do."

"Gosh, I'm sorry to hear it, Patty." Hell, I didn't know what to do either. Wherever you went around here you stepped in another pile of poop. I found myself missing L.A. and the company of people who only worried about the availability of their personal trainers and whether or not their arugula was actually organic.

We finished the elevator ride in silence, then walked back out into the parking lot. I really needed Patty's help dealing with Ted Hendricks and this whole explosion weirdness. I reached over and grabbed her arm. "Patty, I have something I need to talk about. Have you got a minute?" I felt like the only way to register the proper impact and scale of this whole incident was to take her out to the site of the explosion. Nothing would make the point like standing in the center of that crater.

"Sure, yeah... go ahead. I'm sorry I got so wrapped up with my mom. I'm sure you can see how much better she is, but she still has a long way to go before she's well again. You could see she's better, right?"

"Uh, yeah, sure, a lot better... but, uh, well, here's the deal, Patty. It seems like Wilmer Graves and his accomplice were involved in some really weird shit. If I tried to explain you'd never believe it, but there's something you need to see that will spell it out in big, bold, and bone-chilling letters. Are you free now?" The sun was going down and it was getting dark. It was also starting to get cold. If we were going to head out to the crater, we had to hurry.

"Gosh, Frank, it sounds amazing, but I promised Bernie, uh, Deputy Bodie, that I would come back to and catch up on some paperwork. I've been taking so much time off to visit my mom that I've gotten kind of behind, but tomorrow's Saturday and I don't have to work. I could go with you in the morning. How about that?"

"Yeah, okay... it can wait until tomorrow. And thanks, I appreciate your support. I'll see you in the morning."

"No problem, Frank. I look forward to it." At that point she threw her arms around me and gave me a huge hug, then planted a massive wet smacker right on my lips. Okay, there was no tongue action or anything, but I got the message and it was clear as a freight train in a baby's bedroom. The words of the late great Frank Zappa echoed in my brain, "There's no way to delay that trouble comin' every day."

An hour or so later I was back at the Roadside Inn. Looking around I rethought my position on the woe-inducing nature of hospital rooms. I mean, really, compared to my motel room, complete with instant coffee, styrofoam cups, mildewed tile and a toilet flaunting a distinctly flawed flushing technique, the hospital was a fucking Shangri-La. Regardless, the nearness of Patty, the aroma of her soft and inviting femininity, the memory of her eager arms and wet lips, were all having a strong and compelling effect. At this point there was really only one thing to do—jerk off.

In previous times, the solution to a problem like this would have meant a trip to some crummy 7-11 to check out the *Hustler* and *Club* magazines while some swarthy-looking guy that barely spoke English eyeballed you suspiciously. But hey... this was modern times. We now have the INTERNET, a vast cornucopia of erotic entertainment. As any red-blooded guy knows, the latest innovation in this particular arena of joy is tube sites. Tube sites are to porn as YouTube is to NBC—an unlimited supply of teasing, titillation and toe-sucking, or whatever your twisted cravings command.

I had picked up a fifth of Jack Daniels in KC and still had a little over half of it left. After a quick visit to the ice machine, I poured myself a couple of fingers of Jack, unzipped my pants and settled down in front of my laptop. Now, one of the great things about cheap motels these days is free Internet access. Conversely, if you stay in the so-called nice joints, they fucking charge you fifteen to twenty bucks a day to log on; meanwhile every Motel 8, TraveLodge, Choice Inn, etc., is giving it to you gratis. But, while your connection may come sans fee, it is absolutely the worst Internet service imaginable. Okay, beggars and choosers and all that crap, but when it comes to carnal relief, if the poison of your choice is streaming video, a 28K connection won't cut it. But who knows, maybe I'd get lucky.

All right, to put us on firm ground here, I have to confess that my evil of interest is spanking. Okay, I know it's a little kinky and not exactly PC, but hey, depravity is depravity, you grab it where you can, if you get my drift. But sometimes I like to warm up with a little milder stuff—you know, a couple of cute teens doing the old in-and-out before settling down with the whips and heart-shaped paddles.

So I logged on to xHamster.com. Like most tube sites, it contains a fairly massive variety from ho-hum vanilla to bondage, gang-bangs and rape fantasies, but I was easing in so I played it straight. Fairly quickly, I came upon a video featuring the lovely Iona (a.k.a. Merriweather, a.k.a. Katherine, etc.). I doubt that most people are aware of the major boost Internet porn has given to the economies of eastern Europe, and the delightful Iona, with literally hundreds of videos scattered across the web, has certainly been a prime beneficiary. Fresh-faced and eager, one would never expect the pure and innocent features of Iona/Merriweather/Katherine to warp into a mask of unadulterated lust the instant a penis entered her rectum, but the babe has talent.

I clicked on the preview window and the video sprang into action. There was the angelic "teen," lying on a bed wearing a tube top, tight shorts and knee socks, smiling as she thumbed through a copy of *Teen Vogue*. No more than thirty seconds passed before her "boyfriend" entered the room, playfully grabbing her buttocks as Iona squealed with glee. Another thirty or forty-five seconds found him passionately kissing her open mouth and forcefully grabbing her breasts. In approximately two-and-a-half minutes, the young cutie was topless, zealously unzipping the guy's pants and I was experiencing a sharp stirring in my loins. Twenty seconds later, the video froze. I restarted and ten seconds later, it froze again... and again.

You don't have to know much about streaming video to understand my feeling at that point. Whenever a fuck film sucks you in, then suddenly stops, freezing the action, it's frustrating, but if your best friend is rising to the occasion, it's mean and nasty. This can happen for different reasons—the resolution of the video is too high, it's poorly compressed, the connection speed is too slow—so the thing to do is click on another one and hope for the best, which I did. The next video actually made it somewhere between five and six minutes before it stopped, just enough time to reach full erection plus a few solid strokes. The next time it was three-and-a-half minutes, then two, then five-and-a-quarter. To say I was frustrated at this point is similar to saying sharks like mammal meat.

Hey!—no surprise. The "free" Internet basically wasn't worth a shit, at least not for my current needs, but I wasn't without options, the first one being a refill of bourbon, which I hastily knocked back. Next in line was my cell phone. My Samsung Galaxy S4 was a couple of years old, so I couldn't get LTE service, not that they would have 4G coverage in Clinton, but 3G should be okay. I logged on again, this time to tube8. com, another favorite. Okay, I was going from a decent-sized laptop screen down to a fucking postage stamp, but sex primarily happens in your head anyway. I would have to work a little harder, so to speak, but I was up for it... way up.

By now my frustration level was at a point where I needed to just go ahead and get it over with, so I went for the Nacho. Nacho Vidal is this ugly, well-hung dude who absolutely drives them crazy. A babe hooked up with Nacho will be abused, humiliated and slapped around like a baby bunny with a German Shepherd. She will also come about a dozen times. Determined, I clicked on a sordid encounter between Nacho and the inappropriately named Kristina Rose. Kristina is to Iona as Mommy Dearest is to Shirley Temple. If innocence is your thing, don't bother with Kristina Rose, but if full-on debauchery, punctuated by SPANK ME! SLAP ME! PULL MY HAIR! does it for you, then Kristina is the one.

I won't go into all the sordid details, but after fifteen or twenty minutes of Nacho and Kristina on a couch, on the floor, in her ass as he choked her, spanked her, rammed his fingers down her throat, etc., etc., I finally came to a satisfying conclusion. Exhaling a massive sigh of relief, I wiped myself off, knocked down the rest of my Jack and went to bed. Tomorrow and tomorrow and tomorrow... or so said Shakey, the great.

Arriving into Terry's I met Patty for breakfast at ten the next morning. She was not only as cute as ever, but appeared to have spent the whole morning putting herself together, which seemed a little odd since our destination was a crater in the middle of the woods. We ordered our food and chatted, mainly small talk about the weather, her mom and brother, and what it was like growing up in a place like Clinton. Only twenty-three and radiating innocence, Patty dreamed of seeing the world, but my impression was more that of a young woman deeply mired in the gravity of small-town America.

After a few minutes, I noticed a guy in a state trooper's uniform staring from a table across the room. The guy's look was so intense, I quickly found myself becoming apprehensive. Finally, in a low voice, I whispered to Patty. "Don't look, but there's a state cop on the other side of the room staring at us."

Despite my caution, she glanced over at the guy's table. "Oh, him... that's just Duane. Don't pay any attention to him. Duane thinks he's my boyfriend. We hang out some, but we're just friends. I told him about you and I think he's a little jealous, but it's no big deal."

I had a feeling that life was about to become complicated. We finished our breakfast and as I walked up to the cash register, I noticed Duane pushing his chair back and slowly rising to his feet. The guy was fucking huge. He was at least 6'5" and probably went 240. Gradually ambling over in our direction, the big trooper looked like John Wayne sizing up some lily-livered cattle rustler.

Standing next to me, Patty greeted Duane with a distinct

chill in her voice. "Hi, Duane. What do you want?"

"Just thought I'd come over and say hi, Patty. Nothing wrong with that, is there?"

Not bothering to disguise her irritation, Patty sighed. "No, Duane. There's nothing wrong with that. Now go away, okay? Frank and I have some business to take care of."

"So this is the guy?" He could have been talking about a dead skunk. "This is the hotshot reporter from L... A..." Speaking deliberately, Duane added a sound somewhere between a snicker and a snort, loudly punctuating the end of his sentence.

"Duane! I told you to leave us alone. This is official business."

"Yeah, right... official business." Duane turned to me. "So I guess you'll be leaving town pronto... right, reporter dude?"

"It's Franklin, Duane. Franklin Blodgett," I said, holding out my hand. Duane scrutinized it as if eyeing a dead fish covered in moose manure. Reluctantly, the trooper enveloped my palm in his, completely crushing my feeble mitt in the process.

"DUANE..."

"Okay, okay, I gotta go to work anyway.... but I'll pick you up tonight and we can go over to Jimmy's and have a few beers. I think there's a good game on later."

"No, Duane, I'm busy tonight..."

"Busy, what do you mean..." Duane was giving me a hard stare.

"I'm sorry, Duane, but I promised Bernie I'd catch up my paperwork. We'll get together another time."

"But it's Saturday night, Patty. We always go over to Jimmy's." Duane's eyes had not left me. The malice produced by his glare could curdle armor plate.

"I'm sure Jimmy will get by without us for once. Bye, Duane." As I uneasily glanced back and forth between them, Patty stared back at her boyfriend.

Turning away, the trooper frowned, shrugged his shoulders and said, "Yeah, yeah, okay, okay," then looked back at me. Placing an enormous index finger in the center of my chest, Duane sneered, "See you around clown town, hotshot." And with that snappy retort, he left.

After I finished paying, Patty and I also left the café. Watching the state cop roar away in his patrol car, we headed toward my spiffy Sonic. After a few steps Patty remarked, "Duane's not such a bad guy, but I guess he can be kind of a bully at times."

Okay... good news... was I loving this latest development or what? "Yeah, great... he seems like a real sweetheart. I'll bet he gives away free lollipops with every citation. Maybe we should leave before Captain Cojones decides we need an official escort."

"You're funny, Frank. You know, I like you."

"Yeah, I like you too, Patty." Trouble, trouble, boil and bubble. A blind rat could see it coming and guess who was in the crosshairs? Regardless, for better or worse, my path was dead ahead. We got in the car and headed out Highway 18. At this point Patty could no longer restrain her curiosity. "So what's this all about, Frank? Where are we going?"

"Like I said before, it's pretty hard to explain, but it seems that Wilmer Graves and his accomplice, who I'm certain is a guy named Ted Hendricks, were out here just before Graves died."

"And you think this Hendricks guy is the one who tipped us on Graves' body?"

"Absolutely... the call about the body came from Hendricks' home phone, so it had to be him... but some really weird shit went down out here not long before Wilmer Graves died... really weird. I'll show you something. Here... open this glove box, Patty."

I pointed at the small compartment between the seats used to hold CDs, small electronics, whatever. Patty reached over, flipped it open and pulled out several pieces of gold-colored metal. As she picked up the scarred and twisted fragments, the young woman looked at me with a puzzled expression. "What... what is this?"

By now the scenery was racing past the windows of the car. It was cold outside and from the look of the sky, it might start snowing any minute. And since my mood perfectly matched the grim feeling of a bleak winter day, I felt a certain synchronicity between myself and the world around me. Okay, so it was probably an illusion, but what the fuck—this was it. Jump in or go home. Shit or get off the pot, dude. So I took a deep breath and plunged ahead, "Hold on, Patty, because this is where it starts to get strange. What you are holding in your hands are the partial remains of a brand new Cadillac Escalade; Wilmer Graves and Ted Hendricks were seen driving it shortly before Graves died." The young blonde's eyes widened as she stared at the shards of marred and misshapen metal in her hand. I pressed on, "From what I can tell, someone or something blew that Cadillac to holy fuck. That much I'm pretty sure of. What I can't figure out is how Graves and Hendricks survived an explosion undoubtedly designed to eliminate any trace of them and their bodily functions. BOOM! They should've been gone—but for some reason they weren't. Graves died shortly after, maybe from the shock of the explosion or maybe he was just finally worn out. Then Hendricks went back to a café near Adrian where he had left his car and drove away; he called in the tip on Graves' body when he got home."

Patty was stunned. "But... but... who would do such a thing... and why?"

"That's the million-dollar question. At this point I have no idea who did it, but when I spoke to Ted Hendricks, he was scared shitless of something... or someone. In a few minutes, I think you'll see why."

The look on Patty's face said it all. The mental wheels were turning but it was a useless process, an endless, earnest and empty yearning, leading only to a single non-conclusion: cannot compute. The young woman had just been given information so far beyond her comprehension that she had no frame of reference. Confused, Patty sat beside me staring at several oddly shaped hunks of metal previously associated with the outer shell of an expensive automobile. Whatever had transformed them from a sleek and shiny Cadillac into ugly, distorted scraps of paint and metal were outside her grasp, and understandably so. Finally, after a long pause, in a voice slightly above a whisper, Patty spoke, "I... I don't understand."

For the next fifteen or twenty minutes, we sat in silence. Nothing was going to prepare Patty for the scene she was about to see, but at least the drive gave our conversation a little time to sink in. It had begun to snow, lightly at first, but the heaviness of the gathering clouds promised considerably more. Getting out of the car at the site of the explosion would be pure misery. After a long period of reflection, Patty finally broke the silence, "So, you must be taking me to the place where this explosion happened... is that right?" She sounded a little apprehensive, but the kid was smart. She was putting it together.

"Yeah... this whole thing is so wacky, I figured a trip to the bomb site was about the only way for you to get the full impact. We'll be there in a few minutes."

Five minutes later we reached the turnoff leading back into the wooded area sheltering the bomb crater from the rest of the world. As we turned, the snowfall had increased, but more striking was the wind, propelling the flakes in a trajectory almost parallel to the ground. I pulled the Sonic up to the edge of the crater and stopped.

Wide-eyed, Patty sat and stared. Reluctantly, I encouraged

her to leave the car and feel the full effect of what had happened here. "Let's get out, Patty. It looks totally miserable out there, but you need to walk around in that crater. It's really the only way to get a sense of this whole crazy deal."

Immediately assaulted by the wind, we struggled to maintain our footing as we left the car. It had to be blowing thirty to forty miles an hour, slowly rising as the temperature had gradually dipped into the twenties. Why people lived in hellholes like this when God had created Malibu was beyond me.

The snow was starting to fill the small crevices distinguishing the landscape of the crater, but the feeling of devastation was unchanged. As we battled the wind, walking around the barren terrain, Patty's eyes were wide with wonder and confusion. A couple of times she stopped and bent over, picking up a door handle at one spot and what appeared to be a piece of a hubcap in another. Finally, after four or five minutes, she turned and walked toward me, holding out the car fragments for my inspection. "So this was a car? A huge SUV... and it was just sitting in the middle of this crater... and somebody blew it up?"

"Well, technically, there was no crater until the explosion, but, yeah, you're getting the picture."

"But why, Frank... why? It doesn't make any sense. There's nothing around here."

"I don't know, Patty. I haven't figured that part out yet... but I'm freezing my butt off out here. Let's get back in the car."

I had left the engine running with the heater on, so it was nice and toasty in the car. As we sat there with the snow still swirling around us, Patty spoke, her voice tight with urgency. "We have to do something, Frank. We have to tell Bernie or the sheriff... we have to get somebody out here!"

"I know, Patty. That's one of the reasons I had to show this to you. Look... there's obviously a big story here... it's easily the biggest thing I've ever been involved in. But I have a confession to make... I don't have any connection to the *L.A. Times*. I just said that to try and get information on Graves. Your pal Bernie sniffed me out like a month-old rat corpse. I figure if I go back to her, she'll just blow me off, but she'll pay attention to you. But you also mentioned the sheriff... maybe we should go to him... I don't know. What do you think?"

"It's Sheriff Fitch... but he's old and doesn't do anything but play cards... or dominos. He'll just tell Bernie to deal with it. She runs everything around there, so we might as well just deal with her directly."

"Yeah, okay, I guess that's more or less what I expected." I put the car in gear, turned around and headed back to Clinton.

"So why did you lie to Bernie, Frank? I know she likes to act tough, but she's okay. It's just a coverup. She's really kind of shy."

Yeah, they say rattlesnakes are shy, too. "It's kind of hard to explain."

"Try me, Frank. I like you, but this is kind of freaking me out. What are you up to... and if the newspaper didn't send you, why did you come all the way out here from L.A.?"

"Okay... okay... Here's the deal. I'm really not a bad guy, but I'm... well, I'm kind of at a weird point in my life. It's true, I'm not with the *L.A. Times*, but I am a writer... and... and I just broke up with my wife... Louise... and I needed something to do beside sit around my stupid apartment... and drink bourbon... and watch TV... and... and..." My voice drifted away. Maybe I said too much. I mean here I was in fucking southern Missouri spilling out my guts to a twenty-three-year-old kid I didn't even know a week ago. Was this crazy or what?

Patty's eyes were brimming with concern. "I understand,

Frank... sort of... you mean you got on a plane and came all the way to Clinton because you were lonely?"

"Well, yeah, I guess. I saw this piece on the news about Wilmer Graves and all of a sudden, it just hit me... there's a story here... and I needed a story... well, I needed something."

"Okay, I guess that makes sense... in a weird way. So what's next?"

"Well, we have to tell people... Bernie... the sheriff... whoever. And that means I have to give up the Hendricks kid... and I feel kind of bad about that. I have no idea how he got involved in all this and he seems like a nice enough guy, but the bottom line is that somebody blew up that SUV and I don't think it was Ted Hendricks. And anybody crazy enough to totally waste a brand new car, a car that right before it blew up had two people in it, is dangerous... more than dangerous... lethal... deadly... who knows what he might do?"

"Yeah... yeah... of course... you're right."

Lost in thought, we sat in silence for several more minutes until Patty finally spoke, "Look, why don't you take me back to my car? I'll go see if I can find Bernie. She usually works on Saturday, so she's probably around the office. I'll tell her about this and see what she says, but she'll probably want to talk to you. How does that sound?"

It sounded like a gift from the gods. There was no way around it... I figured I'd have to deal with Deputy Dawg again, but if Patty was willing to break the news, it was not a problem. "Sure, Patty, that sounds great. Thanks, I appreciate it."

"I have to go and see Mom after that, but I thought maybe I could cook dinner for you after I leave the hospital... if you want to."

I wondered if I heard right. "What? I thought you told Duane you had to do more paperwork tonight."

"Oh, I can see Duane anytime. I just said that to get rid of him. He'll go over to Jimmy's and drink beer and watch the game and forget all about me. I wanted to spend some time with you, Frank. Can you come over around six—here's the address." Flashing a sweet smile, she handed me a scrap of paper.

Life was suddenly moving much too fast. "Oh... yeah, cool... uh, me too." My head was spinning as Patty kissed me on the cheek. After dropping her off at her car, I hurried back to my motel looking for my friend, Black Jack. I needed a drink.

A few hours later I got in the Sonic and headed over to Patty's. I hadn't had a lot to drink, but I did have a couple of shots killing time before dinner. For some reason the idea of spending the evening with this young woman I barely knew was making me nervous, which was, like, mondo dumbo. Patty was a cute kid and I got the feeling she had a crush on me, but jeez, I was practically old enough to be her father, something she had pointed out right after we met. I figured maybe a little wine with dinner might calm me down, so I stopped at a liquor store and picked up a bottle of Chardonnay. I normally prefer reds, but the chicks usually go for white so it seemed like a safe bet.

Patty had given me directions with the address, so finding the house was easy. It was a little after six, dark and freezing cold when I pulled up and parked at the curb in front. I knew she still lived with her mom, so I wasn't surprised to find a fairly modest, wood-framed house in the middle of a working-class neighborhood. Kicking the snow off my boots as I stepped onto the porch, I reminded myself not to move to Missouri anytime soon.

Twenty seconds after I rang the bell, Patty opened the door. Wow! She looked great, relaxed and casual on one hand, but totally done up at the same time. It may have been cold as hell outside, but the petite blonde was wearing this tiny little top that stopped about three inches above her jeans, exposing her lower abdomen and navel in a way that made my hand yearn for the touch of a soft seductive belly. With no hesitation, Patty threw her arms around my neck and gave me a huge, wet kiss. The windmills of my mind began to move.

"Patty… hey, you look great!… just great!" Drowning in a sea of potent femininity, I took three or four wobbly steps into the house, stopped and looked around. The living room was a total homage to Patty and her younger brother, Tommy Joe. There were photos of Patty playing piano, Patty as a baton twirler, Patty with her Girl Scout troop, etc., accompanied by similar images of Tommy Joe on various sports teams, holding a huge fish, with a girlfriend at the prom and many more. Virtually every inch of shelving, wall space, tabletops and other surfaces were filled with photos of the two siblings covering every age from birth to the present.

"Wow! This room is pretty crazy… it looks like your mom practically worships you guys."

"Yeah, Mom is pretty devoted to us. Being a mother is really about the only thing she ever cared about." Patty took my coat and directed me toward the kitchen. "Would you like something to drink, Frank… coffee… tea… Diet Coke?"

"No, I'm good, but I did bring a bottle of wine for dinner. We could have some of that."

My host returned to the range where she was finishing our dinner. "No thanks, I don't drink alcohol, but it's okay if you have some. Do you want a glass?"

"Sure, great…" She reached in a cabinet, pulled out a

large Mason jar, handed it to me then returned to the stove. After eyeing the jar cautiously, I asked, "Uh, do you have a... corkscrew?"

Patty shook her head sheepishly. "No... sorry."

"Hmmm..." For a moment I looked back and forth between the jar and wine bottle. This was a problem. Setting the jar aside, I stared at the bottle for a moment, then tried again. "How about a knife?"

Patty reached her hand into a drawer and pulled out a large carving knife. "Is this okay?"

"Um... sure... thanks." Silly me, I had forgotten that I was in Buttfuck, Missouri. I graciously accepted the knife, then spent the next ten minutes chipping the cork out of the neck of the bottle, as Patty completed our dinner and moved it onto the kitchen table. Finally, after successfully conquering the cork, I poured two or three inches of wine into the bottom of the Mason jar and relocated to the table. As I sat down, I was surprised to see there were three place settings. "Is someone joining us?"

"Oh, I forgot... you didn't know Tommy Joe is here. He's up in his room. I'll call him down for dinner."

As Patty left the room, my fantasies of a steamy romantic evening were beginning to fade. Puzzled, I turned my attention to the table. Patty, sweet as she was, did not appear to be a mistress of culinary delights. The meal consisted of boiled sausages, canned string beans and tater tots. Oh yeah, there was also a green salad accompanied by a bottle of Wish-Bone dressing. I emptied my wine glass and poured some more.

A few moments later the room was invaded by the thundering hooves of Tommy Joe, closely followed by his sister. "Tommy, this is Frank." The teenager threw his leg over the back of a chair, plopped into the seat and grabbed the plate of sausages without ever looking up. Two of the boiled meat tubes were on his plate and half-eaten almost as quickly.

"Tommy Joe! I just introduced you to Frank!"

"Yeah... where's the mustard?"

"TOMMY! Where are your manners! Frank is our guest!"

At this point, less than eager to test Tommy Joe's conversational acumen, I joined in, "It's okay... it's not a problem..."

"IT IS A PROBLEM!" Patty was pissed. "He has to learn how to be a civilized human being! Tommy, shake hands with Frank!"

Realizing that he was hungry and his sister was not about to back down, Tommy Joe rolled his eye and shoved a limp fist in my direction. "Yeah... hi... so this is the dweeb you've been talking about?"

"Tommy..."

"Yeah, yeah... so you're from L.A.? Big deal..."

"I live in West Hollywood, Tommy. It's a nice part..."

"West Hollywood? Isn't that where all the fags live? You hang out with a bunch of queers?"

"Well, I do have some gay, lesbian and transgender friends, if that's what you mean."

"Yeah, right." Focusing his attention back on his plate, Tommy Joe shook his head in disbelief. It then took him about ninety seconds to devour the rest of his sausages, two servings of green beans and about twenty tater tots. "Thanks for the grub, Patty. I'm out of here... don't wait up..."

The teenager's sister stood and protested, "But wait... where are you going?" but it was too late. Like a starving wolf in search of suckling piglets, the kid had vanished into the night leaving me and Patty looking across the table at each other.

As we finished our meal, my dinner companion told me about her conversation with Bernie earlier this afternoon. Needless to say, with the story originating from me, Deputy Dawg was fairly skeptical, but Patty showed her the fragments of the Cadillac she had collected and urged the deputy to at least drive out and confirm the existence of the bomb crater. After a brief discussion, the deputy agreed to let Patty show her the site of the explosion Monday morning. If there was anything to it, which she doubted, Bernie would want to question me that afternoon. I nodded, thanked Patty, then, with our "business" taken care of, we moved into the living room.

Demure, my young hostess asked if I would light the fireplace so, rising to the call of manly virtue, I said sure. How hard can it be, I thought... Seeing a box of matches on the mantel, I took one out, struck it, held it under a log... and it went out. Undaunted, I struck another, and another, and another... bewildered, I looked over at Patty, barely concealing a giggle. Finally after another minute or so, she took pity, grabbed some newspaper and kindling and lit the fire. We laughed and sat side by side on the couch. The TV was on, showing an old *CSI* rerun or some boring crap, but neither of us was watching; except for the twin flickerings of tube and tinder, the room was dark. The wine bottle was more than half empty as I poured more Chardonnay into my Mason jar, took a couple of sips, then turned to look at Patty. Returning my gaze, her eyes glazed over as her mouth, surrounded by moist and inviting lips, glistened in the firelight.

Pausing to place the jar on the floor, I turned back, immediately kissing Patty full on the mouth. Without hesitation, her tongue found mine and they danced back and forth, igniting the unspoken passion flowing back and forth between us all evening. I slipped my hand under her top and grabbed a breast, eliciting a clearly audible moan as the eager young woman reached her arms around my neck, pulling me closer. Consumed by passion, we slid over, laying side by side on the couch, eagerly kissing, groping and undressing each other. I pulled her tube top down, exposing her breasts to my tongue. With Patty's moans growing louder, she tangled her fingers into my hair, jamming my face against her breasts. Grabbing her crotch, I rubbed my hand against the fabric of her tight jeans, unbuttoned her pants, and pulled them down to her knees, causing both of us to tumble off the couch and onto the carpeted floor.

If anything, the pace of our lovemaking only accelerated as we rolled across the floor ending passionately entwined before the fireplace. Our mouths locked together once more, tongues darting in and out like two snakes in a slavish and savage embrace. Reaching my hand down into her panties, I felt the wetness between her legs, immediately causing Patty to arch her back, pushing her pelvis hard against my hand. Suddenly her fingers were holding my dick, stroking it back and forth causing me to match her moans, the two of us filling the empty air with the feverish music of lust.

Slipping my pants down to my knees, I rolled Patty onto her back, easing my torso between her legs as they locked around my back. Rubbing my hard cock against her panties, I felt her wetness through the thin fabric. After two or three strokes I paused, preparing for the final assault, causing Patty to look up at me, her eyes pleading. "I love you, Frank, I love you..." she moaned. "Do you love me? Do you?"

Startled, the sudden sound of words, questions, vocal assertions, thrust into the midst of our debauched and animal lovemaking, caused me to hesitate... to consider... to take assessment... and just as suddenly I was impaled by the unassailable fact that I didn't love her... that I was wholly propelled by lust to fuck a nice kid who looked like she could be my baby sister... okay, I didn't HAVE a baby sister, but the young woman beneath me was pristine, perfect and pure, an ideal of innocence before it's twisted by lust, distorted by desire, warped by the ravaging fire that only consumes and never fulfills. How could I fuck it?

What was I thinking, I asked myself. It's only sex, but somehow, I found myself outside it, no longer engaged in the act, no longer hurtling ahead, no longer squeezing, pushing and licking as if the fate of the world depended on the sudden and violent discharge of my no longer mighty member.

"What's wrong, Frank?"

The next morning I woke up on the couch, alone. I found a note from Patty on the kitchen table, explaining that she had left for church and would be back a little before noon. I was welcome to whatever I could find to eat.

The previous night, laying nearly naked in each other's arms, I made a pitiful attempt to explain my lack of... what?... staying power? But no matter how much a guy professes exhaustion, alcohol excess or the reality of random dysfunction, there's never an adequate explanation for the failure of one's manly hard... uh, software.

I got up, dressed and was about to check out the kitchen when in galloped Patty's brother, Tommy Joe, apparently having been out all night doing whatever teenagers do. The kid was surprised to see me. "Hey, whoa... what have we got here? Looks like the L.A. dude stayed over... how was it, stud? My sis is a pretty cute trick, huh!"

"Uh, look, Tommy... uh, it wasn't exactly like that..."

"Wasn't exactly like what, cousin? Wasn't exactly like a hot piece of ass... what's the matter... disappointed my big sis ain't like all those hot L.A. babes?

"No... no.. you see..."

"Yeah, I see. Wait 'til old Duane hears about this! WOO HOO! I wouldn't trade places with you for a million buckaroonies... he'll turn you into Silly Putty, dude, then eat your eyeballs out of spite... something to look forward to, huh?"

"You don't understand, Tommy Joe..." But it was too late. The kid had already headed up the stairs three steps at a time, slamming his bedroom door behind him a split second later.

Great... not only did I have a dysfunctional dick, but Patty's brother was going to tell her mad moose boyfriend that I screwed his sister. Talk about lose-lose... if I was going to get my ass kicked, at least I could've gotten some action for it... and it wasn't even 10 a.m. yet. Talk about a shitty way to start your day...

At that point, I figured I'd better move on. I wanted to make it right with Patty, but didn't exactly know what to say... and who knows, the moose might show up any minute. It was time to head for safer ground.

And when you're stuck in Clinton, Missouri, what could possibly be more benign than Terry's Café? By now Terry's was practically my second home... Jesus, did I really say that?... but sure as shit, after walking into the small café and basking in the bouquet of bacon, eggs and hot buttered toast—the awesome aroma of grease—a warm feeling welled up inside of me... okay, maybe it was just hunger, I often get those mixed up, but Terry's suddenly seemed like THE place to be. Of course, before entering I scanned the street for

Duane's Moosemobile, but it was a quiet Sunday morning. The place seemed safe enough.

I ordered my breakfast then sat sipping a cup of coffee, reflecting on the strange events of the last several days. It had been almost two weeks since I first learned about the sad, abandoned body of Wilmer Graves, and during that time I had gone from a casual observer to alarmingly close to... something... something not only incomprehensible, but teeming with twisted implications. And if that wasn't enough, I had gotten myself involved with a young woman who was far too nice, far too naïve and, for some reason, far too interested in me... and worst of all, I COULDN'T EVEN DO IT! Oh shit, I know all the rationalizations and maybe some of them were even true, but nothing makes a guy feel worse than a droopy dick... a poopy pecker... an irrelevant rod... and I couldn't stop thinking about it! It's always the same. You can rip off ten, twenty, screaming, scratching, eyeballs-rolled-back-forever FUCK ME! FUCK ME!s in a row, then it's one wilted willy and... OH-MY-GOD-WHAT'S-HAP-PENED-WILL-IT-EVER-WORK-AGAIN!!!... and it nags the shit out of you until it does. Doubt... failure... feeble... useless... pathetic... lame... all swarming around your brain like bees abusing a legless lamb. I mean, usually when this shit happens, you have a girlfriend or a wife or somebody you're doing on a regular basis, so it's like falling off a horse, hopefully a cute horse, and you just jump back on and everything is okay again, but if you're not with someone... if you're all alone in Armpit, Missouri, and the only bonkable babe is a sweet young thing who works for the sheriff and also happens to have the Hulk for a boyfriend... well, it's not quite as easy as *let's get it on.*

My breakfast had long since arrived but somehow faded into irrelevance. I picked at my food, my mind wracked with doubt, until, with half a plate of cold scrambled eggs, hash browns and bacon staring at me, I gave up and headed toward the cash register. After paying my bill and counting the change, I looked up—WHAT THE FUCK!... a large black-and-white cruiser pulled up in front of the café. Great! After ducking out the back door, I hastily retreated to the safety of my motel room.

After leaving Terry's I found a convenience store where I could buy a fresh fifth of Jack and then proceeded to down most of it that afternoon and evening watching football. A worthless exercise in squandered time to be sure, but I was tired of thinking, tired of being horny and most of all, tired of feeling lonely and, in that regard, the Jack did its job; but television is a lazy diversion, leading to lethargy, despondence and passing out with an almost empty bottle of booze on your chest.

A little later I was awakened by a loud and insistent knock on the door. Barely conscious, I staggered across the room, leaned against the wall and said, "Who... who's... there?"

"It's Patty, Frank. Let me in."

Patty? Patty? The name was familiar but I was having a problem pinning it on a person. "Patty? Patty? Where... where do I know you from... Patty?"

"Frank! Stop joking around! I want to talk to you." The voice was familiar, but still... I couldn't quite place it. "Frank, c'mon... it's cold out here!"

"Okay... okay..." I reached over, unlocked the door and opened it wide enough to peek out. "Oh... Patty, of course... I remember you... come in... come in." I tripped and nearly fell over backwards making room for the overly animated young woman to enter the small motel room.

"Frank... what's wrong with you? What... you... you're drunk! You're drunk, Frank! I was worried and came to see what happened to you... and you're drunk!"

"No... I'm not really... drunk... I just had a few..."

"A few! I see the bottle on your bed... What's wrong with you? Why did you just disappear? We had a nice evening together... I thought we had something going, Frank, and okay, maybe the sex stuff didn't work out, but we can fix that... but you... all you can do is hide out in a motel and get drunk? Is that the best you can do, Frank?" I stared at the floor, then slumped back onto the bed... numb and brainless, I could only think of how remarkably few hiding places the small motel room offered. "Answer me, Frank! Is this the best you can do!"

Briefly looking at Patty for the first time, I saw anger mixed with disappointment... somehow without even trying, I had failed again. "I... I'm sorry, Patty. I didn't mean..."

"You should be sorry, Frank! You should be sorry... I made a nice dinner for you... we were having a great time... and just because you lost your erection... is that what this is all about, Frank? Because if it is..."

"No... Patty... no... well, maybe, just a little... you see..."

"I see... I do see, Frank. I see a man who just broke up with his wife and he's lonely... and wants to connect with someone, but he doesn't exactly know how... is that right, Frank?

"Well, I don't know..." Staring at the bedspread, I noticed how the little rows of tufted cotton balls undulated across its surface like miniature hills and valleys. There was something almost soothing about the regularity of...

"Look at me, Frank... look at me... be real."

In a stupor, my gaze moved from the bedspread to Patty's eyes which were somehow hard and soft at the same time.

And as I looked, we connected, as if the opposite poles of electromagnets were suddenly charged, compelling and driving us together, fueled by forces of friction, desperation and lust.

It was over in a matter of minutes... maybe seconds. The frenzied ripping away of clothing, at least enough to bare the essential parts, was awkward and crude but ultimately efficient. Somehow, even in my feeble and wasted state, I was able to get it up... up enough at least, and in... and three or four strokes later, it was over. And that was it... my tolerance and capacity for dealing with a world far beyond my control was shriveled, shattered and shot... at least for today.

Patty woke me up at 6:15 the next morning. She had to be at work at 7:00 and wanted to brief me on the day's activities before leaving to grab a quick breakfast at Terry's. Toweling herself dry after getting out of the shower, she said, "Did you hear me, Frank? Did you?"

To begin with, the words "morning" and "person" are never uttered in conjunction with Franklin Blodgett, but today was special. A spongy mixture of mush and mud on the best of mornings, my brain was totally paralyzed by throbbing pain, courtesy of yesterday's Black Jack. I replied... weakly, "Huh... whassat..."

"C'mon, Frank... now listen. I'll be taking Bernie out to the bomb crater around 9:00 or 9:30 and I'm almost certain she'll want to see you after that, so you should come to the office around noon. We'll be back by then... got it?"

"Huh... yeah... office... noon... I got it."

"And Frank..."

"Huh?"

"Underneath it all, you're an okay guy. I like you a lot." And with that she threw her arms around my neck, gave me a huge smacker on the mouth and bolted out the door.

"Yeah... I, uh, like you too... uh..." As my voice trailed off, my newly authenticated lover abruptly disappeared. Stumbling over to the window, I barely made out the outline of Patty's Jeep speeding away, but the sun beaming through the curtains hit me like a hammer in the hands of King Kong. Unable to face the day, I wobbled back toward the bed and collapsed, instantly disappearing into a deep sleep.

Two hours later, consciousness creeped back toward the neighborhood of my brain, which was clearly not a good thing. Lurching into the bathroom, I took four ibuprofens, drank a huge glass of water and stumbled into the shower. Laying in the tub, I felt the water washing over and around me like a warm summer rain... in hell. The pain pounded against the back of my eyeballs like an eager invasion of rats, gleefully jabbing away with tiny icepicks.

But as I laid there, the pain slowly ebbed away. And as the throbbing diminished and the mental haze began to clear, my cognitive power slowly returned. So I fucked Patty last night... or she fucked me... or something like that. This was not going to make things better.

Finally, after nearly an hour in the shower, I decided to brave the outside world. Breakfast at Terry's was out. Duane was obviously a regular at the local diner and, having more or less hosed his girlfriend last night, crossing the big guy's path was a no-show on my priority list.

My head still slightly pounding, I hopped in the Sonic and took off. A quick cruise around Clinton revealed Dave's Donuts and suddenly the thought of sugar and fat, washed down with a quart of coffee, seemed like a great idea. If everything worked out as planned, I still had to meet with Deputy Dawg and clearly needed to be semi-coherent.

Desperately seeking refuge, I peeked inside. The place was not only still and quiet, but the sound of classical music softly filtered through the room, reinforcing the feeling of calm. Round and serene, the guy behind the counter, apparently Dave, looked a little like Buddha wearing a white apron. The place was perfect. As I walked in, he was just setting a tray of fresh goodies in the display case. It looked like I had made a good decision.

"Two glazed, one jelly and one chocolate... oh yeah, and a gigantic coffee... thanks, Dave."

"...not Dave... Dave's a stupid prick... here... three bucks... pay now." Thrusting the coffee and confections in my general direction, not-Dave seriously contradicted my worldview. Oh well, he was still round... fat, actually... surly and fat. Not anxious for interaction, I quietly slunk to a table across the room. Determined to jump-start the job of rejuvenation, I kept my head down as the chubby cook rattled dishes, pots and pans in the sink... loudly.

Suddenly, three teenagers came bursting into the room carrying a huge boom box, which, unless I was mistaken, was blaring out the music of Vanilla Ice. VANILLA ICE? Man, the neighborhood was going down fast. I mean, okay, I'm not a huge fan of rap, or hip-hop or whatever, but white guys doing it? No way! And this shit was uncool twenty years ago. At least they could be disturbing my morning with something that's uncool now, like Keisha or Justin Bieber. The kids, white of course, were wearing typical "gangsta" drag: coats about three sizes too big, low-slung pants, black knit caps and sunglasses.

At this point, breaking through the cacophony, came the piercing voice of not-Dave. "Look, I told you kids a million times, Dave won't stand for no music but operas and stuff in here, so turn it off! I don't care, but Dave says it gives the place class, so stop! Okay? You want me to lose my job?" Not-Dave was not happy. Anxiety tightened the skin across his face like a paunchy pink balloon about to burst.

Typically, the teenagers responded by turning up the music even louder, then joining in on the chorus of the song. With all three of them dancing around the room chanting "ice, ice, baby," tension was on the rise. It was a curious scene and one I could have enjoyed, but my hangover was still hanging on so I played it cool, sipping my coffee and eating a little faster.

Meanwhile, not-Dave, his face scarlet and neck tendons erect, was seriously stressed. "Stop it… stop it, you hear!" Unimpressed, the teenagers rocked on, hi-fiving each other in total abandon. At this point, the fat guy appeared to be on the verge of losing it. Wildly waving his arms, he screamed, "OKAY, THAT'S IT! NO JELLY DONUTS! YOU HEAR ME! NO JELLY DONUTS!"

Laughing hysterically, but not missing a beat, the three teenagers instantly morphed their chant of "ice, ice, baby" into "No jelly donuts!" Gleefully gyrating around the room, their voices rising as the tension grew, the kids simply ignored the bulging and irate cook. Surreal and absurd, their rallying cry of "No jelly donuts! No jelly donuts!" crackled through the small space, as the donut guy's impotent rage vainly attempted to match the teenagers' youthful bravado.

Then, to my surprise, I recognized one of the kids as Tommy Joe, Patty's brother. Slinking down behind my vat of coffee, I hoped he wouldn't notice me across the room and it worked, but not for long. Coffee or no coffee, I couldn't take much more and was about to make a move for the door, when the donut guy suddenly pulled a gun out from behind the counter. "OKAY!" he screamed, "I WARNED YOU! I WARNED YOU!" Taking aim at the biggest kid, the cook was about to squeeze the trigger, when Tommy Joe lunged, grabbing his arm and causing the shot to go wild as the bullet shattered the front window of the donut shop.

As I ducked under the table, I watched Tommy Joe wrestle the revolver away from the fat guy, then, with the terrified cook cowering on the floor, Patty's brother pointed the gun right at the man's head. Jumping up, I screamed, "NO, TOMMY JOE, NO!" Hearing his name, the teenager abruptly looked in my direction, resulting in instant recognition. With the spell of anger and rage broken, the kid stared at the pistol with a puzzled expression, then threw it at the floor, causing the weapon to discharge. Grabbing his head, the wounded cook's scream was chilling as he lurched forward, passing out on the floor. With a pool of blood slowly gathering around the donut guy's skull, the teenagers vanished like lizards in the tall grass.

After calling 911, I did what I could to care for the unconscious cook. Finding a couple of towels behind the counter, I wiped the blood away and tried to make the guy comfortable, not that he could tell. While the injury didn't appear to be life-threatening, the cook's left ear was pretty much nonexistent, the bullet having ripped it off before bouncing off his skull and embedding itself into the ceiling. The head wound, gruesome as it was, created a mess in terms of blood loss, but it could've been way worse.

Waiting for the ambulance, I sat on the floor with the injured man's head in my lap. I was positive that one of the kids, the one who grappled for the gun with the donut guy, was Tommy Joe, but the way the teenagers were dressed, I couldn't swear to a positive ID. Plus, it was Patty's brother; I really didn't want to rat the kid out, especially since it was an accident. Man, this Missouri shit was just one mess after another.

Ten or twelve minutes later, the ambulance arrived, closely followed by a pickup equipped with a siren and a flashing light. A couple of guys wheeling a gurney immediately entered the shop, followed by the one and only Deputy Dawg.

"Well, well, what have we got here? It's my major man, Scoop—the Ace Reporter... on the scene again. You get around, don't you, Slick? But ol' Billy here ain't lookin' so good... givin' him a head massage or what? Speak up, son, I can't hear you."

Well, she certainly hadn't lost any charm. As the two emergency guys lifted not-Dave, or ol' Billy according to the cop, up onto the gurney and checked his life signs, I rose to my feet, took a deep breath and spoke, "Look, Deputy Bodie, I just came in to get some coffee and donuts... that's all."

"Coffee and donuts, huh? And then what happened? Did tough ol' Billy pick a fight with you... I don't see nobody else around. Or did he catch you with a hand in the cash box?"

I didn't care for the tone of her questions. "I'm not exactly sure what you're getting at, Deputy, but I was just sitting here minding my own business when three teenagers came in, blasting rap music out of a boom box. Ol' Billy, as you call him, took offense and it accelerated from there. Just ask Billy... he'll tell you."

The deputy slowly looked over at the donut man whose eyes were open, staring blankly at nothing, a major amount of drool quickly collecting at the side of his appallingly open mouth. "Well, as soon as ol' Billy stops catchin' flies, he might agree with you, but until then, you're the only suspect, er, witness, I got, Scoop, so tell me some more. Are you sayin' these teenagers shot Billy? Were they tryin' to stick up the shop?"

As the two guys wheeled the cook outside and into the ambulance, I walked back to my table. With her hand on her holster, the short cop's eagle eye never left me, but I was determined to finish my coffee—even if it was cold. Picking up the cup, I took a sip. attempting to explain, "No, it was nothing like that, officer. The whole thing was an accident... Billy tried to stop them and they started making fun of him. He escalated the whole thing by pulling that gun." I pointed at the donut guy's revolver still laying on the floor.

The peace officer approached the pistol, then bent over, inserted a pen in the barrel and picked it. With an eternity of *CSI* episodes under her belt, the delight inherent in this gesture was obvious. Holding the gun out in front of her, the deputy spoke with deliberation, "Yep... looks like Billy's gun all right. So you say they shot him with his own weapon?"

"No, no... he pulled the gun, then struggled with one of them. The kid took the pistol from Billy, then threw it away. It went off when it hit the floor. Like I said, the whole thing was an accident."

"And what did these kids look like? I assume you could identify them if you saw them again?"

Now it was starting to get tricky. Up to this point, I hadn't lied... yet. I took another deep breath and tried to look calm. "Well, they looked pretty typical, if you know what I mean. You know... dressed like kids from the 'hood... oversized coats and pants, black cap pulled down and sunglasses... it could be hard to ID them for sure." Staring at my cup of coffee as I spoke, I couldn't tell if she was buying it or not.

"Uh-huh... I see... kids all look alike these days... right?"

Looking up from the cup, my eyes rose to meet Deputy Bodie's. "Well... not exactly, but sort of." I had the feeling she was going for it.

The peace officer paused for a moment, as if pondering our last exchange, then spoke, "Okay, Scoop, that's enough for now. Let's go down to the office."

"What... are you arresting me?"

"Frank, if I wanted you in custody, you'd be lying on the floor, hands cuffed behind your back right now... get it?"

Surprised that she actually knew my name, I took a moment to check Officer Bodie out. She was about four-and-a-half feet tall with a strong resemblance to a bowling ball, short but solid enough that I had no desire to challenge her. "No problem, officer. Do you want me to follow you there?"

"No, I'll follow you... and take your time, Slick... take your time."

A short time later, I pulled up in front of the sheriff's office with Deputy Bodie right behind me. I figured Patty would be inside, and wondered how to react. Should we be formal with each other... casual?... warm?... or what? Our "relationship," such as it was, was anything but out in the open, which was fine for me; but more than that, I was uncertain about the donut shop thing and Tommy Joe. Apprehensive, I opened the door and went in.

Patty was surprised to see us. "Frank... Bernie? How did you guys get together?"

The deputy responded, "There was a shooting over at Dave's Donuts... not exactly sure what happened, but your friend here seems to be implicated, although he says he was just a witness. Of course, nobody but Billy was around... and he was unconscious when I got there." She eyed me suspiciously. *Implicated?*... I didn't like the tone of this. I was just getting over yesterday's hangover and already felt like I needed another drink.

Patty was stunned. She looked at me. "Frank... you were involved in a shooting? what... what happened?"

Rolling her eyes, the deputy nodded at me and said, "You tell her, Scoop... it's your story."

I repeated the incident to Patty, omitting the part about

her brother, but she wasn't letting go easily. "That sounds like it could be some of Tommy's friends... you... you don't think he was one of them, do you?"

Both women were staring straight at me, waiting for a response. "Uh, no, I don't think so... I mean, you know, they had these caps on and sunglasses and all... and it happened really fast."

Deputy Dawg jumped on it. "You mean you think one of them could've been Tommy Joe... is that what you're saying?"

I stared out the window. "Well... no... not exactly." Uncomfortable, I tried to buy some time. Turning to Patty, I asked, "Do you have any coffee... I could really use a cup of coffee right now."

Smelling fear, the little deputy was not letting up. "Well, what do you mean... exactly?"

Patty handed me a cup of coffee and I quickly took a gulp. It felt like boiling fucking lava gleefully melting my tongue. Closing my eyes against the pain, I swallowed hard and gasped, "Shit! Fuck!," as it burned its way down my throat. My head was spinning.

"Are you all right, Frank? Do you want to sit down?"

I slumped into a chair and took a moment to compose myself. "Sorry... sorry... I didn't expect it to be so hot."

Still suspicious, the deputy grabbed a chair and pulled it over. Sitting beside me, her short little legs dangling back and forth, Deputy Dawg was ready to crank up the old third degree, but Patty got me off the hook. "It's okay, Bernie, I'll talk to Tommy Joe about it. I'll get a straight answer out of him."

The deputy hopped down and walked across the room. "Okay, but I get the feelin' Ace ain't comin' completely clean on this deal. Billy was unconscious when they took him to the emergency room. I'll go down there after lunch and get a statement." Shuffling papers on her desk, the short cop was obviously annoyed.

Patty changed the subject. "So did you guys talk about the bomb crater at all?"

The deputy snorted in disgust. "Bomb crater... bomb crater? HA! Patty showed me your big mystery this morning. You got a lot of imagination there, Scoop."

"Huh?" Okay, I can appreciate a good skeptic, but c'mon, it was right in front of her. I was getting pissed. "So what did you think it was, Deputy Da... er, Bodie? An excavation for a kiddie swimming pool... an alien landing site?"

"Well, you got me there, Frank... it's true, I don't know what that thing is. And yeah, something happened out there. I can see that, but who knows what it was... maybe some farmer's digging a watering pond for his cattle... or somebody's prepping the land for biofuel crops... or maybe it was more 'teenagers' playing around with fireworks."

"Biofuel! Fireworks! Are you nuts?" I shook my head, then looked at Patty who just shrugged her shoulders and prompted me to go on. Deputy Dawg was proving a tough nut to crack. Taking a deep breath, I calmed down and continued, "Okay, look... I haven't been exactly wasting my time here for the past week and, hey... I'm sorry about the whole *L.A. Times* thing. I have written a couple of articles for them, but that's all. I only said that to get some information. I was convinced that there's a story here... and there is!"

At that point I spent the next fifteen minutes laying it all out: Wilmer Graves' crime spree, Hazel, the waitress in the café near Adrian, Graves and Hendricks driving away in the Cadillac, the farmer and his pig, Ted Hendricks' total meltdown when I confronted him with Graves' death and finally, the bomb crater, complete with scraps of a vaporized Cadillac Escalade.

"I mean, c'mon, Bernie... something weird happened off Highway 18 and, okay, I may not have it all figured out yet, but whatever's out there, it's not a goddam cattle pond... or teenagers playing with fireworks."

"Yeah, yeah, I hear you, Frank... I checked out those pieces of metal Patty showed me. They could be fragments of an SUV, but this is a pretty cockamamie story you're throwing at me... I mean, get real... who destroys a brand new car in the middle of nowhere... and why?"

"Okay... okay... I haven't figured that part out yet, but if you saw the expression on Ted Hendricks' face... I mean, the kid was scared shitless... of something."

Pushing away from her desk, the deputy briefly paced around the room before turning back to me. "You know we don't have any budget for crazy shit like this." At least she was finally thinking about it. After a short pause, the little cop spoke again. "Okay, so you say this Hendricks guy lives in the 'burbs of Kansas City?"

I nodded. "Yeah, Blue Springs."

"Okay, I know a guy on the force up in KC. I'll see if I can get him to pick Hendricks up and bring him down here for a chat. How does that sound?"

"Great, Bernie... thanks. I think you'll find it pretty interesting."

"We'll see... I have to get back to work now." The deputy opened a drawer and took out a magazine. "Oh yeah, and don't leave town, Frank... okay?"

"Sure, Bernie, sure..."

"And one more thing... and I'm only passing this on because you're such a sweetheart."

Headed for the door, I stopped and turned back, a puzzled look on my face. "Huh... what's that, Bernie?"

"I got a call from the morgue saying Wilmer Graves' widow showed up this morning to claim the body. She's coming by to pick up his effects in a couple of hours. I thought you might like to talk to her."

After leaving the sheriff's office, Patty and I went to lunch. Since I wasn't feeling so swell about Terry's, we went to Cobb's Bar-B-Que, a little hole in the wall specializing in smoked meat. Cobb's had about six tables and seemed to do most of its business as take-out. At this point the place was a little rundown, but with autographed B&W photos of country and western stars hanging on the walls, the joint obviously enjoyed quite a reputation back in the '50s and '60s. The photos gave Cobb's a kind of authentic atmosphere, but the smell of smoke was so pervasive, it made me nervous. I kept feeling like the place was on fire.

Of course, Patty knew the owner, happily greeting the young man as he took our order. "Hi, Junior. How's Louie doing?"

"Not so good, I'm afraid, Patty. It looks like Louie's had another setback. The doctors aren't so sure if he's gonna pull through this time. Who's your friend?"

"Oh, this is Frank... he's a reporter from L.A. Frank's working on a story about that dead guy we found out on Highway 18 a couple of weeks ago. I'm really sorry to hear about Louie. I hope he makes it. My mom is doing a lot better. I think she should be coming home in a few days."

"That's great, Patty. Nice to meet you, Frank."

After taking our order, Junior went back to prepare the food. Patty said that Louie, his dad, was actually the owner, but his son had taken over when Louie retired a few years ago. When I mentioned the photos, Patty said that Cobb's Bar-B-Que was famous all over the Midwest; consequently country stars made sure their buses came through Clinton, and Louie always got them to sign photos when they came in. Looking closer I saw pictures of Johnny Cash, Patsy Cline, Buck Owens, and Jim Reeves along with many others. I was never a country music fan, but it was pretty impressive for a tiny joint in the middle of Missouri.

Still feeling the effects of last night's bourbon, I needed food. While the meeting with Bernie had ultimately gone okay, dealing with the testy little fart was an emotionally draining pain. That, plus a week away from home and the constant sensation that the restaurant was on fire made me more than a little edgy.

Not feeling so social, I sat in silence until Patty finally spoke up. "I saw Duane when I went to breakfast at Terry's this morning." I had a bad feeling about what was coming next. "He knows about us, Frank. I'm not sure how he found out, but him and Tommy Joe are pretty close, so that could be it. Clinton is a pretty small town, after all." Yeah, right... too small to hide in and too bored to ignore... people talk, as they say.

"Gee, Patty that's great news. It does a lot for my sense of security and well-being to know that a highway patrolman the size of a truck wants to kick my ass. I'll sleep well knowing that I could be reduced to a whimpering puddle by tomorrow morning."

"Duane's not that bad, Frank. He can be a little pushy, but he's just a puppy underneath it all." Yeah... a puppy with the disposition of a rabid bear.

At that point our food arrived and it was awesome. At least the condemned man ate a hearty meal.

As soon as we finished, Patty and I headed back to the sheriff's office. As we opened the door I immediately spotted an elderly woman with a walker sitting by Deputy Bodie's desk, accompanied by a young female companion appearing to be in her early twenties. Aware of my interest in speaking to Graves' widow, Bernie introduced us. "Mrs. Graves, this is Frank Blodgett, a writer from Los Angeles. Mr. Blodgett wants to talk to you about your husband."

As the woman struggled to rise from the chair, I walked across the room and extended my hand. "Please, please, don't bother to get up, Mrs. Graves... it's okay," I said. About halfway up she paused, reconsidered, and settled back into her seat. Looking up, she reached out her hand and we greeted each other. "I'm pleased to meet you, Mrs. Graves."

The old woman's movements were slow and labored but her eyes were bright. "Call me Mildred. I'm happy to meet you, too, Mr., uh, Blodgett?"

"That's right... Franklin Blodgett."

"That is such an unusual name. Are there many Blodgetts in Los Angeles?" Soft-spoken and heavily accented, Mrs. Graves' voice registered an unaffected grace and dignity often known to older people in the South.

"No... not really. It's a not a common name." Despite her disability and lack of education, Mrs. Graves had a calm, centered quality, as if the troubles of the world were nothing more than raindrops, kept at bay by a gracious and well-behaved umbrella. "I'm sorry to bother you at such a difficult time, Mrs. Graves, but I'd like to talk to you about your husband... if that's okay."

She nodded, then spoke, "Why of course, Franklin, but please... call me Mildred... oh, I'm forgettin' my manners." She gestured at the bored-looking young woman sitting next to her. "This here is my niece Eurline. She helps me out quite a bit." I reached over and shook the younger woman's hand. "Now, how can I help you? What would you like to know about Wilmer? He was such a sweet man."

With a history of violent behavior and over fifty convictions, Wilmer Graves was not a man many would describe as "sweet." The old woman was either deep in denial or she enjoyed a significantly different relationship with Wilmer Graves than the rest of the world—maybe it was a little of both. "A number of people have tentatively identified Mr. Graves as the perpetrator of several robberies during the week before he died. Can you tell me anything about this recent series of crimes, uh, Mildred?"

"Oh dear... I'm afraid it's all my fault, Franklin... all my fault, just as sure as I'm sittin' here."

"I beg your pardon. Are you saying that you persuaded your husband to commit these robberies?" Mildred Graves did not strike me as the Bonnie Parker type.

"Oh heavens, no. It's just that I have this bad hip." She patted her left side. "And Wilmer, bless his heart, he was jus' trying to raise some money so's I could get an operation. That's all.... but I never told him to be robbin' no one."

"I see... uh, Mildred, it seems that Mr. Graves had an accomplice in these robberies. I'm fairly certain it was a young man named Ted Hendricks. Do you know how your husband became acquainted with Hendricks... and how long he had known him?"

Reflecting on my question, the older woman paused for a moment, then replied, "Well... I'm afraid I just can't recall any Ted Hendricks... can you tell me a little more about him?"

"Hendricks is quite tall and very young. If you had ever met him, you'd probably remember. He's also involved in the computer business so he seems like an unlikely crime partner for your husband."

"Is he a Christian boy... this Ted Hendricks?"

"Uh, I really can't say, Mildred. Why do you ask?"

"Well, you see Wilmer spent the last twenty years of his life in the service of Jesus Christ, so I thought maybe that boy could've heard one of Wilmer's sermons and they met that way is all." She briefly paused again then continued, "Poor Wilmer, he was so disappointed in himself, what with all his relapses and everything. He tried so hard, but he just couldn't help hisself."

"When was the last time you saw Wilmer, Mrs. Graves, uh, Mildred?"

"Well... let me see. I think it was just about a month ago. Yes... Wilmer had a doctor's appointment... his health was really goin' down you know... an' he left to go to the doctor's an' he jus' never come back."

"I know your husband was using oxygen... a bottle was found next to him. Did he have other health problems?"

"Well, his kidneys was failin' him for one thing... the doctors told him he would have to go on one of those artificial kidney machines soon. An' of course he had high blood pressure and diabetes... he musta took about fifteen or twenty pills a day. There wud'n no doubt about it, Wilmer was a mess..." The old woman paused for a moment, then looked straight at me. "Uh, excuse me, Franklin, but why is it that you're askin' me all these questions about Wilmer... him bein' deceased now an' all."

"That's a fair question, Mildred... you see, I'm a writer and writers need stories... we need something to write about. And when I read about your husband being found all alone out on that highway with nothing around but an oxygen bottle and a gun, I was moved... it seemed that there had to be more to it, so I came out here to write Wilmer's story." Despite her circumstances, something about the old woman, a certain inner calm, compelled me to say more, to reveal myself in an unguarded way. I hesitated, gathering my thoughts, then continued, "And to be totally honest, I'm at a point in my life where I really need something... something I can care about. And I can't exactly say why, but uncovering and telling your husband's story seems to be fulfilling that need. I'm sorry if it sounds strange, but I can't explain it any better than that."

The old woman, her eyes reflecting concern, seemed to be searching my soul. "I understand, Franklin. We all need somethin' to believe in even if that somethin' is plum crazy to ever'one else. Just look at me... I believed in Wilmer for almost fifty years an' he musta broke my heart a million times... now how crazy was that?"

"And what was it, Mildred... what made you hang on when your husband was in and out of prison for decades?"

Momentarily overwhelmed by a lifetime of memories, the old woman appeared to be on the verge of breaking down. Examining her weary expression, I wondered if the residue of unfulfilled expectations was too much for her to bear, but she quickly regained her composure and continued, "Well, I always wanted children of course, but it didn't take too long to realize that wud'n gonna be so good with Wilmer, what with him always bein' in prison an' all, but the thing was... the thing was, Franklin... I loved him... an' sometimes there jus' ain't no explainin' love... it's a gift that dud'n offer any explanations."

We sat there for a moment in silence. There were more questions I could have asked and I still couldn't grasp how Graves' wife managed to endure such a seemingly intolerable situation, year after year. Finally, after another minute or so, Eurline, the old woman's niece, broke the silence. "We got a long drive ahead of us, Aunt Mildred... we should probably be startin' back home now."

Lost in thought, Mrs. Graves looked up, first at her niece then at me. She paused again as if she had one last memory to ponder, then responded. "Yes, of course, Eurline... you're right... we need to be headin' on home." She struggled to her feet, positioned herself behind the walker, then turned to me. "It was so nice to meet you, Franklin. If there's any way I can be of any further help, you jus' let me know... okay?"

"Yes, of course, Mrs. Graves, er, Mildred. I really appreciate you taking the time to speak to me." And as I watched the old woman carefully making her way across the room, the meaning of her decades-long relationship with a man who lived the majority of his life behind bars suddenly became clear to me, and the answer was quite simple: hope. For an uneducated woman in the South, especially one without children, hope had to be a precious commodity, becoming even more so as she aged. And every time Wilmer Graves was released from prison, hope bloomed anew. Each re-entry of her husband into Mildred Graves' world carried the promise that this time it would be different. This time Wilmer would live what he preached... this time he'd get a job and they'd build a life together... this time he wouldn't get drunk, rob another gas station and go back to prison. And that hope had fueled her for almost fifty years, but now Wilmer was dead and the hope died with him, and its loss was as sharp as a bright but worn-out old woman slowly trudging across the room.

Time is funny. Some weeks occupy the mental real estate of years, while years can vanish into the memory bank like shit sucked into a sewer. It was only mid-afternoon but the day already felt like three weeks. What the fuck—time for a drink. Surprisingly, my brief time in Clinton had been so packed, I hadn't seen the inside of a single bar, much less found a favorite. Driving around town I'd spotted several joints and this was the time to check one out. Fatty & Jim's, a promising little spot, popped up on the mental radar so I parked the Sonic out front and went in. The bar was deserted except for a middle-aged couple hunkering down in a booth. Dark and faintly smelling of smoke, Fatty & Jim's was clearly old-school—my kinda place. As I plopped myself down on a stool, the bartender slowly made his way in my direction. "What'll it be, bud?"

Feeling the need of something special, I splurged, "Woodford Reserve... rocks... if you got it."

The guy behind the bar was bald, average height, overweight and obviously a pro at minding his own business. "Woodford, it is..." the barkeep replied, calmly pulling a bottle out from under the bar and blowing the dust off.

My mood lifting up at the sight of the premium bourbon, I reconsidered, "Hey Mac, make it a double, okay?"

"Sure... no problem." The guy poured me a generous double, then retreated to a small portable TV at the other end of the bar. Sipping my Woodford, I mulled over the day's activities. The meeting with Mildred, Wilmer Graves' wife, had gone well, but left me more than a little depressed. A pleasant, intelligent woman, Mrs. Graves was left facing an empty and barren future with absolutely nothing to look forward to. Okay, maybe it was no different than before, but Wilmer's death had eliminated her illusions, leaving a wounded, open and aimless core.

Despondent, my thoughts moved on to Patty and her brother, Tommy Joe. With no parental guidance, the kid was headed for trouble. Sure, Patty could offer a little support, but she was a clerk in the sheriff's office in Clinton, Missouri, with no fucking future herself. Most likely, Tommy Joe would never give a shit about anything; he'd drop out of school, hang around with his dumb-ass friends chasing pussy, taking drugs and getting fired from shitty jobs until he wound up in jail... or worse. Talk about depressing.

Oh yeah, then there was Duane, the beefy state trooper who wanted to kick my butt for bonking Patty. What a fucking mess. Sipping my bourbon, my mind moved on to Bernie, Deputy Dawg, the midget gatekeeper who could make this whole crazy trip worth it if she just pulled her head out of her ass. Well, at least she was following up on Ted Hendricks.

Pondering the ultimate negativity of it all, I was just about to order another drink when I had an idea. It was still light outside; I could drive back out to the bomb site and search for more evidence, something solid that Bernie couldn't dispute. Okay, it wasn't much, but it beat sitting by myself in a dark bar, wallowing around the rim of self-pity and despair.

So I paid for my drink and left, but first I stopped by a liquor store and picked up a pint of Jack Daniels. It was a long drive out to the crater and I could use a little pick-me-up. Hopping in the Chevy, I cracked the Jack, took a couple of slugs and headed out Highway 18.

Passing the time listening to old R&B, it wasn't long until I parked the car at the edge of the crater. The sun was beginning to set and it was already cold as hell. After taking another slug of bourbon, I jumped out of the car and headed out into the large bowl-shaped area. Most of the searching done by Patty and me was near the center of the crater; maybe, by searching around the edges, I could find something we missed.

Walking the perimeter, I surveyed the area as thoughts from the conversation with Bernie bounced around my brain... Cattle pond? Biofuel? Fireworks? She had to be fucking nuts. I mean, okay, at this point here was no definitive evidence that an explosion had happened here, but all you had to do was look around... the way the vegetation at the edges fanned out from the center... the way the debris segregated itself into larger and larger pieces as it moved from dust in the center to large chunks at the rim... I was certain that bomb experts, technicians trained in the use and management of explosives, would have no problem finding the residue of Semtex, C-4, PBX or something even more powerful. Nothing else could create this kind of destruction.

It was cold and getting dark. Irritated at not bringing a flashlight, I obviously couldn't continue much longer. About to give up, I suddenly tripped on a rock and, attempting to block my fall, felt something hard and rectangular beneath my outstretched hand. Lifting it up, I squinted in the dim light, barely making out the shiny, silver block letters, spelling out "E...S...C...A...L...A...D...E"... Jackpot! It was the nameplate of the Cadillac. Okay, it still didn't *prove* an explosion happened out here, but that was just a formality. The SUV was definitely here. Deputy Dawg had to listen to me now.

Desperate for the car heater, I hurried back to the Chevy, jumped in and started the engine. A couple of swigs later, I put the car in gear, pointing it back toward Clinton. Finally, something seemed to be going my way.

It was dark, and darkness on a two-lane highway cutting through the heart of Missouri in the middle of winter is blackout city. With nothing to look at, I zeroed in on my headlights disappearing into the dark, but, with no stimulation—no truck stops, diners or Starbucks ahead—my focus began to fade. Maybe it was the cumulative effects of an overly draining day, maybe it was the lack of sleep, and yeah, okay, maybe it was too much goddam bourbon, but whatever the reason, the next thing I knew the Sonic was racing off the road and into a drainage ditch. Slamming on the brakes, I managed to slow the car's exit from the roadway, but not before hammering headlong into a dirt embankment on the far side of the ditch.

I was fucked.

Oh well, at least I had almost half a pint left. Okay, I know they say alcohol doesn't actually warm you up, it just feels that way; but if I was going to get frostbite and maybe buy it, I wanted to feel as little pain as possible. Unscrewing the cap and slugging down a little more Jack, it occurred that someone could drive by, but, with the car in the bottom of a ditch, they probably wouldn't see me. But I also couldn't risk standing on the highway in the cold in order to flag a passing car. This was not good.

It was getting colder. Luckily the engine was still running, so the heater worked, but I'd never make it though the night with less than a quarter of a tank of gas. And of course there was no cell phone coverage—unless someone came along, I'd probably freeze to death long before the sun came up. Luckily I wasn't hurt, so I got out of the car to inspect the damage, and seeing how the right front wheel had crumpled underneath the chassis told me the Sonic would never get out the ditch without a tow truck, but that wasn't all. Inspecting the rear of the car, I smelled gasoline; getting down on my knees, I reached underneath and felt a steady stream of gas dripping from the tank.

Thinking fast, I came up with a plan. If I could start a fire, someone might spot it and see me down in the ditch. Grabbing an empty coffee cup from the car, I positioned it under the leak, thinking I could use the dripping gasoline to start a fire. With no shortage of fallen trees and broken limbs nearby, I worked fast, breaking off branches and grabbing newspaper from the car, then doused the pile of tinder with gas.

I didn't have any matches, but there was a cigarette lighter in the car. Wadding a piece of paper, I soaked the end with gasoline, then ignited it with the lighter. Holding the flaming paper above my head, I climbed out of the car, tossing the torch onto the pile of kindling. As intended, the mass of dead wood and paper immediately burst into flames, but, as I walked from the car to the pile of firewood, I neglected to notice a stream of liquid leaking from the cup. Standing in stunned surprise, I watched as the flame abruptly erupted along the trail of gasoline and back into the ditch, immediately engulfing the Chevy in flames. Dumbfounded, I collapsed onto the ground between the two fires; stunned into oblivion, I slowly drained the remains of my Jack Daniels. It wasn't getting any better.

As I sat there feeling the effects of bourbon numbing my brain I tried to recall everything I could remember about freezing to death. It seems that hypothermia happens in three stages, with the most curious behavior coming in stage three when the victims often exhibit an apparent self-protective action known as terminal burrowing, where the individual, at this point incoherent, attempts to enter a small enclosed space. This behavior is often accompanied by another completely counterintuitive reaction known as paradoxical undressing. Finding naked people frozen to death has often caused potential rescuers to erroneously believe that a deceased person has also been a victim of a sexual assault, an especially curious confluence of personal misfortune.

At that point, as I amused myself with the thought that Patty and Deputy Dawg might discover my naked body curled up in the burned-out trunk of my rented Chevy Sonic, a pair of headlights suddenly appeared on the highway just above the ditch. Amazed at my good fortune, I stumbled to my feet and staggered up the embankment just in time to recognize a distinctive black-and-white cruiser. Not knowing

whether to laugh or cry, I then noticed an even more familiar figure emerging from the highway patrol car and walking
my way. It was Duane.

My hands cuffed behind my back, I soon found myself
riding in the back seat of the highway patrol car. I can't say
that Duane was exactly gentle with me, but then I don't exactly remember and don't know that I would have blamed
him if I did. There were a few bruises on my upper torso
and back, which occurred when I "tripped," according to
the report made by the law officer. I do recall submitting
to a breathalyzer test and hearing Duane's laughter as he
announced the results to no one in particular.

I also remember that, after applying the handcuffs down
near the ditch, the highway patrolman went back to his car
and returned with what had to be a digital camera, because I
can still see a surreal series of flashes lighting the pitch-black
area around the burning Sonic. Almost as if in a dream, I
watch myself stumbling around in the darkness only to have
the world suddenly transformed into brilliant luminescence
for split seconds at a time, but whenever it happened, the
center of the lighted area stood out, tenaciously retaining
the blackened outline of an oddly bent and vaguely vehic-
ular shape.

Moments later, I was roughly thrust into the back seat
of the cruiser, after which I apparently passed out, because
the next thing I remember is the car stopping in front of
the sheriff's office. My brain completely fogged by bourbon
and sleep, I could only make out snatches of a conversation
between Duane and Deputy Bodie exchanging clichéd com-

ments like "throw the book at the asshole" and "I knew he was no good" followed by brief bursts of smug laughter.

At that point the door of the cruiser burst open and I was hauled out onto the sidewalk. Dazed and confused, the two law officers tried to pull me up to my feet, but it was no use. Attempting to regain my balance, I took a step or two then stumbled into the highway patrolman who grabbed me like a doll, dragged me into the small building, then out to the cell in the rear. With Duane propping me up, Bernie opened the cell door. Barely conscious, I felt the handcuffs being removed just before I was pushed into the tiny jail. Stumbling across the room, I tripped and fell on the bed which felt oddly lumpy. Still trying to orient myself, I looked around and noticed a pair of feet sticking out from under a rough wool blanket, then as my eyes traversed what seemed to be a body stretching out forever, a head emerged from the other end of the blanket.

People see strange things when they're drunk and sleepy, but I'd swear the head bore an uncanny resemblance to Ted Hendricks.

PART TWO
THE STORK

I woke up several hours later,
hung over again. Peeking out from
the blanket through a blur of pain
and nausea, all I could see was
something towering over me. With a
very erect posture, the something
was pacing a small area next to my
cot. The something was disturbed.
The something was Ted Hendricks
and he was screaming at me.

"He called me Stork! STORK! I hated that!"

Maybe I was still dreaming... a particularly unpleasant dream.

"STORK! Do you know who The Stork was? DO YOU?"

If this was a dream, it was time to wake up. "I beg your pardon? Stork?"

"DON'T CALL ME THAT! It was Willy... Willy called me Stork."

"I'm sorry... but I'm not following you."

Sluggish and dull, I could only watch as Hendricks, his fury poorly concealed, paced the room like a horny giraffe, back and forth, until his own mindless incoherence reached around and tapped him on the shoulder. Pausing, he looked back and while his eyes were pointed in my direction, they saw something else, something from his past. Dialing it down, the disturbed content screener continued, "Willy... he was a huge Oakland Raiders fan... Ted Hendricks... he was a football player for the Raiders back in the '80s... they called him The Stork... he was tall, like me."

It was difficult, but a light was flickering in the fog. "So you're saying Wilmer Graves called you..."

"STORK!"

"...and that's why you're so upset?"

"I'm upset because I'm in jail... AND YOU FUCKING PUT ME HERE, RIGHT?"

The fog was indeed beginning to lift, but the unsightly something lingered, a specter of rage, tension radiating from it like stink around a troubled skunk. As it hovered over me, clenching its teeth, I stammered, "Uh, well, you see..."

"Of course it was you. WHO ELSE?"

I battled back. "Wait a minute... you did accompany Wilmer Graves... Willy... on a series of crimes, right? You guys were sticking up convenience stores, donut shops and formal wear rental places... right?"

The ominous specter diminished. "Well, sort of... but it wasn't really like that."

"Like what? Like you didn't point a gun at people and say 'GIVE ME ALL YOUR MONEY!'... if it wasn't like that, then what was it like?"

"That was Willy... not me. I mostly drove the car. I hate guns."

"So why did you help him... and how does a guy like you get involved with a degenerate old fart like Wilmer Graves to begin with?"

"You don't understand... Willy was... he was..."

Seemingly stricken by a sentimental moment, Hendricks froze, staring into empty space, then collapsed on his bunk, sobbing. Like a falling fat man greeting concrete, Ted Hendricks' mood was shattered. Between blubbers he blurted out again and again, "You don't understand... you don't understand..."

I felt a little sorry for the kid. Yeah, he was guilty of something, but he just wasn't a criminal type. Walking over to his cot, I put a hand on Hendricks' shoulder. I sounded like fucking Father Flanagan or something but I couldn't help myself. "Maybe it would help if you talked about it."

He looked at me, tears welling up and oozing out around the corners of his eyes. "My grandfather... my grandfather died a few weeks before I met Willy, and it was weird but they were so much alike... at least to me... well, of course Dido wasn't a criminal or anything..."

"Excuse me... Dido?"

"That... that was the name I had for my grandfather... I called him Dido... Dido practically raised me. My dad was a heroin addict and after he OD'd, Dido took me in... I was just a kid... we were so close, Dido and me... then when Willy showed up, not long after Dido died, it was like getting him back in a funny way... yeah, okay, Willy wasn't your typical grandpa type, and they both had these gruff person-alities... but underneath they were kind and loving..."

The kid was starting to open up.

"Sometimes I think Willy was even more generous than Dido..."

"Uh... Correct me if I'm mistaken but didn't Wilmer Graves shoot the manager of a donut shop for thirty-six dollars? That's a funny kind of generosity."

"Oh that... that was just an accident... the guy should've just given Willy the money... once Willy robbed a 7-11 then turned around and gave half the money to a kid on the street... then he waved his gun at the kid and said, 'Go to school! Go to school, kid, or you'll wind up like me!' And he laughed... Willy had a great laugh. He was always doing stuff like that..."

"So how did you meet Willy? I mean... well, you guys are a pretty unlikely pair..."

"Oh, yeah... sure, I know what you mean... it was Margo... it happened because of Margo... or at least, I thought it was her."

"Wait, are you trying to say you met a career criminal, a guy with over fifty convictions, through your girlfriend?" The kid's story was odd, but it was about to blast off into an uncharted realm of pure, unadulterated weirdness.

"No, no, it was nothing like that... it was..."

As he searched for words to explain an unheard-of con-fluence, a combination of the absurd, profane and prepos-terous, a pained look came over Hendricks' face. "Well... no... you see..." After an extended and painfully long pause, when the content screener finally spoke, his voice was barely above a whisper: "I... I thought she was fucking a monkey."

As he told his story, I could see Ted Hendricks standing in the doorway of a cheap motel room several weeks earlier. He walks to his car and retrieves the box I had seen in the back seat of his car, the box labeled "eSPY – HI-TECH SPYING MADE EASY." He carries it back into the room, then sits at a small desk and immediately opens a laptop computer. Quickly locating a folder labeled "INAPPROPRIATE!," Hendricks then finds a sub-folder titled "YouTube_Flagged." Navigating through the folder's vast array of files, he focuses his attention on one labeled "Chimp_Woman_XXX." Clicking on the file causes the familiar YouTube contextual fields to appear surrounding a video; a bright red "RESTRICTED!" warning appears at the bottom of the picture. The image in the video field appears to be a static shot of the exact same motel room, and as the tech screener watches, the video shows a young woman enter, followed by a full-grown male chimpanzee. The woman wears tight jeans and a halter top; the chimp is wearing a striped T-shirt.

The image is fairly lo-res and while she never directly faces the camera, the woman does bear a passing resemblance to Margo, Ted Hendricks' girlfriend. Not only that, her clothing is similar to the outfit Margo was wearing during my encounter with the couple at their house in Blue Springs. After handing a banana to the primate, the young woman undresses, climbs onto the bed and gestures for the chimp to join her. As she embraces the monkey, kissing him fully on the mouth, Hendricks angrily slams the laptop shut.

The tech worker then turns his attention to the box containing the amateur surveillance equipment, but his hands are shaking so badly, it takes him several moments to open it. He spreads its contents out on the bed, but a familiar urge soon reappears, compulsively seizing his scarred and shadowy soul; anxious, the young man obsessively returns to the laptop, pauses for a moment, then opens it again. Resuming play, the video shows the young woman disrobing the chimp, then as she fondly rubs his back, her other hand reaches around and down between the monkey's legs. Unable to take any more, Hendricks slams the laptop shut again, abruptly turning back to the spycams. For several minutes, he continues this back-and-forth pattern of slowly distributing the tiny cameras around the room, checking the functionality of each as he does, then periodically returning to the obviously disturbing video.

As this curious and compulsive task nears completion, Hendricks hears a loud noise outside. Carefully placing the final spycam on the desk, he crosses the room and opens the door just as a 1980s-era Cadillac abruptly pulls into the parking spot of the room next door, its flopping flat tire and roaring muffler demanding attention. With the young techie watching, the Caddy comes to a halt and an older man tumbles out, sprawling onto the asphalt parking lot. Tethered to an oxygen bottle, he struggles to his feet, waving a large handgun in the air as he does. Then, just as the man regains his footing, a Highway Patrol cruiser, siren screaming and apparently in pursuit, blindly roars past the entrance to the motel.

Mesmerized by the curious scene unfolding in front of him, Ted Hendricks can only stand and stare as the man jerks his head around, surveying the scene for potential danger. With no one else in sight, his eyes quickly land on the young man watching him. Breathing heavily, the old man barks, "WHATCHA LOOKIN' AT? HUH?"

Startled, Hendricks considers retreating to his room but the old man, surprisingly quick and still waving the huge pistol, is on him in a flash. With the gun poking his ribs, Ted looks down at his shriveled and gnarled adversary. Judging by his piercing eyes and full head of gray hair, the man is probably not as old as he *looks, but his shaking hands and hacking cough suggest neglect and years of self-abuse.*

Anxious and overwrought, the old man makes a split decision. "Quick, kid! Back in the room! You're gonna help me... or else! UNDERSTAND?" Brandishing the weapon with practiced bravado and flair, the barrel of the gun barely reaches Hendricks' chest as the old man forces him back into the motel room, then collapses in a fit of coughing as the door slams shut behind them.

A few hours later Wilmer Graves and Ted Hendricks are parked outside a Selix formal wear rental shop in the Kansas City suburb of Raytown. The shop is in a strip mall slightly isolated from the other stores, making it a perfect choice for Graves' next caper. Having abandoned the old man's stolen Cadillac at the motel, Hendricks is now chauffeuring the ex-con in his ten-year-old Honda.

"Okay, kid, out... we got a job to do. C'mon..."

Hendricks looks around nervously. "Uh, I'd rather not, Mr, Graves... if you don't mind, I'll, uh, just wait for you here in the car."

"Mind... MIND? Are you fucking crazy, kid? You think I'm gonna let you haul ass as soon as I'm in that fucking shop? Hell no! You're comin' with me, SO GET THE FUCK OUT!"

Self-conscious, the high-strung Hendricks exits the car spastically pivoting his head around, as Graves, pistol tucked into his waistband and oxygen bottle in tow, steps out onto the sidewalk. Muttering under his breath, the old man snarls, "Cool it, kid. You look like some pansy-ass little girl... relax and act natural... like me. C'mon..." Hitching his pants, drooping under the weight of the huge handgun, Graves nods at his young companion, then follows him into the shop.

The store is deserted as the odd pair enters. With no other customers and anxious to please, the clerk approaches the pair, then hesitates, a look of concern on his face. Wasting no time, the old man immediately retrieves his pistol, waves it in front of the terrified man and fires a shot at the ceiling. The noise is deafening. Cowering, the clerk falls to the floor, his hands covering his head. Radiating terror, the man's shrill voice instantly fills the void following the sharp sound of gunfire, "I GIVE UP! I GIVE UP! JUST DON'T SHOOT ME!"

With the wide-eyed Ted Hendricks looking on, Graves screams, "SHUDDUP, FAGGOT!" as he thrusts the gun into the back of the clerk's head. "SHUDDUP AND ACT LIKE A MAN! Now gimme all your fucking money! MOVE, FAGGOT!"

On his hands and knees the man scurries like a bug across the floor to the cash register. Timidly he rises to his feet, opens the register drawer, pulls out a handful of bills and shoves them toward Graves, standing on the opposite side of the counter. As the old man reaches out to grab the money, he's seized by another coughing fit, causing him to discharge the gun a second time, filling the small room with an ear-splitting roar as the bullet ricochets off the floor, shattering a large plate glass mirror. Terrified, the clerk immediately falls to the ground again, dropping him from Graves' line of sight as the old man, on the other side of the counter, struggles to regain his composure. Immersed in the chaos of noise, gunsmoke and broken glass, the gunman suddenly realizes he has lost track of the clerk and panics.

Screaming, he yells, "WHERE ARE YOU, FAGGOT? WHERE ARE YOU? YOU CAN'T GET AWAY! YOU HEAR ME? SHOW YOURSELF... SHOW YOURSELF, FAGGOT!" then fires the gun two more times. Meanwhile, Ted Hendricks, who has remained remarkably calm throughout the entire ordeal, stands near the end of the divider with a clear view of the scene, including the cowering clerk tightly squeezed into a corner behind the counter.

As the smoke and acrid stench of gunfire waft their way

through the cramped and confined space, an eerie silence en-velops the room. Each unable to see the other, Graves and the clerk are frozen in indecision for a long uneasy moment until Ted Hendricks, boldly breaking the silence, finally releases the tension. Appalled and frightened for the safety of the petrified clerk, he points at the terrified man and shouts, "Mr. Graves... please... he's right there on the floor... the poor man is scared to death. I think it's time to leave now."

Jolted back to reality by his young companion, Graves snaps into action. "Huh? Oh... yeah... you're right... we gotta leave... c'mon." With that he grabs his oxygen bottle and heads out the door.

Moments later, anxious to leave the crime scene, Ted Hendricks steps on the accelerator as the Honda merges into traffic, but the old man cautions him. "It's okay, kid... back off. We ain't in no hurry."

Still upset, the young man glances over as his companion calmly reloads his pistol. Radiating tension, Hendricks speaks up, "I don't understand why you gave that clerk such a hard time, Mr. Graves. Anyone could see what a harmless little guy he was."

"It's easy for you to say, kid, but I've done this a hunnerd times... th' first thing you gotta do is let 'em know who's in con-trol. I know what I'm doin' here."

"But you were abusive... verbally abusive... and there was no reason. He would've given you..."

"You mean that faggot shit? Look, I ain't got no problem with the fags... I've known plenty of 'em in prison... good folks, most of 'em..."

"But it was total chaos back there... you could've shot the guy... maybe even killed him."

"Okay... okay, maybe it got a little out of hand... just for a second or so... but nobody was hurt... he'll be okay."

They ride in silence for a few moments until Wilmer Graves speaks again, "But hey, you was a standup guy back there, kid. You kept your head and got us out when it got crazy and I appreciate it... much obliged, kid... I owe you one." After a brief pause, Graves breaks the silence again, "So what's your name, son... I can't just keep callin' you 'kid.'"

"It's Ted, Mr. Graves... Ted Hendricks."

"TED HENDRICKS! THE STORK! You gotta be kiddin' me... I knew there somethin' special about you, kid... TED HENDRICKS! No shit..." Completely baffled by the old man's reaction, the young man still feels a certain warmth of affection at Wilmer Graves' obvious embrace of his name.

Each feeling the afterglow of their strange bond, the curious couple search for a motel where they can unwind and spend the night. After traveling a few miles in silence, the old man speaks again, "Hey kid... just call me Willy, okay? Don't nobody call me Mr. Graves, 'cept my lawyer. Just call me Willy... okay?"

"Sure... Willy."

Completely absorbed, I've listened for the past hour as Ted Hendricks told the story of his initial encounter and involvement with Wilmer Graves. And as he spoke, missing pieces of a puzzle I had been wrestling with for the past two weeks were falling into place. My head was throbbing and my throat felt like a dirt road in hell, but I had to keep the kid talking.

"So why did you stay with him? I mean as weak and sick as Graves was, surely you realized you could have taken the gun from him... or just run away. You must have known you were incriminating yourself... becoming his accomplice. Why did you do it?"

Obviously conflicted, Hendricks sat, unmoving in the dim light of the jail cell. When he finally spoke, his voice, coming from deep within, barely rose above a whisper. "I... I just couldn't do that to him. He needed me... maybe like no one ever needed me... I just couldn't send him back to jail... or leave him to die. I... it looked like he didn't have much longer. I thought about Willy a lot over the past couple of weeks. I keep wondering if there was anything I could've done... I mean, his health was obviously bad, but I could have taken him to a doctor or tried to call his wife... or something... I just... I didn't expect it to happen so fast..."

Deep in thought, Hendricks laid back on his bunk and stared at the ceiling. The kid's mood was darkening. Now that Graves' reluctant accomplice was finally opening up, I didn't want to lose him so I probed a little deeper. "Earlier you said you were primarily the driver while Graves was doing the actual robberies. How long was it before he left you alone in the car? Before he actually trusted you?"

Lost in guilt and recrimination, Hendricks laid there for another thirty or forty-five seconds until he finally sat up and turned back to me. "It was funny, you know... the way he was tough on the surface, but not really like that all." And as he spoke, I could see Wilmer Graves coming alive in his mind and the kid's spirit seemed to lift. "It happened pretty fast... like the next day... kind of caught me off guard, but I guess by then Willy didn't have much choice." He paused, mentally reconstructing the events, then continued, "We were hungry, so Willy ordered this huge pizza... I couldn't believe the stuff he ate... the pizza was, like, half pineapple and half Kung Pao chicken..." Drifting into reminiscence, the kid was warming up again. "Oh yeah... then he put ketchup on it... he always carried a bottle of ketchup with him...

Willy put it on everything... then he started watching TV... horrible stuff... you know, *Duck Dynasty*, *Celebrity Apprentice*, *Project Runway*... junk like that, while I worked on my laptop, but pretty soon I could see he was nodding out... oh yeah, he smoked nonstop, too. There he was, this crazy old guy, on oxygen, smoking and NODDING OUT IN BED! HE BURNED TWO HOLES IN THE BEDSPREAD WHILE I WAS WATCHING... and he kept jerking awake, then jumping up and pointing that crazy gun at me... until he finally had to go to sleep, but he was nervous about me being in the same room, so he took my belt and tied my hands. I couldn't relax with my arms behind me so I watched Willy sitting on the floor, blocking the door with the gun in his lap. I could tell he was uncomfortable, too, but it wasn't long before he nodded out again, then slumped over on the floor. I closed my eyes and tried to sleep but I heard something and looked up... and there was Willy, just standing at the foot of the bed... staring. He was sleepwalking... as I watched, the old man wandered around, bumping into a chair, tripping over a stool, talking to himself... still dragging his oxygen bottle behind him... it was kind of creepy... then he turned and walked into the bathroom, very deliberate like. Curious, I got up and followed, but just as I reached the door, Willy climbed onto the toilet, then stepped up on the tank, almost like he was climbing stairs. He was just about to topple over backwards when I lunged in behind him, awkwardly breaking his fall and causing both of us to land in a pile on the floor. At that point Willy woke up, but he was still groggy. Staggering back to the bed, he collapsed, falling back into a deep sleep. The next morning when he untied my hands, I said, 'Willy, you know you really didn't have to do this.' He gave me a kind of hard look, then shrugged his shoulders and that was it. Later he said I was the best getaway man he ever had. It was kinda sweet, in a weird Willy way."

As Hendricks continued to speak about his relationship with Wilmer Graves, he recalled a conversation he and the old man had the following day. Willy was in a reflective mood as they sped down the highway.

"Hey Stork, you got a girlfriend?"

"Please, Mr. Graves... Willy... I'd rather you didn't call me that."

"Yeah, whatever... you got a chick, kid?"

"Well, yeah... Margo... we've been involved for about a year now. Why do you ask?"

"Oh, I been thinkin' about Millie, my ol' lady. You know Storkie, there ain't nuthin' like the love of a good woman. Hell, I spent most of my life in the joint, but no matter how many times I fucked up, that woman always stood by me... but you know, sometimes... sometimes I have to wonder why." The old man pauses, lost in thought for several minutes, then continues, *"But Millie's health ain't so good these days. She needs a new hip... that's why I been pullin' these jobs lately... to make some money for Millie's operation... but the thing is, well, I promised Millie I'd go straight when I got out... you know, I feel real bad about that, but I had to do it... that woman'd do anything in th' world for me."* Despondent, the old man broods for several minutes, then, apparently remembering something, his mood abruptly brightens and he changes the subject. *"Hey Storkie, so what was you doin' in that motel when I came along? You wud'n gettin' some nookie on the side, was you?"*

Pleased with his little joke, Graves chuckles in a knowing way, but, blindsided, Hendricks is caught completely off guard. While not exactly hitting the target, the old man's question definitely nicks a nerve. Flustered, the content screener stammers out a response, "Uh, no… no… nothing like that… it, uh, had to do with my work."

"Work? I ain't never heard of no work that folks do in a cheap motel 'cept prostitutes… an' Stork, you sure as shit don' look like no whore to me. What kinda work you do?"

"I work in the tech industry. What do you know about the Internet and computers, Willy?"

"I know it's a damn good place to watch porn… hell, I hear you can see a woman fuck a donkey on the Internet."

Again the old man's inadvertent comment hits a little too close to home. His face flushed, Hendricks' embarrassment is unnoticed as the car rolls down the highway; maintaining his composure, the tech worker continues, "Well, it sounds like you know more about what I do than I expected. I'm what they call a content screener, Willy, and it's my job to look at photos and videos flagged by users as 'inappropriate.'"

"No shit… I guess you must see some pretty weird stuff."

"Weird? Weird is nothing… we're talking torture, sadism, bestiality… Every horror and atrocity imaginable shows up in my inbox. There's a lot of sicko bottom feeders out there, Willy."

As the significance of Hendricks' words sinks in, a look of revulsion creeps onto the old man's face. Disturbed by the idea of a garbage dump for depravity and filth, he's nevertheless curious. "Like what… what have you seen?"

"Willy, I see humanity's capacity for inflicting pain, documenting it, then holding it up for the world to see as pretty much infinite… are you sure you want to hear this?"

The old man pauses for a moment. Having lived most of his life among society's castoffs, men who have inflicted measureless acts of malice upon their fellow humans, Graves feels like he's seen it all, but still, he can't help wondering how deep the bottom is… how low does mankind go? After a brief pause, the ex-con takes a long drag off his cigarette and replies, "I'm hooked, Storkie… Fire away. Hit me with your best shot, dude."

"Okay, you asked for it. I'll start off with a couple of easy ones... first there was the guy who made a crucifix out of cow dung. It was thirty feet tall and mounted on a frame of dogwood, just like Jesus' cross. He said it was supposed to bridge the gap between Christianity and Hinduism. Of course, there was nothing illegal about it... not even borderline. Then there was the one who posted photos of his collection of two thousand dog testicles. And get this... He called himself the Rover Remover... no joke... his mission was ridding the world of unwanted dogs. And then there was the deranged foot fetishist... he posted pictures of severed human feet... there must of been forty or fifty and plenty of photos of what he did with them... the cops took special interest in that one... oh yeah, there was also the rat skinner... only live rats, of course, and documented in high-definition video... and I shouldn't forget the website dedicated to barbecuing babies. There were no documented killings but there must have been two hundred recipes... smoked babies, grilled babies, baked babies..."

Having heard enough, the old man protests, "Okay, okay, that's enough... that's enough."

Divulging his list of depravities brought a tone of world-weariness to the tech worker's voice. "There's more, Willy... always more... more than you can imagine... more than... anyone's mind... can..."

Tentative and vague, Hendricks' voice drifts into a meaningless void.

That night they were sitting in another motel room with the content screener back on his computer and Wilmer Graves watching TV. As a particularly obnoxious commercial invades the space, the old man mutes the television, causing Ted to look up. Becom-

ing more intrigued by his companion, the tech worker asks, "Willy, have you ever tried to go straight? You must have held down a job at some point in your life... what did you do?"

The career criminal frowns, a minor acknowledgement of his ongoing failure to deal with the world on its terms. "Yeah, Stork, I had a job... a few of them, but the one I remember most was when I tried to be a bricklayer... it was my first job... I was seventeen and apprenticed with this guy named Edgar... ol' Edgar was a brick mason an' a pretty decent dude, but right from th' start he was raggin' on me. 'No, Willy...' an' 'That's not right, Willy...' an' 'Do it this way, Willy...' I mean, the guy was just doin' his job... I knew that, but after a couple'a weeks of listenin' to him bitch an' complain while I was haulin' bricks up an' down a ladder in that hot fuckin' sun, all of a sudden I jus' stopped an' I said 'That's it! I can't take this shit no more! I quit!' Well, like I said, Edgar was an okay dude... I could see in his eyes that he cared about me, but he jus' did'n get it... so he sat there, lookin' at me an' shakin' his head an' finally he says, 'You know, Willy... everybody's gotta do something... Otherwise you can't pay your rent... you can't buy shoes for your kids... can't even eat...' Then he stopped for a minute and stared at me with this real sad look in his eyes, an' he reaches over an' grabs a brick... he holds it up right in front of me an' says, "Willy, at some point in life you gotta be real... this brick is real. It has substance and if you learn how to use it, it can give you a lifetime of comfort and security, but you can't eat it... you're a good kid, Willy, but you can't eat bricks.' Well, that jus' pissed me off, so I picked up a hammer an' grabbed that brick an' broke the fucker up in a hunnerd pieces... an' I ate it... with ol' Edgar watchin' the whole time... that night I pulled my first job an' stuck up a 7-11... Hell! Ain't nobody gonna tell Willy Graves what he can't do."

"So this was, what... two days into your involvement with Graves and you were getting to know him pretty well."

Hendricks got that faraway look in his eyes again. The affection he felt toward Wilmer Graves was apparent. "Yeah, Willy was pretty special. I never knew anybody quite like him."

The kid was telling me a lot, but I kept feeling like we were just scratching the surface; obviously a lot more happened back there, so I questioned him again. "What can you tell me about 'Beasley'? When we first spoke, back at Starbucks, you said something like 'I should be looking for Beasley.' What can you tell me about him?" The look on the kid's face as soon as I mentioned Beasley's name was like someone stabbed him in the stomach with a steak knife. "What's the matter, Ted? You look sick." But that was it... like he was a faucet that somebody just turned off. Clamming up, the tech worker abruptly turned his back to me and tried to go to sleep.

After Hendricks had been so open about his relationship with Wilmer Graves, I wondered if maybe I'd shut him up for good, but at that point, I had other things to think about. The cell we occupied was behind the main building. The barred room was obviously a makeshift addition to an office never intended to accommodate prisoners in addition to the sheriff and his staff. Covered with a tin roof and partially exposed to the Midwestern winter, the jail was heated by couple of propane patio heaters. Wedged into its crudely constructed nook, the cell with its two small cots, leaking sink, and open, uninviting toilet, was your basic shithole—literally.

More than anything else, I needed a plan to get out and

of course, that meant Patty. It was 8:30 in the morning and the young clerk should be at work, but I had no idea if she knew I was back here or not. Duane sure as hell wouldn't tell her, and for all I knew Bernie might not either. My friends in this dumbfuck town numbered exactly one, and when I stopped to think about it, there weren't many back in L.A. eager to bring me a get-out-of-jail-free card either.

The situation needed drastic action and since I truly in fact felt like DOGSHIT ON A STICK, it should be a piece of cake. Falling on the floor, I began to moan, "OOOOOOO-OOOAAAAAAAAHHHHHH! OOOOOOOOOOOOOAAAA-AAHHHHHH!!!" I did that for a couple of minutes, gradually getting louder, but nothing happened until Hendricks finally rolled over, stared at me for a few seconds and said, "Shut the fuck up!" My plan obviously wasn't working so I opted for the heavy artillery. Back in college I roomed with a guy affectionately known as Barry the Ep. Barry was a card-carrying epileptic, consequently I had seen my share of grand mal seizures. It was time to throw a fit.

Arching my back, I tensed every muscle in my body, clenched my teeth, and began to breathe—loud, fast and rhythmic—through my mouth. I guess the act was pretty convincing because Hendricks was on me in an instant. "My God! Are you okay?" I breathed that much louder, adding a slight wheeze to enhance the effect. Apparently experienced with seizure victims, Hendricks took a sock off and stuck it in my mouth to keep me from biting my tongue. Sucking sock, I almost threw up but the act was working. The young techie immediately yelled for help and almost instantly, the back door of the office opened—and who should pop out but Patty. BINGO!

Approaching the cell with a confused look on her face, she stopped just outside the door, looked down and said, "Frank? Is... is that you?" With no hesitation, I dropped the epileptic bit, sat straight up and said, "Patty! It's me... you gotta help me get outta here!" Startled and confused, both Patty and Ted Hendricks froze, staring in stunned silence.

Patty finally spoke up, "Frank... what are you doing? And why are you in jail?"

"I'm sorry, Patty, but I can explain. Okay, I fucked up. I was checking out the site of the explosion and wrecked my rental car driving back to town. It was stuck in a drainage ditch in the middle of nowhere and I started drinking... okay, I had already been drinking, but it was cold... and then I set the rental car on fire, but hell... I was fucking freezing and who should come along but your buddy, Duane... I mean, yeah, he rescued me and all, but then he threw me in this fucking jail cell... and who should I find in here but Ted Hendricks! He's the guy I was telling you about... Wilmer Graves' accomplice... he knows all about Graves' death and the explosion and everything! It's just... it's just..." I was exhausted, burned out, fried, and as I plopped back down on my cot, the world was spinning around me like a record stuck in a groove repeating over and over, "FUCK ME! FUCK ME! FUCK ME!..."

Somewhere a curtain seemed to be closing... the world was getting dark and the last thing I remembered seeing was Patty and Ted Hendricks standing there, still staring at me. I don't know which was more wide open, their eyes, their mouths or their blown fucking minds.

Several hours passed before Patty brought a doctor who promptly pronounced an irrefutable diagnosis: hangover. He then prescribed two Alka-Seltzers and told me to sleep it off, which I did. When I woke up it was déjà vu all over again, as Ted Hendricks towered over me, his irritation immense—and rising.

"So you already knew about Willy and me... and the explosion. Why didn't you just come out and say it, instead of pissing around like a fucking retard?"

"Look, I was trying to get you to talk about your involvement with Graves back at Starbucks, then later at your house, so don't play dumb... and yeah, I found that crater, but I have no idea what caused the explosion... and why. But I know it has something to do with somebody named Beasley. You made that much pretty clear. So what gives, kid?"

Repressing his anger, Ted Hendricks was silent as a tense moment soaked the tiny cell. When he finally spoke, his voice was a hiss, "Willy was the only other person who ever called me 'kid,' and it felt kind of affectionate when he did it, but you make it sound condescending."

"Look, I'm sorry, but there's a story here... your story... and Willy's story... and I want to tell it, but you have to help me, ki..., uh, Ted. Something bad has happened... bad and scary as shit... and maybe I can help, but you gotta let me in... okay?"

As Hendricks stared at the floor, another long silence ensued before he finally looked up and spoke again, "Okay, I guess it starts with PAGWAG."

As Ted Hendricks returned to his story, he and Willy are back in another motel. It's late at night as Graves counts the money he got from robbing a donut shop while the young techie works at his computer. After their last conversation, the old man has become fascinated by his companion's job. "Hey Storkie! So what kinda

weird shit are you findin' out there on them interwebs now?"
Wearing the portable headphones he often uses when he works,
Ted is oblivious to his roommate's question, causing the ex-con
to hobble across the room and yell, "YO STORKO! I'M TALKIN'
AT YOU, DUDE!"

Removing the headset, Hendricks looks up from his laptop.
"Huh? Oh sorry, Willy... yeah, well, I've just been looking at
something you might find interesting. It's a Facebook page for a
group called PAGWAG. The letters stand for Purity And Grace is
Water And Guns. PAGWAG's agenda seems to be guarding and
protecting our water supply..."

"So what's wrong with that? I mean, good water... that's
cool. Right?"

"Well, sure... nobody gets upset about clean drinking water,
but their idea of protecting our water supply is to create a special
security force of ten million armed militia who will have the re-
sponsibility of defending every reservoir, dam, aqueduct and water
treatment plant in the country. This force, which PAGWAG calls
the Water Warriors, would be financed by a special tax on cell
phones because they believe that radiation from cellular networks
is contaminating the water supply." At this point, Hendricks paus-
es and looks up from his laptop. "Are you sure you want to hear
this, Willy? It's pretty wacky stuff?"

Graves finishes counting the money, looks up and nods yes.
"Yeah, yeah, Storky... keep readin'... makes a lotta goddam sense
to me. Go on..."

The tech worker gives his companion a questionable look,
then turns back to his computer. "Okay, if you say so... Up to this
point, everything I've mentioned is more or less standard right-
wing, nutso conspiracy theorist dogma. With minor variations,
I see this stuff all the time. It's so common in my work that it's
not even entertaining and definitely not dangerous; these guys
never have any money and even less motivation to actually do
anything, but this one is different. The deeper you go in this, the

stranger and more disturbing it gets." Hendricks pauses and looks up again.

"Keep goin', Storky... I'm listenin'."

"Okay... do you know what fluoride is, Willy?"

"It's that shit they put in toothpaste, right?... gets ridda bad breath an' makes your teeth white or somethin'... right?"

"You're close, Willy... that's a good guess. Fluoride is a chemical compound that's been known to reduce cavities. That's why they put it in toothpaste."

"But wha's this floor-ride got to do with th' Packywhack? I don't get it."

"I'm coming to that part... so, in addition to putting fluoride in toothpaste, some places also put it in the water supply... in very small amounts... and PAGWAG believes that this fluoride, in addition to cellular radiation, is threatening our water."

His frustration growing, the ex-con frowns, then interrupts, "But what's wrong..."

"Hang on, Willy, I'm getting to the weird part. Do you have any idea what one of the main sources of fluoride is?"

"How would I know where that shit comes from?"

"Tea... fluoride is found in tea, Willy."

"TEA! I never drink that crap... I don't drink nuthin' but coffee... instant Maxwell House..."

"Uh, yeah... stay with me, okay? So what PAGWAG plans to do is dump thousands, hundreds of thousands, of tea bricks into the Colorado River, which would then greatly increase the fluoride content of L.A.'s water."

Displaying a look of pained confusion, the old man stammers, "But... but why the fuck would they do that? I mean, the Packywhacks are all about clean water... right?"

"You got it! That's what's so weird about this, Willy. PAGWAG is both in favor of pure, clean water AND wants to pollute the Los Angeles water supply with massive amounts of fluoride."

Graves' expression is one of total dismay, "But, but..."

"I know it's confusing, Willy, but it's all spelled out in PAG-WAG's manifesto right here on their Facebook page. From their perspective, the population of Los Angeles is primarily made up of celebrities and other parasites, who they see as scum... the underbelly of our culture, but they also understand that this celebrity class is highly influential. Okay, here's the deal... while a little fluoride is good for your teeth, too much of it creates a condition called dental fluorosis, which makes your teeth turn brown. So the purpose of this fluoride contamination is to give BAD TEETH to everyone in L.A., and once that happens, the parasites will support PAGWAG's agenda of cleaning up and protecting the water supply. I mean, their plan is completely demented, but it's not without a certain twisted logic. Think about it—whoever heard of a celebrity with brown teeth? It's kind of fascinating."

"But you're gonna report 'em, right? They can't get away with this shit... can they?"

"Well, they haven't actually done anything illegal yet, but even so, there's really nothing to worry about. It's like I said before, PAGWAG's agenda may be a little more creative than most of the whack jobs out there, but in one sense, they're all the same... they never have any money, so they're ineffective. Unbalanced, sure, and maybe even crazy, but they're ultimately harmless."

Continuing his story, Hendricks said the next day they pulled their final robbery.

Stopping outside a liquor store, Willy speaks, "This shud'n take long, kid. Just wait out here with the motor runnin' an' I'll be right back." The tech worker watches as the old man struggles to remove himself and his oxygen tank from the car, then, standing outside the door, he pulls out his pistol, takes a deep breath and enters. *No sooner does the ex-con disappear inside the small building than a huge pickup drives up and parks next to the Honda. As the young tech worker watches, a very large, overweight man exits the truck and immediately enters the liquor store no more than sixty seconds behind Willy Graves.*

Sensing trouble, Hendricks leaves the car, its motor still running, approaches the store and peeks through the window. Peering into the dark interior, he's horrified to see the big man standing near the door pointing a gun at Willy across the room; Graves is positioned by the cash register, his pistol also drawn and aimed at the clerk. Shouting voices can be heard through the window, but the sound is too muffled to be clearly understood.

Anxious, Hendricks pauses for a moment then quickly retrieves his iPod and headphones from the Honda. Convinced that the man hasn't seen him, the tech worker places the headphones on his ears, playing the music loud enough that a distinct buzz can be heard by anyone nearby. The music is "Constantinople," a song by The Residents, and Hendricks immediately begins to sing along as he enters the liquor store, blithely swaying to the music. "Here I come, Constantinople, here I come, Constantinople…"

As the tech worker enters the room, both Willy and the big man are screaming, each demanding that the other surrender and drop his weapon. Terrified of finding himself in the line of fire, the clerk cowers behind the counter. Deliberately looking away from the ongoing conflict, Hendricks appears oblivious to the tense standoff as he casually approaches a large display of liquor bottles still singing, "All the leaves are off of the oak and all the sheep have followed…"

As soon as the big man sees the tech nerd, he yells, "HEY BUDDY! HEY! THERE'S A ROBBERY GOING ON! WE NEED YOUR HELP!" Seemingly unaware, the content screener sings louder as he casually picks up two half-gallon bottles of bourbon and heads toward the checkout counter, "HERE I COME, CONSTANTINOPLE, HERE I COME…" Increasingly tense and frustrated, the fat man continues screaming, "HEY! HEY BUDDY! LOOK OUT! WE

GOT A SITUATION HERE! HEY! BUDDY! HEADS UP!"

Looking up as he nears the anxious man, Hendricks, pretending to suddenly grasp the situation, stops singing and cries out, "OHMYGOD!! WHAT'S HAPPENING!!" The tech worker then drops the liquor bottles, causing the glass to shatter around the big man's feet, soaking his pants and shoes with bourbon. Shocked, the fat man jumps back, losing his balance and falling awkwardly, giving Ted Hendricks just enough time to lunge forward and grab the man's gun.

Shaking as he holds the pistol above the fallen fat man, the neophyte gunman screams, "STAY DOWN! UNDERSTAND!?! DOWN ON THE FLOOR! FLAT!" then raises the revolver and fires it, creating a deafening roar and shattering three liquor displays. At the same time, the recoil from the pistol causes Hendricks to lurch backwards, tumbling into yet another stack of bottles, scattering booze and broken glass around the room. Jumping to his feet, the tech worker quickly regains his composure, aiming the gun at the big man and yelling, "DON'T EVEN THINK ABOUT IT, FATSO!" Stunned, the big man lays quivering on the floor, his clothes speckled with blood and drenched in whiskey.

Standing on the other side of the room, both Wilmer Graves and the store clerk watch in stunned silence as the unexpected scene chaotically unfolds before them. After a moment of shock and awe, Willy quickly regains his composure and shouts, "WOOHOO! STORKO! YOU THE MAN! WOOHOO!"

Shocked by his own bravado, Hendricks' reaction is noticeably restrained compared to Willy's ecstatic response: "Uh, well, something, uh, had to be done, Willy. I mean, I looked through the window and... well, you were in a hell of a mess."

Moments later, the pair is speeding away as the adrenalin induced by their near disaster begins to ebb. Still shocked at his comrade's audacity, Willy chuckles, "Stork, my man, where you been hidin' all them balls, dude? Woowee! You shudda seen the look on that fat guy's face when you snatched his piece an' then KABOOM!"

Still reeling from stress, the young tech worker is tense and edgy. Regardless, he can't suppress a slight smile as he responds, "Well… you said to let them know who's in charge."

Remembering their stickup of the formal wear shop, Graves laughs, filling the car with his raucous heehaws. "Yessiree! You done that, Storky… you sure as hell done that!"

"I felt kind of sorry for the fat guy though. I mean, you were robbing that liquor store and he was just trying to help. He probably goes in there all the time."

The Honda grows quiet for several minutes as they drive along the interstate looking for a motel. Graves finally breaks the silence, but when he does, the tone and subject of his words have changed dramatically. "Hey Stork, I keep thinkin' about those Packywhacks, and you know… I don't like 'em, no siree. I mean it just ain't right to be fuckin' around with folks' water."

Dusk quietly announces the end of the day as lights twinkle on and the sun slowly disappears. Reflecting the mood of his companion, Hendricks speaks, "I agree with you, Willy, but like I said, they're probably harmless… nuts maybe, but harmless nuts." He pauses for a moment, remembering something, then continues, "That reminds me… I've been checking out the PAGWAG website and I think their base might be right around here somewhere."

"No shit! Maybe we should find 'em… straighten 'em out a little." Willy holds up his pistol and smiles.

"Well, I don't know about that… They're fairly secretive so I don't exactly know where they are, but they do mention 'The Kingdom' several times and they also refer to some nearby landmarks, like Greer Spring in the Ozarks."

"So you really think the Packywhacks are close by?"

"I think there's a good chance. A few years ago Callaway County, less than fifty miles away, got a lot of attention for having the third best drinking water in the country, and… the nickname for Callaway County is 'THE KINGDOM of Callaway.' I don't know but it seems like the kind of place where you might find a group like PAGWAG."

"But what about Beasley? I thought you were gonna talk about where he fits into all this." The kid's story was interesting, but he seemed to be losing focus.

"Just hang on, okay? I'm getting to it but I wanted to give you some background first."

Maybe I should've kept my mouth shut… I mean, he was talking and that was great, but I didn't have a clue as to where this was going. We sat in silence for a minute, then I remembered something that had been bothering me. "Ted… I hate to change the subject but something you said earlier keeps bugging me. I know this has to be a sensitive subject so if you don't want to talk about it, it's okay but… I gotta ask."

Since I interrupted him, Hendricks had grown quiet again. A moment later, his eyes rose to meet mine. The kid was smart. The odd expression on his face made me wonder if he already sensed what was coming. Speaking slowly and deliberately, the baby-faced young man replied, "So… what? What is it?"

I took a deep breath and jumped in. "Uh, well, it's about your girlfriend, Margo. I mean, what makes you think she would fuck a chimp? She's fucking gorgeous… the most beautiful woman I ever saw. If she wants to get laid, there's no way she has to…"

The sight of Hendricks' utterly crestfallen face made one thing devastatingly clear: I had blindsided him like an anvil abusing an ant. I felt like a jerk... but then I'd never let that get in my way before. "Look, Ki..., uh, Ted, I'm sorry if I upset you... if it's too painful, don't talk about it."

As Ted Hendricks slumped back on his bunk, shadows surrounded his face making him look much older than his twenty-eight years. He pondered my question briefly before finally responding, and when he did, his voice was slow and cautious, "No... I probably should talk about it. I haven't spoken of this to anyone else and..." As the kid begin to choke up, I reached out and touched his shoulder, but he shrugged me off. "It's okay... no, it's not okay, but I need to get it out, even if it's just to a jerk like you." He paused again, staring hard at me, then continued, "You see, Margo has always liked animals... okay, considering what I already told you, that has to sound ironic but she REALLY likes animals. I'm sure you remember Archie, our chihuahua... well, sometimes I thought she loved that goddam runt way more than me... and then there was her hamster... and her turtle... and her parakeets... I knew she loved me, but the competition for her attention was fierce... but when she aimed her love light at me, it was like sitting in the sun on a rainy day... and when that happened, I was THE ONE... the ONLY one... and nothing else mattered... but then the light began to dim... I don't know why, but she grew distant... detached... unavailable... Margo is a lab assistant for a pharmaceutical company that experiments on chimps... she's totally conflicted about her work. She hates seeing the animals in cages, separated from their mates and family groups, but she also thinks it's great that someone like her can be there to take care of them, make their lives better... but then lately... around the time she grew distant, she began to talk about this one chimp... he's a full-grown male and she said there was just something really special about him... a kind of warmth and intelligence... she said she could see it in his eyes... eventually, she talked about the goddam monkey so much, I started feeling kind of jealous... OF A FUCKING CHIMPANZEE!" Composing himself, Hendricks paused again, then continued, "Then that video showed up on YouTube. Okay, I know you can't totally recognize the woman... but who would shoot a video like that... and then post it on YouTube... and the camera's static, like it's on a tripod, so she must have shot it herself, BUT WHY?... I know I'm obsessing on this but I can't help it... I can't help it..."

At this point I was pretty much in shock myself. When Hendricks first told me about Margo and the monkey, I couldn't believe it. I almost cracked up, but the kid was serious. Now, hearing Hendricks talk, he almost had me buying it. I mean, this was fucking nuts. I wanted to offer some sympathy or support or whatever, but what do you say: hey-Ted-I'm-so-sorry-to-hear-that-your-girlfriend's-bonking-a-dumbfuck-chimp? Somehow that seemed a little inappropriate, but I needed to say something, so I blurted out, "So the whole deal with the spycams was all about clarity... finding out, one way or another?"

"It... it was the only thing I could think of. I mean, I couldn't confront her on it. What if it's not her? She'd never speak to me again... and I couldn't blame her."

We sat in silence for a few moments, each mulling his own unique and twisted version of reality, when the back door of the jail suddenly opened. It was lunchtime as served by Deputy Dawg. Things were looking up.

Missouri is not noted for its jailhouse cuisine, but the break was welcome. My head was still swimming. The freakish affair continued to tease my mind but sharing more feelings with Hendricks on the subject of primate interbreeding was a no-go. Maybe I could point him back toward Beasley. "So, Ted... did it turn out that PAGWAG was headquartered around there?"

"Huh? Oh yeah." With little hesitation, he took me back to a few hours after the liquor store robbery.

The young techie and his ex-con companion are driving through a small town when Willy spots a grocery store. "Hey Stork, let's stop at this Piggly Wiggly. I could dig some barbecue chips and Dr. Pepper." It's the middle of the day and the parking lot of the small shopping center is busy. After looking for a spot near the store, Hendricks finally pulls into one next to a conspicuous and oddly painted car. With darkly tinted windows and covered with a desert camo design, the stretch Hummer is so striking that Ted and Willy are compelled to take a closer look, and as they do, both men are immediately struck by a single distinguishing feature: a bold PAGWAG logo emblazoned across the car's door. Riveted by the now familiar design, they look at each other in silence, their mutual recognition obvious.

Willy Graves is the first one to speak, "That's it, ain't it? The Packywhacks... they're here." He looks around suspiciously. "What're we gonna do?"

"I don't know, Willy. I mean... what can we do?"

Standing together in the parking lot, they watch as a third man, slowly pushing a shopping cart, advances toward them. The man, appearing to be in his mid-fifties, wears a Desert Storm jacket and pants, combat boots, and wraparound sunglasses, while protruding between his lips is a camo-colored cigarette holder. Completing the look is a black beret covering his freshly cropped military haircut; a government-issue M1911A .45 caliber automatic pistol conspicuously rests in a holster strapped to his waist. Drawing closer, the man inserts a cigarette into the holder, and as he does, the clenching of his jaw reveals a set of dark brown and mottled teeth. Standing next to Ted's ten-year-old Honda, the pair continues to watch as the man opens the rear hatch of the Hummer, places his groceries inside, then turns back to face the smaller car. With a look of disdain frozen on his face, he steps up to the Japanese car, strikes a match on its roof and lights the cigarette. Pausing to inflate his chest, he then snorts, spits in the general direction of the small car, climbs into the Hummer and drives away, never acknowledging the two men still standing in the parking lot.

Willy is the first to react: "C'mon... we gotta follow that fucker."

Hendricks quickly slides in behind the steering wheel as Willy struggles into the seat next to him, laboring to move the oxygen bottle onto the floor in front of him. As soon as the car door closes, the old man yells, "Let's go, Storky! The asshole's gettin' away!"

Shifting the Honda into gear, the young tech worker pulls out of the parking lot and speeds off in the direction of the Hummer. Soon the large and highly visible SUV can be seen up ahead. Maintaining a discreet distance, they follow for several miles until they pass a sign proclaiming "Kingdom City." A few miles past the tiny village, they watch as the Hummer turns in to a dirt driveway and stops, allowing a large iron gate to open. Moments later the car disappears, the gate closing behind it. Stopping just outside, they survey the ominous and clearly secured compound surrounded by a razor wire-topped chain-link fence. Arching across the entrance is a large sign loudly displaying a now familiar logo, PAGWAG.

"So Beasley is some kind of right-wing, para-military nut?"

"Yeah, you could say that, but that was just the beginning. The guy is something else... weird... scary weird... but I had other stuff going on. At that point, Willy and I had been together for five days and I was pretty conflicted. I claimed sickness and signed in to my job remotely... that way I could keep up with my work, but as far as Margo was concerned, I had disappeared. Despite the distance between us, I knew she was worried, so the pressure to get back was huge, but what about Willy? I was really attached to the old guy... yeah, he was crooked as a snake but I couldn't just dump him. So anyway, I guess that's when the whole Beasley and PAGWAG thing started getting to us. I mean, okay, the guy was a total asshole... nothing indicated illegal activity at that point, but the fucker was up to no good... and yeah, he took our minds off Margo and robbing donut shops... I guess he was kind of a distraction, although I didn't see it like that then... we talked about him later in the motel room."

A few hours after discovering the location of the PAGWAG compound, Ted and Willy are talking. "You still think that guy's harmless, Storky? He don't look so harmless to me."

"I don't know, Willy. Yeah, he looks kind of threatening, but I don't buy it... Like I said, these guys talk big, but they don't back it up."

"All puff an' no stuff, huh? I don' know, Stork... I feel something evil in that guy... an' I'm always right about this stuff. I tell you, he's evil and we gotta stop him. I think we should go back to that Packywhack place an' check it out... maybe follow him an' see what he's up to. Besides, I been countin' my money an' I pretty much got enough for Millie's operation, so I don't need to be pullin' no more jobs... whatcha think, Storky?"

"Yeah, I guess so, Willy. It won't hurt to check him out. We'll go over there in the morning after breakfast. Oh yeah, I also got his license number... I'll see what I can find out with that."

There's no activity in the PAGWAG compound when Ted and Willy arrive the following morning. Parking the Honda where it can't be seen, the tall techie pulls out a pair of binoculars, leans over the top of the car and watches as Beasley walks out the front door, pulls the .45 from its holster, then empties its clip, firing into the empty air. Apparently satisfied, he enters a fresh clip in the gun butt, climbs into the Hummer and slowly approaches the gate.

While his partner was spying on their adversary, Graves remained in the car. Alarmed by the sounds of shots, he whispers loudly, "What the fuck, Storky? What's that asshole doin'?"

As he reenters and starts his car, Ted's expression reveals a feeling of apprehension, "I don't know, Willy... the guy must be gun-crazy. I don't think we should get too close."

Guarded, he follows the Hummer at a safe distance as it passes through Kingdom City before stopping in front of two large warehouses just outside of town. Not wanting to arouse suspicion, Hendricks continues past the parked SUV as Beasley exits and approaches one of the buildings. A few hundred yards beyond is a gas station; pulling in, the content screener watches as the older man unlocks and enters one of the metal buildings. A few minutes later, a semi-tractor truck stops beside the big car and, as it does, the metal door rises and Beasley instructs the driver where to unload the shipment. Using a forklift, the man lifts two pallets from the truck bed and deposits them inside the warehouse.

As he fills his tank, Hendricks watches the unloading process, then enters the station and speaks to the attendant. "Hey buddy, my friend is looking to rent some warehouse space around here. Do you know anything about those buildings down the road?" He points at the warehouses. "Think there might be some space available over there?"

The attendant, a man in his seventies, is obviously in no hurry. Moving like his legs are marooned in molasses, he lumbers out from behind the counter, walks to the window and stares at the two metal buildings. Deep in concentration, the man almost appears to be seeing them for the first time. "Oh, those buildings... huh... don't know so much about them buildings... belong to a newcomer... he just built them about a year ago... don't nobody seem to know much about him. You oughta just ask him. That's his car down there... only one like that around here. They say he's got a hot tub in the back of that car... Can't say as how I believe it... why would anyone want a goddam hot tub in a car? Can you imagine how that goddam water would splash around... I heard he carries a lot of guns in it, too... strange guy if you ask me, but nobody does... wife died a couple of years ago so nobody asks me nuthin' anymore. Where you from an' why the hell would you want to rent warehouse space around here? There's a buncha warehouses over by Doobie Creek. I used to live over there a few years..."

"Uh, it's not important. My friend inherited some, uh, furniture and he needs a place to keep it for a while." Convinced that the old man could maintain his monologue indefinitely, the tech worker is anxious to leave, but the old man continues.

"Furniture, huh? I inherited some furniture one time from my uncle... Uncle John Harold... He was a hemophiliac... raised guinea hens, too... sold 'em to restaurants... that furniture was under his house when he died... can you believe that?... all covered with dirt... looked like shit, but it cleaned up real nice... my wife really liked it... she died of food poisoning... damnedest thing..."

"Uh, I'm sorry, but I have to leave... my friend is not feeling well... sorry..."

Exiting the gas station, Hendricks watches as Beasley leaves and locks the warehouse, returns to the Hummer then drives back in the direction of Kingdom City. Feeling abandoned and ignored in the car, Willy's greeting is less than pleasant. "So where the fuck you been, Stork? Look, the sunufabitch is leaving... we can't let him get away."

"Hold on, Willy... he's not going too far. We know where he lives now... and you could spot that car anywhere, but we'll follow and see where he goes." Anxious to find out more about the enigmatic Beasley, the pair tails him for a while but after a series of mundane stops at the post office, hardware store, and dry cleaners, they've had enough.

Bored, Willy remarks, "We need another plan, Stork. We ain't learned shit doin' this. Whaddaya think of those warehouses? What's goin' on back there?"

"I don't know. The guy at the gas station said he just built them a year ago. He must have something he needs to store... and a lot of it, judging by the size of the buildings. But we still don't know that he's done anything illegal. Maybe they're full of hay."

"I don't think so... I got a feelin' about them warehouses. Let's go back over there and look around."

As they arrive back at the warehouses, Willy checks out the narrow corridor separating the two buildings; not seeing any security devices, he instructs Ted to park in the passageway so he can check out the rear of the building. Slowly approaching the corner, he peeks behind the warehouse, notes a motion detector over the back entrance and returns to the car. "Nuthin' to it... it's a goddam PIR sensor... passive inf'ared... easy to fool... an' I can pick that lock in half a flash... piece of cake... let's go."

It's late afternoon and Ted is sitting at his computer in the motel room he and Willy have occupied for the last two days. The TV is on, as always, but Willy has fallen asleep.

Inane and mindless, the sound of the television drones on, but

Hendricks, staring at his laptop, blocks it out with headphones. A close look at the screen reveals a website called DMV FILES, a site where the owner of any license plate number can be identified. After consulting his notes, Hendricks enters the license number of the Hummer and pays the fee. Almost instantly, as he stares at the laptop, the Hummer's owner flashes before him: Crawford Beasley.

Next, the young techie brings a Google search engine up on his home screen and enters "Crawford Beasley" into the search field. Again, the result is almost instantaneous: POWERBALL WINNER CRAWFORD BEASLEY CALLS MISSOURI HOME! "Any place is home when you have 267 million dollars," says Beasley.

For a long tense moment, Hendricks' eyes remain locked on the screen.

It's 10 p.m. when Ted and Willy drive up and park in the corridor between the two warehouses. Ted is speaking as he stops the Honda, "I don't know, Willy, but you may be right about the nut job... his name is Crawford Beasley... and get this... the asshole won the lottery... 267 million dollars... that may not make him evil, but it'll buy a lot of pain."

"I told you... I told you... I got a bad feelin' about the dude. His goddam teeth are almost black! Weird... creepy... c'mon, let's see what's inside there."

After getting out of the car, they grab two mylar thermal blankets from the back seat and drape themselves like kids in ghost costumes at a school Halloween party. Peeking out through holes in the silver blankets, Willy instructs Ted on how to fool the PIR sensor: "Goddam thing works on body heat... the mylar will block the sensor but just to make sure, we need to move real slow... got it?" Looking like cartoon spooks, the ultra tall Hendricks and short Graves, oxygen bottle in tow, slowly glide, as if in a dream, toward the rear door of the warehouse. As they reach the entrance, the ex-con raises his blanket, giving him access to the lock which he immediately picks. Still pulling his oxygen bottle behind him, the old man enters the building, looks around with a flashlight and signals his partner to join him. "Just like I figgered, there ain't no more alarms in here. Everything's on the outside. Let's check it out."

Holding two small flashlights, they discover the warehouse is two-thirds full of neatly arranged pallets, which are then stacked three high. Row after row of nearly identical bundles, all exactly like the ones delivered earlier and all bearing the same cryptic Chinese characters, create a series of pathways crisscrossing the warehouse in an orderly pattern. Unable to control his curiosity, Willy finally hobbles over to one of the stacks, reaches up and pulls one of the sealed packages down. Ripping it open, he finds its contents are also wrapped in plastic which he tears away. Holding the dark rectangular object up to his nose, the old man exclaims, "TEA?"

Hendricks, shining his flashlight on his partner, steps up, grabs the rectangular shape and takes a deep whiff. "You're right! It is tea… a tea brick." At that point the young tech worker steps back, looks around and suddenly comprehends the astonishing reality: covertly stored in this warehouse in northern Missouri are thousands and thousands of tea bricks. Shoving the brick back up the top of the stack, Ted Hendricks looks at his comrade in crime, his eyes wide with dismay, and speaks, his voice quivering with disbelief, "Let's go, Willy. We gotta get out of here. I have to think about this."

At that point, as Deputy Bodie reappeared, Hendricks spoke up, "How much longer are you going to hold me, Deputy? The officer who brought me here from Kansas City said this was a routine matter... just a few questions. He didn't say anything about a jail cell. Am I being charged with anything?"

"No, Mr. Hendricks, there are no charges against you... yet. Sheriff Fitch just came in, he will see you now. Yeah, we need to ask you some questions. There's nothing to worry about... as long as you haven't done anything."

Looking a little sheepish, the tall content screener rose and walked to the cell door. "Uh, yeah, okay."

Trailing behind Deputy Dawg, Hendricks disappeared into the sheriff's office leaving me alone in the cell, my mind beyond boggled at the sheer amount of bizarro information it had absorbed in the last twelve hours. Needless to say, there was more than abundant room for skepticism, but then, as they say... who makes this kind of shit up? Not Ted Hendricks. It just wasn't in the kid's character. Whatever else he might be, underneath it all, Hendricks was a straight arrow. And wacko as his story was, it plugged the holes of my own investigation like a gold filling in a monkey's molar.

Hopefully, they weren't going to release the kid immediately. I pretty much had the whole picture by now but a few details were still missing... details I wanted to hear first-hand.

Soon they were back. Bernie, skeptical as usual, eyed the young techie suspiciously as he re-entered the cell. "Okay, Mr. Hendricks, you'll be released as soon as your girlfriend gets here, but we will be checking your story, so don't take any vacations in Mexico... understand?"

Obviously nervous, the kid stammered out a reply, "Y-ye-ah... sure, I, uh, understand... no problem, deputy."

"So how did it go, Ki... uh, Ted? Were they rough on you? Deputy Dawg is a bitch, for sure."

Distracted, it was a moment before Hendricks replied, "Huh? Oh, no, it wasn't so bad. They mainly just asked me about Willy and the explosion, but I denied everything. It seems like they don't have much to go on, but they're trying to figure it out... then they let me call Margo... she was furious, but she's coming to get me... she'll be here in a couple of hours. It won't be a fun ride home."

"Yeah, I'll bet... but at least you're getting out of this dump." We sat in silence for a moment until I finally blurted out, "But what about the explosion? You haven't told me what happened with the explosion yet."

Still distracted, Hendricks was slow to reply and when he did, it was obvious that his mind was still on Wilmer Graves. "Willy... poor old Willy. It was just too much for him." He paused again, reflecting, then continued. "Willy and me... you know, neither one of us drank alcohol... at all... not a drop. It was kind of weird how we connected over that."

Returning to a moment several weeks earlier, Hendricks and Graves are driving down a two-lane highway when Willy suddenly blurts out a question. "What about your ol' man, Stork... what was he like?"

Taken off guard, the tech worker hesitates for a moment then responds, "Well... both of my parents are dead... Mom when I was a baby and my dad OD'd when I was eight, so I don't remember too much about my father." Uncertain, Hendricks continues, a puzzled tone in his voice, "Uh... why do you ask, Willy?"

"Oh, I don't know... I was thinkin' 'bout my ol' man for some reason... the asshole... I hated his fuckin' guts."

Not knowing how to respond, Ted focuses on the highway. As both men stare straight ahead, the car remains silent for several moments until Willy speaks again. "He beat me... beat me with a belt... me an' ma both. He wuz always drunk when he done it... an' he drunk a lot... tha's why I don't never touch th' stuff... makes me sick t' think about it."

"I'm sorry... I didn't know..." Hendricks reaches over and turns up the heater, then continues, "You know, it's funny... I don't drink either."

"No shit! How come, Stork?"

"It was my grandfather, Dido... he raised me after my parents died... Dido was a great guy." Hendricks pauses and looks over at his companion. When he continues, a feeling of warmth softens his voice, "Actually, you kind of remind me of him, Willy."

"Huh?" Caught off guard by Ted's unexpected comment, the old man looks back with skepticism. "Are you shittin' me, Stork? You're jokin' right? Nobody says nice shit like that to me."

"No... It's true... you're not as tough as you act, Willy... just like Dido."

Uncomfortable, the old man turns the conversation back toward his companion. "Uh, so you don't drink 'cause of Dido?"

"Well, yeah, but it wasn't just that... I actually did see Dido drunk once. It was weird."

"Did he whup you? Was that it?"

"No... no... nothing like that. You see he had this dog, Charlie... Charlie was just a mutt, but Dido sure loved him. Then one day he found Charlie lying in the road... hit by a car. Poor old guy couldn't move... looked like his back was broken. Dido took him to the vet but it was no good... they had to put Charlie to sleep. As soon as he got home, Dido went straight to his closet and dug out a bottle of whiskey... I.W. Harper, and then drank the whole thing... straight... and he went nuts. He just, like, exploded in this insane rage, destroying everything inside his little house. First he broke all the dishes and glasses, then he went after the furniture with a chain saw... after that, he drug everything outside and burned it in the back yard... I tried to stop him, but I was just a kid... he was about to set the house on fire when he passed out... he apologized the next day... we never talked about it again, but I never had much interest in alcohol after that."

The car grows silent for a few moments then Hendricks continues, "But... you... you said you don't drink because of your father?"

"Yeah... yeah, I still don't know why I even thought of him... the fucker... I guess he beat on me 'til I wised up... I was fourteen... my ma done run away six months before... hell, that only made him meaner... then all of a sudden one day, it was like, that was it... wud'n gon' take any more... you know, it's funny... the only thing he ever did worth a shit was play banjo... an' he could play that fucker, sure as hell... I jus' kept thinkin' about that goddam banjo an' how it was all he cared about... how much he loved that fuckin' banjo... so one night when he was out playin' with his buddies, I piled up all this furniture and stuff in front of the door... he was boozed up out of his mind when he got home... yellin' and screamin' an' beatin' on the door... 'til he finally come 'round to the back where I was waitin' ... I'd turned off all the lights an' he comes stumblin' in, blind fuckin' drunk... I knew I had him... you see my ol' man was a fisherman an' he always had these gill nets around... you know, fixin' holes in 'em an' stuff... so I spread one of 'em out on the kitchen floor an' put a rope up by th' door... soon as I hears him stumblin' in, I jerked on that goddam rope an' tripped him... asshole fell right in that goddam net... all fucked up an' confused... he was already tangled up in it when I flipped the light on and tied that rope aroun' an' aroun' an' aroun' him... then I beat the shit outta him with that goddam banjo... he just laid there on the floor blubberin' while I pulled out my dick an' pissed on him... I left after that...

157

never saw th' sunuvabitch again." The old man sits in silence for a few moments, then continues, "You know, Stork, I never tol' that story to nobody else."

As the weight of Willy's confession sinks in, the only sound is the winter wind rushing outside the windows of the Honda accompanied by the dull roar of tires rolling along asphalt. Finally, breaking the silence is Ted Hendricks' voice, its tone soft and sympathetic: "Wow... I don't know what to say, Willy. I guess your childhood was pretty rough... did you ever see your mom again?"

"Naw... I was on my own after that." The old man flips his cigarette out the window and immediately lights another one. "Seems like you didn't have it so great either..."

"I guess so..." Moved by the melancholy of the moment, Ted hesitates, then acts on some nameless, inner compulsion. "You know... I like you, Willy... I think you're a pretty good guy down inside there."

A lengthy interval follows before the old man finally responds, "Thanks, kid... thanks, I appreciate that... you're okay, too."

As the car continues down the highway, the two men sit in silence, each lost in his own version of a world where the sad and unseen pieces of tired and untold stories never quite fit together.

I didn't know what to say. I had asked Ted Hendricks about the explosion and got a weird story about Dido's dog Charlie and Wilmer Graves urinating on his father. Not knowing exactly how to respond, I hesitated, but before I could speak, Hendricks came back to Earth—at least the Clinton, Missouri, jail cell version of it.

"I'm sorry... it's been such a crazy day. You wanted to hear about the explosion and I'm just rambling on... can't

stop thinking about Willy, I guess... I... I must have loved him. It's weird..." Stopping again, Hendricks sighs deeply, then continues, "But yeah... the explosion..."

As the kid spoke, he and Willy Graves are having breakfast in a small café in Kingdom City. "So whaddaya think, Stork? Look, you're the one that was followin' all that Packywhack weirdness, but those warehouses are full of fuckin' tea, right? And tea is full of floor-ride, right? And the guy WON THE FUCKING LOTTERY, RIGHT? I mean, yeah, he's a bozo, but he's a bozo with a bazoo-ka... two hunnerd million bazookas if I remember right."

"Yeah, you're right, Willy. Beasley is dangerous and he has enough money to do something really crazy. It's scary... what can we do?"

They sit in silence finishing their breakfast until the old man speaks in a loud whisper, "Don't look! But we're bein' watched... guess who is lookin' through the window."

Hendricks rises and calmly walks to the bathroom, and as he does, the content screener's back faces the front of the café, but when he leaves the toilet moments later, he's looking straight at the plate glass window facing the front of the building. Immediately outside, staring though the glass, is Crawford Beasley, impassive and still clinching the cigarette holder between his tobacco-colored teeth. Dressed in full paramilitary drag, his right hand resting on the butt of his pistol.

Sitting down, his back to the window again, Hendricks tries to finish his breakfast, but his hand is shaking as he raises a fork full of scrambled eggs to his mouth. "He sees us. What do we do, Willy?"

"Cool it... I don't think he knows nuthin'. We wuz just a couple of guys in a parkin' lot two days ago... why would he remember us? An' whut would he do anyway... blow th' whole goddam café away? Jus' cool it, Stork. He'll go away in a minute."

Moments later, Willy nods toward the window and says, "See, he's already gone. It wud'n nuthin'. Just weird that he happened to be there, that's all."

Ted turns and looks at the window. No one is there. "Yeah, I guess so."

As they finish and pay their bill, the young techie speaks again. "You know, Willy, I keep thinking we screwed up back in that warehouse. We have to tell somebody about this and we need some evidence... we should have taken one of those tea bricks with us. At least we'd have something to show the cops or the FBI or... I mean, I'm not all that anxious to go back, but we need something to prove we haven't made all this crazy shit up. What do you think?"

The old man pauses for a moment, then responds, "Yeah, I guess you're right, Stork... I mean, I ain't talkin' to no FBI, but I guess you can... seems like somebody should... so yeah, let's go back and get a fuckin' tea brick."

It's shortly after sunset when Ted and Willy return to the two warehouses owned by Crawford Beasley. As the Honda turns off the main road and prepares to pull in between the two buildings, it suddenly stops. Looking at each other suspiciously, the pair is surprised to see a semi-tractor truck parked behind the warehouses blocking the end of the passageway. Obviously uncomfortable, the ex-con speaks, "I don't like this, Stork... that truck wud'n here before."

"I know, Willy... I don't like it either. Wait here... I'm gonna check it out." Parking the Honda at the opening of the corridor, Hendricks exits the car, walks out to the road and looks around. The area is deserted. Returning to the Honda, the techie gets in and says, "I don't know, Willy... yeah, it's weird but there's nobody around... I guess it's okay." He drives the car up into the shadows between the two buildings and cuts the motor. The air is *dead and this leaden atmosphere mirrors a total lack of movement and sound.*

Donning their silver sheets again, the strange twosome is moving toward the rear of the buildings when Willy stops and whispers, "I'm sorry, Stork, but my goddam prostate's actin' up... I gotta pee. Look, I'll let you in the buildin' an' you grab the tea brick, okay. You don't need me and that'll give me a few minutes to take care of business, then we can get the fuck outta here."

"Yeah, okay, Willy... whatever you say."

Using his flashlight, the old man quickly picks the lock and opens the door, allowing Hendricks to enter the metal building. Standing in the shadows, the ex-con relieves himself, then quietly waits for his partner's return. The autumn air is cool. As he waits, Graves lights a cigarette and watches the smoke as it joins his frosty breath creating tiny clouds that curl and waft their way up and into the night. Taking another deep drag and exhaling, his attention fixates on the puffy abstraction leaving his lips until a distant sound grabs his attention. Holding his breath, the old man cocks his head and listens to the faint hum of a motor, quickly growing louder... and louder. Alarmed, it's obvious that something is approaching and as the noise reaches a dull roar, Willy ducks down behind the Honda just as a large vehicle enters the opening between the buildings. In the dark, from his position hidden behind the small Japanese car, Graves is unable to make out the vehicle, but one thing is clear: the Honda is trapped.

Uncertain, the old man removes the pistol from his waistband and waits, as the car blocking the exit sits in silence. Suddenly the entire area is washed in light accompanied by the sound of electronic deadbolts sliding into place, breaking the silence with an ominous, grinding noise. Not only is the Honda pinned between the two larger vehicles, but Ted Hendricks is now apparently trapped inside the warehouse. Outwardly calm, despite their dire circumstances, Willy listens as footsteps circle the new vehicle, then stop as the opening and closing of a hatchback is heard, fol-

lowed by a crackling electronic sound. Eerie, harsh and abrasive, a voice, amplified through a bullhorn, slices through the night air.

"HAHAHA!!! YOU DUMBFUCKS! YOU IDIOTS! YOU PATHETIC EXCUSE FOR SUBHUMANS! DID YOU ACTUALLY THINK ME UNAWARE?... THAT I DIDN'T KNOW YOU WERE FOLLOWING ME? HAHAHA! WHAT UTTER AND SHEER STUPIDITY! HOW MUCH DID I DELIGHT AT YOUR NAÏVE AND MORONIC IGNORANCE? HOW EASY WAS IT FOR ME TO ATTACH A GPS TRACKING DEVICE TO THAT WRETCHEDLY ANTIQUATED JAP CAR? HUH? HUH? OKAY, NO MORE MISTER NICE GUY! I'M ROLLING UP THE DOOR AND GIVING YOU EXACTLY THIRTY SECONDS TO LEAVE MY BUILDING, CRAWLING ON YOUR HANDS AND KNEES! UNDERSTAND?"

As the large metal door rises, footsteps are heard approaching the entrance to the warehouse. After a few moments of silence, the amplified voice pierces the silence again.

"ALL RIGHT IMBECILES! YOUR TIME IS UP! I'M COMING IN! WHEN THIS DOOR CLOSES BEHIND ME YOU WILL BE TRAPPED LIKE INSECTS IN A CESSPOOL, QUIVERING AND COWERING AS I TRACK YOU DOWN LIKE THE DESPICABLE DOGS YOU ARE! ARE YOU READY! ARE YOU READY TO DIE, DOGS? HAHAHAHA!!!!"

The sound of footsteps is heard again, quickly followed by the noise of the rolling metal door closing with a screeching thud. But, as silence dominates the aural landscape again, a single throbbing drone purrs quietly in the background. In his haste, Crawford Beasley exited the Hummer with its engine still running. Rising up from behind the Honda, Willy cautiously approaches the large vehicle and peeks inside. Noting the key in the ignition and the absence of anyone nearby, he enters the cab, carefully placing his oxygen bottle on the seat beside him, shifts the car into reverse and backs up to the front of the warehouse. Sitting right outside the closed metal door, the old man then *triggers the car's air horn, blasting its intrusive screech across the nocturnal landscape.*

Inside the warehouse, as the chaos erupted, Ted Hendricks climbed on top of a stack of tea bricks. From this perch, ten feet above the ground, he is able to follow the progress of Beasley as the older man methodically searches for intruders, until, without warning, the uber-loud horn of his Hummer penetrates the closed door, immediately followed by the roaring throb of its engine.

Stunned, Beasley rushes to open the closed metal door; and as he does, Willy, watching the steel barrier rise from inside the Hummer, guns the motor again, then steers the huge car back in the direction of Kingdom City. When the metal door finally opens, Beasley, carrying his bullhorn in one hand and his pistol in the other, is shocked to see his car driving away. Dumbfounded and drunk with disbelief, the middle-aged man feebly chases the Hummer down the highway.

"STOP! STOP! YOU HEAR ME? THAT'S… THAT'S MY CAR! YOU CAN'T TAKE MY CAR! DO YOU HEAR ME! YOU CAN'T TAKE MY CAR! HOW… how…" as he lowers the bullhorn, Beasley's voice assumes a faintly flaccid and fragile tone. "… how will… I… get home?" Approximately one hundred feet from the warehouse, the quasi-military devotee stops and stares, his beloved Hummer gradually growing smaller in the distance.

Back at the warehouse, Ted Hendricks stands for a moment in the open doorway, watching the curious interplay between Crawford Beasley and his rapidly disappearing Hummer, but, quickly realizing his opportunity, the techie rushes back to his Honda, slides in behind the steering wheel and speeds away, driving in the opposite direction. Hearing the sound of the escaping car, Beasley immediately turns and fires wildly, aiming several shots in the general direction of the Honda, but, immersed in his own futility, he slowly lowers the gun as his head erratically pivots back and forth, following the flight of the two departing vehicles.

It's several hours later as Hendricks and Graves rehash the hectic events of a wild day while eating barbecue in their motel room.

"Gimme that hot sauce, Stork… damn, these ribs are bitchin'."

"Yeah, sure… no problem." Hendricks grabs a white foam container of coffee-colored sauce and hands it to his companion. After taking a bite of chicken, he pauses then looks over at Willy eagerly gnawing on a sparerib. "Hey Willy… you hid that Hummer in a great spot… good job."

"Thanks… I spotted that dirt road when we were following the dumbfuck yesterday… he'll never find it up there."

They eat in silence for a few moments until the younger man stops and speaks again, "But, uh, what do we do now, Willy? I mean Beasley's a nutcase… And shit, he's dangerous as hell, but we're not the ones to stop him… and I have to get back to Margo… and my job."

"Yeah, I know…" Reflecting, Graves pauses for a minute as he lights a cigarette, then continues, "I been thinkin' 'bout this, Storky… I mean, we got the dude's car an' he's gonna want it back, right?"

Eyeing his roommate uncertainly, the content screener responds slowly, "Yeah? What're you thinking, Willy?"

"Look… you gotta get back to your life an' I gotta get back to Millie… I think I got enough dough to get her operation now, but I wanna get her somethin' special… really special… you know what I mean?"

His uneasiness growing, Hendricks responds with apprehension. "No… I don't know what you mean, Willy… and I'm getting a bad feeling about this…"

"Now don't be gettin' yur panties all bunched up… ol' Willy ain't steered you wrong yet, have I?"

165

Dumbfounded as he looks around the cheap motel room littered with empty food cartons, cigarette butts and dirty clothes, Hendricks briefly considers the shameless gall saturating the ex-con's question. "Well, I don't know about that, Willy..."

"Okay, okay, I'm a shitty housekeeper... so what? Here's the deal... Millie's gonna be all pissed off if I just show up with a fist full of money from doin' a buncha stickups, so I gotta surprise her... take her mind off all them jobs I been pullin'..."

"Yeah?..."

"Yeah... so Millie has always had this thing about Cadillacs... she calls 'em a sign of real class... an' I been promisin' to get her one for years..."

"What are you saying, Willy."

"A trade... a simple trade... no big deal. We give Beasley his Hummer back and he gives us a Caddy... an Escalade... a gold one."

"WHAT? ARE YOU FUCKING CRAZY? We're dead meat if Beasley sees us again! He'll burn us alive and throw the ashes in the trash... no way I'm going near that guy!"

"C'mon Stork... think about it... all's we hav'ta do is figger out some kinda swap where he drops the Caddy off then leaves... we'll make it someplace where we can watch but he can't see us... then after he's gone, we get the Cadillac an' tell him where to find his goddam Hummer... nuthin' to it... piece'a cake..."

"I don't know, Willy... It's crazy... I don't want to have anything to do with that guy... I mean, who knows what he might do... no, it's just too crazy."

"Look... you want outta this whole deal, right? An' I gotta get home one way or 'nother... I mean, I gotta get back to Alabama and I ain't gettin' on a Greyhound with this goddam oxygen bottle... Just help me do this one thing an' I'll be gone back to Millie an' you can go home an' call up the FBI about Beasley... or whatever the fuck you wanna do... okay?"

As the ex-con takes a deep drag on his cigarette, a tense mo-

ment passes between the two men. Obviously uncomfortable with the old man's plan, Ted nevertheless sees its logic—and potential outcome... maybe.

"I don't know... let me think about this a little, Willy... okay?"

"So you guys actually stole Beasley's Hummer, then traded it back to him for the Escalade? Shit! That takes some balls!"

"Yeah, well, Willy had plenty of nerve... maybe too much."

Hendricks checked his watch. It had been nearly an hour since he phoned Margo—she would be showing up soon, but he hadn't gotten to the end of his story. I needed to hear about the explosion. "So how did you work out the swap? Facebook?"

"Yeah, it was easy enough to arrange with private postings. That café right outside of Adrian was the perfect spot. Willy and I waited inside for Beasley to show up and drop off the Cadillac."

Ted Hendricks is fidgeting with his food as his companion lights another Camel. "Willy, you're not supposed to smoke at this table."

"Hell, Stork, we ain't in no goddam Califuckin'fornia... nobody gives a shit 'bout a little smoke aroun' here." The old man coughs into his napkin, then resumes his meal, alternating be-

tween a bite of hamburger, a sip of coffee and a drag on his cigarette. A few minutes later Hazel, the waitress, approaches their table.

"How you guys doin' over here? Can I getcha somethin' else?" Noting the nervous Hendricks, she glances down at his barely eaten burger and comments, "What's the matter, Shorty... not hungry... or you prefer Gaines-Burgers? Haw! Haw! Haw!" Her fake laughter echoes against the hard walls of the small café.

Obviously startled, the young techie looks up. "Huh... what?"

"I'm just jerkin' your chain... you are one long drink a' water, kid, sure as shit... I'll bet don't nobody call you Shorty... huh?"

"Uh, no... not for a while... uh, could I have a coffee, Hazel?"

"Sure, kid... No problemo..."

The waitress returns with Hendricks' coffee and refills Willy's cup. They sit in silence for a moment as the content screener continues to pick at his food, occasionally sipping the hot steaming brew. Bored, the ex-con finally speaks, "Hey! I'm pretty excited about that Caddy, Stork. Ol' Millie gon' shit in 'er pants when I drive up in that baby." He coughs again. Willy's chronic smoker's cough appears to be getting worse.

"I have a bad feeling about this, Willy... Beasley gave in too easily. I don't trust it."

"C'mon, Stork... give it a rest. You been bellyachin' 'bout this all day. I tell you, there ain't nothin' to it." The old man takes a long drag and continues, "Shit man! This is it! I can feel it! My life ain't been nuthin' but fuck-ups an' bad breaks up to now, but this is it... things is finally goin' my way."

The two men are sitting at a table by the window with Willy monitoring the parking lot outside. As Ted Hendricks picks up a cold french fry, stares at it for a moment, then drops it on his plate, the old man speaks up excitedly, "Stork, look... look... there it is!"

With Willy and Ted watching intently, a large gold-colored car pulls into the parking lot followed by a taxi. After the Cadillac slips into a parking spot, Crawford Beasley, as always in *full Desert Storm drag, steps out of the Escalade, pauses for a moment to survey the scene, then enters the back seat of the cab and drives away.*

"That's it! That's it! Ain't it beautiful, Storky? Let's go check it out!"

"Wait, Willy, hold up. We gotta make sure Beasley is gone. We're not going anywhere for at least an hour, so take your time."

"An hour! What th' fuck, Stork… that guy ain't doin' shit as long as we got his car."

"Yeah, you're probably right, Willy, but once we tell him where it is, he could be after us pronto. Let's give him plenty of time to get away."

"Fuck him! Forget about the goddam car. We don't owe him nuthin'!"

"Yeah, I agree, but a deal's a deal… look, this was your idea… and the asshole did deliver Millie's precious Cadillac. Order some pie or something… drink another cup of coffee. We gotta kill some time."

With the old man feverishly chain-smoking and drinking coffee, another forty-five minutes goes by as the café slowly empties. Hendricks finishes his meal, opens his laptop and begins to catch up on his email. Finally, the last customer pays his bill, leaving Ted and Willy as the only ones left in the small café. Ready to close up, Hazel returns to their table, "Hey, dudes! Leavin' is tough when we're havin' so much goddam fun, but I'll be turnin' into a pumpkin pretty soon and it ain't a pretty sight… if you get my drift."

Picking up the repartee, the old man responds, "I hear you, Hazel… hell, I been trying to get this young stud outta here for a hour, but he keeps tellin' me what a hot piece a' ass you are… I think he's hopin' to get lucky."

"Yeah, yeah… I bet he's got a dick the size of Texas, too. C'mon, guys, I gotta close up an' go home."

As the young techie pays their bill, the ex-con drags his oxy-

gen bottle to the door, then steps outside. Standing in the empty parking lot, Willy pauses to look around as Ted joins him. "He's gone, Stork... just like I told you... the asshole wants his goddam car back... he's not gonna fuck with us."

It's just after ten o'clock and the night air is cool and calm as the two men approach the gold car. Peeking through the window, the old man squeals with delight. "Look at that, Stork! It's the most beautiful goddam thing I ever saw. Millie's gonna fuckin' love it. Whaddaya think, dude?"

The tech worker cautiously opens the door and looks around the large interior. The new car smell is all but overwhelming. Sliding into the driver's seat, he notes that the car has been driven a total of thirty-eight miles. "I... I guess it's okay, Willy. Let's get out of here."

Fifteen minutes later, as the big car speeds down the highway, Willy Graves speaks up, "Uh, sorry, Stork, but my goddam prostate's doin' it again. Can you pull off the road so's I can pee."

"Yeah, it's okay, Willy. I guess I'll go ahead and tell Beasley where he can find his car. I'll use my phone to notify him on Facebook. There's a side road up ahead."

The dirt road that Hendricks turns onto is so narrow, he has to drive two hundred yards to find a space large enough to turn the big car around. As he stops the Cadillac in the center of the small clearing, Graves gets out while Hendricks creates the Facebook posting. He finds the PAGWAG page and privately posts the location of the Hummer, then pauses for a minute and suddenly jumps out of the car. Willy has just finished urinating and is stuffing his penis back into his pants when he hears Ted shouting, "Hey, Willy... I gotta check something. If Beasley put a GPS tracker on my Honda, there could be one on the Escalade, too. Wait a second while I look around."

It's cold and the old man is shivering, but he does as he's told. Ted Hendricks quickly crawls under the Cadillac and examines the underside of the car with a small flashlight. "Hurry the fuck up, Stork… it's goddam cold out here." The chilly night air is deadly still as the old man wraps his arms around his body, slowly bobbing up and down trying to keep warm.

"Okay, okay… this shouldn't take too long."

Suddenly, without warning, as the young techie crawls out from under the car, the doors lock and the lights flash; at the same time the stereo system begins blasting a curious piece of music. It's the William Tell Overture in all its Lone Ranger glory. With the familiar refrain echoing through the night air, Hendricks rises to his feet as he and Willy stare at each other, their faces frozen into odd and befuddled shapes. Then, after a taut and unnerving minute, the sound of Crawford Beasley's voice, reminiscent of the recent incident at the warehouse, echoes with a sinister sneer.

"HAHAHA! YOU IDIOTS THOUGHT YOU HAD ME, DIDN'T YOU? YOU THOUGHT I WOULD JUST FOLD MY TENT AND CRAWL AWAY LEAVING YOU WITH A BRAND NEW CAR FOR YOUR TROUBLE! WELL, THINK AGAIN NINCOMPOOPS! THINK AGAIN, BECAUSE YOU ARE CURRENTLY LOCKED INSIDE OF AN AUTOMOBILE THAT WILL BE BLASTED TO ATOMS IN EXACTLY NINETY SECONDS. DO YOU HEAR ME… THAT'S EIGHTY-FIVE SECONDS NOW AND COUNTING DOWN. I ONLY WISH I COULD SEE YOUR…"

As the snide and condescending voice of Crawford Beasley drones on in the background, Ted Hendricks shouts at his partner, "Run, Willy, run! We gotta get out of here." Picking up his friend's oxygen bottle, Hendricks half-pushes and half-carries the old man back out toward the highway as Beasley's malevolent countdown continues.

"SEVENTY-FIVE SECONDS, DOLTS! HAS A FEELING OF

SHEER TERROR TOTALLY AND COMPLETELY OVERWHELMED YOU YET? I DO LOVE THE SIGHT OF A FACE DEVOURED BY PURE UNADULTERATED PANIC! SEVENTY SECONDS..."

Tripping, Willy's frail body is once more seized with a spasm of uncontrolled coughing as he hits the ground. Helping the old man up, Ted urges him onward, "C'mon, Willy... c'mon... we gotta get away from that car!"

"SIXTY SECONDS, YOU NITWITS... NOW IT'S FIF-TY-FIVE... HAVE YOU TRIED BREAKING THE WINDOWS YET? THEY'RE PURE BALLISTIC POLYCARBONATE! YOU COULDN'T GET THROUGH THEM WITH A SLEDGEHAM-MER! HAHAHA! FORTY-FIVE SECONDS AND COUNTING..."

Helping Willy to his feet, they stumble along until the tube leading from the ex-con's oxygen bottle gets caught on a twig, pulling the plastic cannulas from his nose as he falls to his knees, gasping for breath.

"THIRTY SECONDS, LOSERS... TWENTY-EIGHT, TWEN-TY-SEVEN... HAVE YOU GIVEN UP YET! ARE YOU PRAYING TO SOME NONEXISTENT DEITY... A GOD THAT IGNORES, MOCKS AND HUMILIATES YOU... WHILE LAUGHING AT YOUR PATHETIC AND SNIVELING CRIES! TWENTY SEC-ONDS, NINETEEN..."

Bending over, Ted sticks the nosepiece back in Willy's nostrils, picks him up and lurches another twenty feet before collapsing behind a boulder at the side of the road. As both men gasp for air, the relentless voice of Crawford Beasley nears the end of its countdown.

"THE TIME HAS COME, YOU SLIME-SUCKING SEWER SCUM... ARE YOU READY... FIVE, FOUR, THREE, TWO, ONE..."

And then... nothing.

Silence...

The silence of a tomb. The silence of a morgue at midnight. The silence of a cemetery occupied only by rotting cadavers, snakes and snails...

Until... a faint sound is heard from the car stereo, now one hundred feet away. Once again, the sound is both familiar and completely unexpected. It's the theme from Star Wars and after an achingly long thirty seconds, the music fades leaving the sneering voice of Crawford Beasley to cut through the night one last time.

"SURPRISE!"

The sound of the explosion is beyond ear-splitting... beyond brain-rearranging... beyond anything Ted Hendricks had experienced or knew he was capable of experiencing. The sky lights up like lightning but it's a million bolts hitting all at once followed by a rush of air that flattens trees, eradicates bushes and reduces the Cadillac to rubble.

Stunned, the young content screener slowly rises to his feet, scanning a scene of total devastation. Looking down, he immediately senses a void, a lack of life force in Wilmer Graves' limp and motionless body. Crawford Beasley's insane desecration of life was almost complete... but somehow he had survived.

Despite the futility of the act, Ted is compelled to drag Willy's body back out to the road but that's as far as he can go. Dumping the old man's corpse, along with his oxygen bottle and the huge pistol still death-gripped in Willy's fist, by the side of the road, he stops and stares at nothing, unaware of the tears streaming down his face or the involuntary convulsions propelling them down his cheeks and onto the ground.

Finally, with no other choice, he looks back one more time at the lifeless heap that had become his friend and begins the long trudge back to the aging Honda still parked at the café.

PART THREE
BEAST-LEY

So here I am… in jail… in Clinton, *DUMBFUCK*, Missouri. Lying on this *DUMBFUCK* cot, I can feel every *DUMBFUCK* bump and lump on this *DUMBFUCK* mattress, thinking about how many other *DUMBFUCKS* have laid here and pissed and shit and thrown up and maybe even croaked right on this bed… It's been a week… or has it been more… two weeks… three… It's all so hazy now… But yeah, Ted Hendricks' girlfriend Margo eventually showed up, scowling, pissed off and more beautiful than ever, and took the kid home. Patty got my stuff from the motel and brought my laptop, allowing me to document Willy & Ted's Excellent Adventure while it was still fresh on my mind…

But that was several days ago... I haven't seen her since.

I think it's midnight... maybe later, I don't know... The world outside my cell is a void... a vacuum... a cipher. I know nothing more today than I did yesterday... or the day before... or the day before... My pal, Deputy Bodie, brings me three meals a day. I ask about a trial... and a lawyer... and Patty. The midget bowling ball gives me this little shit-eating grin, then slides the tray under the door and splits... I'm beginning to think this is what forever feels like. I mean, what's to stop me from lying on this cot in perpetuity... like they tell you when your rich aunt dies and they want you to buy this stainless steel casket that goes in the concrete vault and protects her from the worms... IN PERPETUITY! But you don't give a shit about the old bag, you just want the money. HA! My mind teems with these thoughts—perverse, morose, depressing, but they fade, oh yeah, THEY PALE COMPARED TO THE DARKNESS... the huge black blob of nothing that floats, shimmering like an ebony amoeba right there in front of me. Every time I close my eyes it's waiting... amorphous, fluid and shape-shifting like a jellyfish made of mucus waiting to mold its evil malignancy to my face, my mind, my soul, my... I keep thinking ATTACK IT! ATTACK THE BLOB, FRANK! MAKE A WEAPON! TAKE THAT PLASTIC SPOON AND MORPH IT INTO A MACHETE, YOU IDIOT! SWING IT! SWING IT, FRANK! CUT THAT FUCKER INTO A MILLION LITTLE PIECES! BUT HO! WATCH OUT! IT'S CREEPING UP YOUR ASSHOLE, FRANK... OH NO! IT'S AFTER YOUR DICK NOW! IT... IT...

"FRANK! FRANK! FRANK! WAKE UP! YOU'RE HAVING A NIGHTMARE!"

I sat up, expecting to see, who else, Ted Hendricks towering over me, weaving back and forth, his rage tangible, but somehow the kid had mutated into Patty... what a pleasant surprise.

"You were swinging your arms around like crazy, Frank.

It looked like... well, you were about to hit your penis, so I woke you up."

"Uh, yeah, good call. Thanks, Patty." Not convinced that I was actually awake, I looked at her hard then shook my head. Red flags were popping up like crazy in my sleep-addled brain. Still not convinced, I tentatively continued, "So, uh, what are you doing here, Patty... if, uh, this is really you..." Desperate for some sign of recognition, I squinted, staring straight at her, and continued, "I mean, you kind of disappeared and I thought..."

"I know, Frank... I'm sorry... you must have felt like I deserted you. It... it's been a rough week." Unable to disguise the pain in her eyes, she looked away, taking a few moments to compose herself before going on, "I'll explain later, but right now I have to get you out of here. Grab your stuff, Frank... let's go."

"But wait... it's the middle of the night... where are we going?"

"C'mon, Frank, we have to hurry..." Projecting a feeling of urgency, Patty picked up my laptop and coat. Aggressively pushing me through the open cell door, she continued, "Look... you want to get out of here, right?"

"Yes, but..."

"But what?" Anxious and frustrated, the young clerk stopped, her eyes radiating a sobering combination of care and concern.

"But... what's going on? Are... are you breaking me out of jail? Is that what's happening?"

"Frank, we don't have time to talk about this now. Bernie is trying to get you charged with domestic terrorism..."

"WHAT?" This couldn't be real. I had to be dreaming.

After a short but tense ride, we pulled up in front of the house where Patty lived with her mom and brother. Stopping the car, the young woman sat behind the steering wheel for several seconds, her eyes staring straight ahead, the engine still running. As I turned and looked, attempting to read her blank expression, the emotional weight of some huge unknown burden was clear.

"What's wrong, Patty? I appreciate the jailbreak, but I don't understand why you're doing this. You're taking a big risk here, and…"

"My mom died, Frank… five days ago. We buried her yesterday."

"What? Shit… I'm so sorry to hear that, Patty. It must be horrible for you and Tommy Joe." I reached over and tried to put my arm around her, but she just sat there, impassive and still, like a rock in a block of ice.

"Tommy Joe is gone. He disappeared right before Mom died." Pausing and turning around, she looked straight at me, making eye contact for the first time since I woke up in the cell. "It was him, wasn't it… He was the one that shot Billy in the donut shop, wasn't he?"

Piercing my persona, her eyes were somehow searching, soft and strong. "Well, yeah, it was him… I mean, he is your kid brother after all… how could I rat him out to Bernie. The gun went off by accident. He didn't do it on purpose. What else could I…"

My voice trailed off as I watched Patty's breath, slow and deliberate, in and out. The kid's world was coming apart. As I reached over and stroked her shoulder again, this time she yielded, ever so slightly, to my touch.

"It's okay, Frank. It's okay… It's…" She paused, feeling the weight of her words as they blocked her tongue, filling her mouth with memories she could no longer control, then, suddenly, spontaneously, spilling back out into the air, "It's not okay… It's not… It's not…" Sobbing uncontrollably, Patty melted into my shoulder, her chest heaving as her breath convulsively jerked in and out. "It… will… never… be… okay… again."

Cloaked in chaos—empty bottles, paper plates and cups, unwashed serving dishes, half-eaten casseroles, and other byproducts of social grief—Patty's working-class home had recently hosted a wake for the young woman's mother. Shell-shocked into oblivion, Patty left the house as it was and, frantic to restore order to an unfocused and floundering life, she had apparently hitched her wagon to my mess, a dubious decision at best… but desperation makes strange bedfellows… or something like that.

After roaming around the disarray for several minutes, I walked into Patty's bedroom where she was finishing pack-ing her suitcase. "I know things are moving fast, Frank, but we don't have much choice."

"There are always choices, Patty, and… Well, maybe you should give this a little more thought. I mean… you have a life here… okay, things aren't so great right now, but…"

"No, things are not great and they're not gonna be great. Is a clerk's job in a sheriff's office great? Is marrying Duane and having his kids great? Is a dead mother and a runaway brother great? You tell me, Frank… and what about you? How will you feel buried in Leavenworth as a domestic terrorist?"

"That's crazy, Patty... there's no way Bernie can get away with that."

"Don't count on it, Frank... you don't know what she's been up to. Bernie has you and Ted Hendricks pegged as co-conspirators. She says the explosion was a plot gone wrong. Did you know the President was in St. Louis for a re-dedication of the Gateway Arch last week? She says you guys were planning on blowing up a car bomb and bringing down the arch... maybe even killing the President. She's got it all figured out, Frank. Oh yeah, apparently you wrote a glowing review of something called *The Anarchist Cookbook* book a few years ago? Right? Well, she found that, too."

"But... but that was just satire... a joke... it was nothing... a joke... a..." As my voice trailed off, a foul flavor ascended from my stomach to the base of my throat, forming a fetid pool that gurgled and brayed, gleefully exuding the rancid odor of panic. Yeah, it was crazy, but what was I going to do? Hire an expensive lawyer... yeah, sure. If Deputy Dawg got a prosecutor to buy into this crap, I'd be stuck with some crummy public defender who'd probably be happy to watch the smart-ass L.A. guy sail off down the river. He and Bernie might even build the boat together.

"Okay, you convinced me. What do we do?"

As far as crazy, convoluted shit goes, the plan was fairly simple. We were headed back to Blue Springs, where we had to talk Ted Hendricks into taking us to Beasley's compound. Then, after signing up Hendricks, we would somehow sneak into the whack job's heavily guarded and fortified stronghold, gather gobs of evidence while avoiding detection, escape unharmed, and facilitate the mad bomber's capture and prosecution... nothing to it... right? Right? RIGHT!?!

Since Ted Hendricks would be at work all day, there was no reason to arrive at his place before late afternoon. Also we had no idea when Bernie and the authorities would connect Patty's absence with my disappearance, but I figured it wouldn't take long and

Patty's old Jeep was a dead giveaway. Staying off the freeway and using back roads, we stopped at a diner on State Highway 58 for lunch.

"So what's the story on your mom, Patty? It's okay if you don't feel like talkIng about it, but she didn't seem so bad the last time I saw her." I was lying, of course; for all I could tell, the old bag COULD'VE ALREADY BEEN DEAD, lying in that hospital bed, but the kid was carrying some heavy baggage and I thought she might need to unload.

Looking at me from across the table, Patty's pain and anguish were obvious. This time she maintained her composure, but as she spoke, the tears still welled up around the corners of her eyes. "It was a staph infection, Frank. Thanks for asking... it came out of nowhere with no warning... no warning at all. Mom was a fighter, but her health was never great... she smoked, like, two packs a day... and always seemed to have a cough... or a cold... or a sore throat..."

As Patty went on about her mom's poor health and consequent death, I thought about how differently we perceived the dead woman. To the daughter, her mother was a courageous warrior who came up unlucky... hitting a bad streak that ended in a fatal staph infection, something she would surely have survived if the hospital had managed her care properly. But I saw the middle-aged woman as a burnout, a single mom with a thankless, low-paying job, who took shitty care of herself. Okay, I didn't actually know her, but all the signs pointed to a short, miserable life. Of course, I didn't say that to Patty. Let her see the dead woman as a damaged saint, a flawed diamond in a massively imperfect world—what's the harm in that? Regardless, thinking about this shit was depressing. I needed a drink. We all have our illusions and at that point, I needed to find mine. We were just finishing our burgers.

"I noticed there was a bar next door when we came in. You want to stop in and get a drink?"

Patty frowned. "I told you I don't drink alcohol, Frank."

"Oh yeah, sorry."

"But you can have one if you want."

Her voice was saying one thing but her tone and downcast eyes said something else. Well, what the fuck... It had been well over a week since I'd had a drink and this fugitive from justice shit was stressful. I deserved a little pick-me-up. "Okay, I'll make it a quick one. We won't be in there long."

The bar was typical of the kind of places you often find attached to diners and greasy spoons. It was dark, almost empty, and decorated in a thoughtless, almost haphazard, way. The most notable motif was a recurring pattern of ancient *Mechanics Illustrated* calendars, apparently someone's collection from the '50s and '60s. From several random spots around the room, a bevy of young beauties, their faces and hands artistically smeared with grease, passionately fondled wrenches, screwdrivers and spark plugs.

I immediately felt at home, but I can't say the same for Patty. Her seeming estrangement from the bar's laid-back ambience had me wondering if this was a virgin excursion, while also prompting me to check out the joint with fresh eyes. Yeah, it was relaxed, but it was the kind of diversion that took its value from consciously going against the grain of everyday life. It was like a sex shop—you don't go in one if you've just knocked off a hot piece, and you don't enter a bar at peace with the world after two hours of hatha yoga.

Objectively, they are often dreary, drab and mundane, especially bars like this one. Regardless, I realized my brain was working overtime processing worthless information, a sure sign that I needed a drink. Waking up the bartender, a dead ringer for Kojak, I ordered a bourbon on the rocks. As he placed the tumbler of amber liquid in front of me, a tingle of anticipation charged up my gut. Immediately reaching for the glass, I hesitated, restraining myself from knocking that sucker back in one gulp. Carefully controlling my compulsion, I calmly took one, then two sips, sighed deeply, and leaned back into my bar stool. Suddenly remembering my young companion, I turned to face Patty, closely observing the mechanics of my bar behavior.

A long tense moment passed before she finally spoke, "Are you an alcoholic, Frank?"

Later as we approached Blue Springs, Patty's question was like a stubborn hangover, looming over the short trip. I had done my best to dodge the obvious, rationalize and justify my behavior and generally weasel my way out of an uncomfortable situation, but I guess the five shots of bourbon that I consumed during the two hours we spent in the bar, were answer enough. As I hemmed and hawed, ducked and dodged, Patty smiled and nodded. I hadn't fooled her for a minute. I knew it and she knew it, but the pleasant young blonde's polite Midwestern upbringing kept her from calling me the lush we both knew I was.

It was 7 p.m. when we pulled up in front of Ted Hendricks' small house with the now familiar Honda sitting under the carport. Since the kid would undoubtedly greet me like a loud and uninvited uncle, Patty immediately hopped out of the car, walked up the sidewalk and rang the bell. The tall content screener quickly appeared and, even though she didn't carry a badge, Patty promptly flashed her ID from the Clinton County sheriff's department. Recognizing her from their earlier encounter in the jail cell, Hendricks was initially taken aback, nervously scanning up and down the street. Assured that Patty was alone, Ted turned his attention back to the young clerk, who by this time was explaining the plan. Guarded, the techie nevertheless listened politely, slightly bent over and nodding his head, until the focus of the conversation reached me. Instantly stiffening, he rose to his full majestic height, scowling at the Jeep as if suddenly aware the car concealed two tons of day-old sheep shit. Frantically shaking his head, with Patty imploring him to hear her out, Hendricks turned back toward the interior of the house.

This was it! If ever a time for action existed, the moment was NOW! Without hesitation, I leaped from the car, shouting Hendricks' name, took two steps toward the house and tripped over a lawn sprinkler, falling and planting my face on the sidewalk. For the second time in less than two weeks, I had broken my nose on Ted Hendricks' property.

Talk about déjà vu. Five minutes later I was once again sitting at the table in the techie's breakfast nook with Hendricks Scotch-taping toilet paper over my nose, only this time it was Patty, not Margo, making the coffee and staring at me from across the kitchen.

Obviously unhappy, Ted Hendricks applied one last piece of tape, stepped back to admire his handiwork and spoke, "I don't seem to be able to get rid of you, Mr. Blood-Jet, neither you nor your bloody nose... but I'm afraid I'm going to have to ask you to leave."

I felt like a fool. Okay, I know, this was not exactly virgin territory, but whatever... it was time to suck it up. If I couldn't convince the kid to join us, I might be facing an unwanted vacation in Leavenworth. Desperate, I lurched ahead, "Look, Ted, I'm not sure exactly what Patty has told you, but..."

"It doesn't matter what she said, Mr. Blood-Jet, I've got enough trouble already... Margo left me yesterday and I could be facing charges over Willy's crime spree. Whatever you're selling, I don't need!"

"But..."

"Forget it! I don't need any more problems! My life is a fucking wreck and you are at least partly to blame! Please! Finish your cup of coffee and leave. Am I not being clear!?! I WANT YOU TO GO!"

Discouraged, I picked up my cup and stared at the black steaming liquid in silence. Fear, anxiety and outright panic urged me to press on but the kid's locked jaw and set-in-stone scowl said forget it. My neck was in a noose and someone was kicking the crate my toes were precariously perched upon. Back in the darker recesses of my mind, a tiny voice was speaking. It said the kicker was me.

Suddenly there was a knock at the door. A loud knock, accompanied by an even louder and painfully familiar voice. "State Police, Mr. Hendricks. I need to talk to you." It was Duane! Punch-drunk with panic, I bolted for the back door, but my young cohort stopped me.

"Stall him as long as you can, then let him in, Ted. I'll take care of the rest. Frank, you come into the bedroom with me." Having no idea what Patty was up to, I protested but she quickly put a hand over my mouth while pushing me into Hendricks' bedroom. Quickly undressing, she grabbed the techie's robe and motioned for me to crawl under the bed. Speaking in a loud whisper, she told me, "Just stay under there and keep quiet, Frank... I'll take care of Duane... Okay?" Nodding uncertainly, I dropped to my knees and slithered beneath the bed. Still a little drunk, I laid there in the dark, clueless and confused. Patty's plan had better work, otherwise I was garbage... dried-up donkey dung... offal in an onion patch... you know, bad shit. Meanwhile, we followed the uneasy confrontation in the other room.

Standing behind the closed door, Hendricks responded, "What do you want, officer?"

"Open up, Mr. Hendricks, we have reason to believe there's a fugitive in there."

"You're wasting your time, officer. There's no one here but me."

"A suspicious car is parked in front of your house, Mr. Hendricks. A car we have reason to believe was used in the recent escape and flight of a dangerous felon. Please open the door!" Stalling for time, the kid didn't respond, so Duane pushed on, "It wouldn't be hard for me to break through this door, Mr. Hendricks. DON'T MAKE ME DO IT!"

Accepting the inevitable, Hendricks reached for the doorknob but only after securing the night latch. Opening the door to the limit of the short chain, he peeked through. "Do you have a search warrant, officer?"

"I don't need a warrant, Mr. Hendricks... not if I have just cause to believe you are harboring a fugitive and I do. NOW... OPEN... THE... DOOR! I'm losing my patience!"

Taking his time, the content screener slid the chain free, swung the door open and stepped back. "See... there's no one here, officer."

"I'll be the judge of that, Mr. Hendricks." Placing a hand

on the butt of his gun, the state trooper stomped into the small living room and looked around.

With perfect timing, Patty took Duane's entrance as her cue. With her hair suggestively disheveled and obviously wearing nothing beneath the techie's robe, the young blonde boldly burst into the room. "ARE YOU STALKING ME, DUANE? WHAT THE FUCK ARE YOU DOING HERE?" Wide-eyed and completely off guard, the trooper took two halting steps backward and stared, his mouth open in disbelief. "ANSWER ME, DUANE! WHAT ARE YOU DOING HERE? THIS IS SEXUAL HARASSMENT!"

Flustered, the cop stammered, "But... but... Patty..."

"But what, Duane? You haven't answered my question. WHAT ARE YOU DOING HERE?"

Reluctant to face his indignant lover, Duane turned to Ted Hendricks. "I... I thought you said there was nobody here but you..."

Unwilling to let the floundering fish off the hook, Patty bore in, "I told him to say that, Duane. Now please apologize for interrupting us and leave."

Subdued and without the benefit of his normal bravado, Duane tentatively pushed ahead. "I... I'm sorry, Patty, but somehow that sleazeball writer escaped last night and since you and him were, uh, kinda tight... uh, we thought... well, Bernie and me... we thought..."

"You thought I helped him escape? Is that what you thought, Duane? Are you fucking crazy?"

Composing himself slightly, Duane continued, "Okay, then what are you doing here... with this guy?" He turned and looked at Hendricks suspiciously.

"Not that it's any of your business, Duane, but Ted and I made... friends, while he was in Clinton. I wanted to get know him better, so I drove over..." The gutsy chick then walked over to Hendricks and grabbed his arm, while leaning her head against his shoulder affectionately. "DOES THAT ANSWER YOUR QUESTION, DUANE?"

His face turning the color of rancid watermelon, Duane's battered ego had had more than enough. "Uh, yeah, I get it, Patty, but…"

"BUT WHAT, DUANE!?! FOR FUCK'S SAKE. LOOK AROUND IF YOU DON'T BELIEVE ME! Ted and I have nothing to hide."

By this time the totally demoralized trooper couldn't get out fast enough. "Yeah… yeah… okay… okay…" After quickly scanning the bedroom and the kitchen, Duane skulked out, got into his patrol car and roared away.

A few minutes later we were back congregated around the kitchen table. The good thing about the Duane episode was that it served to focus the tightly wound Hendricks and, more importantly, put all of us on the same page. At least for the moment, the relief of having deflected Duane's attempt to bust Patty and me left us more or less bonded, but I had to connect with the kid before he retreated into his uber-defensive shell. Of course having Patty at the table, with her tousled hair and cleavage seductively framed by the lapels of Hendricks' robe, didn't hurt. Suffice it to say, none of this feminine pulchritude was lost on the suddenly attentive Ted Hendricks.

Feeling the moment was now or never, I went for it. "Ted, I understand that you don't want any part of our crazy Beasley caper, but there's something you should know before we leave."

With his eyes still riveted to Patty's shapely form, provocatively outlined under his robe, Hendricks muttered, "Yeah, what's that?"

He bit. I could already feel him weakening. All I had to do now was reel him in. "Ted, you're probably not aware of it, but Deputy Bodie is trying to use the explosion to pin a domestic terrorism charge on me and…" Cocking an ear, the kid looked up. "…she's got you pegged as my accomplice."

"WHAT!?!" The hook was set. Ted Hendricks was fully engaged. It wouldn't take much more, especially after I began pulling the kid's heartstrings over poor Willy's treatment at the hands of the heartless Crawford Beasley. I had only planned on asking Ted to take us to Beasley's compound; Patty and I could take over from there, but something was telling me that Hendricks might just be sticking around. It wouldn't take long to find out, and the more I watched the kid ogling Patty, the more confident I became.

Five minutes later, Hendricks declared himself in. "Okay, I'll take you guys to the compound, but that's as far as I go. Okay?"

Spending the night at Hendricks' place would have been easy enough, but Patty insisted it was too risky. "Look guys, we may have fooled Duane, but he's not a total idiot. Once he's had time to think it over and report to Bernie, he'll be back… and we won't be so lucky next time."

It didn't take much to convince me. The thought of Duane's stormtrooper boots reducing the door to splinters was plenty. "Yeah, I agree… We gotta get outta here. Ted, didn't you say Beasley's compound is near Kingdom City? How far is that?"

"Not far... about two hours on I-70. I have to get some stuff... It'll only take a couple of minutes..." Rushing, the kid took two steps toward his bedroom then paused and turned back. "Hey! I'm okay showing you guys how to get to Beasley's compound, but I should probably print a map, too. That way, if we're separated or something, you'll still be able to find it."

"Yeah, okay... just hurry... Duane could be back any minute."

Brimming with urgency, we burst into action. Ted printed the map, then packed while Patty grabbed her clothes and hurried into the bathroom to change. A few moments later the techie emerged from his bedroom carrying a bag and a laptop. As soon as the others returned to the kitchen, I spoke up, "Look... Patty's car is easy to spot, so we should stick to the back roads, and leaving now means it's late when get to Kingdom City... and I'm hungry. Let's get something to eat, stop in a nearby motel and drive on over to Kingdom City in the morning. Ted, you lead and we'll follow. Does that sound okay, guys?"

With both Patty and Ted nodding their approval, we grabbed our stuff and headed out the door.

It was almost 9 p.m., but so much had happened since we arrived at Ted Hendricks' house, it seemed much later. After heading north out of Blue Springs on State Highway 7, we turned east on U.S. 24, soon finding ourselves in the town of Buckner, MO. Nowhere burgs like this shut down early, so finding a motel and a greasy spoon was crucial. Wasting no time, we went for Sam's Tiki Town, an oddball Polynesian-themed motel, connected to an unappealing bar-restaurant. After checking in and opting for the De-Lux Suite, two beds and a fold-out sofa, we hurried to the restaurant, where the grill had just shut down. Starving, we faced a plethora of grim and grimmer choices: barbecue potato chips, cereal, a tired salad bar, cold premade sandwiches and pickled eggs. Playing it safe, Patty got the Sugar Frosted Flakes while Hendricks beat me to the last roast-beef-on-a-French roll. Reeling, I made the monumental blunder of ordering a day-old cheese sandwich.

Thoughtlessly, I peeked inside. Between the two slices of white bread, was an even blander mass, a thick viscous substance I uncomfortably categorized as a cross between frozen mayonnaise and marshmallows. The second mistake was biting into it, the effect of which was a mouth packed with albino tar, instantly encasing my oral cavity while effectively gluing my teeth together. Patty and Ted, engaged in a spirited conversation, were apparently oblivious to my fate until I grabbed a knife and wedged it between my teeth, desperately attempting to force the orifice open.

Her eyes widening, Patty was the first to notice, "Frank, are you okay?"

Pointing at my jaw with one hand while twisting the knife with the other, the only remark I could muster was, "UUUMMMMMOOOUUURRR!"

Looking up from his plate, Hendricks mumbled, "He seems to have a problem." Rising to his full nearly seven-foot height, Ted loped around the table, approached my chair and bent over, closely inspecting the problem area. As I continued to emit unintelligible sounds, the kid spoke again, "It looks like something is stuck in his mouth... Is that correct, Mr. Blood-Jet?"

Nodding my head frantically, I motioned for him to grab another knife and, with each of us prying different sides of my mouth, we finally forced it open, allowing the gooey white mass to escape onto the tabletop with a sickening PLOP! Looking up at me like an ashen squid embryo, I quickly scooped the pile of saliva-coated detritus into my napkin and threw it away.

"I think I need a drink." Lurching over to the bar, agreeably labeled "Larry's Liquor Locker," I ordered a bourbon on the rocks, as Patty and Ted returned to their conversation. They were talking about apples.

Up to this point my "relationship" with the uber-cute blonde had remained ill-defined and fuzzy. There was no doubt the chick had a crush on me and also freed me from the grasp of Deputy Dawg. Yeah, I was attracted to her big-time and we had "done it"... once... sort of... But somehow a widening gap appeared between us after Patty's earlier "alcoholic" comment. Now as I sat in another bar indulging my intemperance with a second, then a third whiskey, I watched as my companions discussed the merits and shortcomings of Honeycrisps versus Granny Smiths and Gravensteins. And as I watched, I had the clear impression that apples, just as in the Garden of Eden, provided nothing more than the subtext of a deeper, more primal conversation.

Thirty minutes later, as I was finishing my fourth bourbon, listening to Ted debate the virtues of heritage varieties compared to newer hybrid fruit, the bar announced closing time. Walking back to our room, the budding connection between my partners remained on full display, as well as an ongoing source of confusion to my manly virtue, currently blind, bewildered and hiding in the dark.

The next morning, keeping to the back roads, we continued our trek to Kingdom City, but rather than creating a conspicuous presence in such a small town, we opted to stop in Mexico. No shit... there is actually a burg in the state of Missouri called Mexico, a.k.a. "The Fire Brick Capital of the World." Hey!—don't ask me. But with Mexico only seventeen miles north of Kingdom City, Beasley's compound would be easily accessible without drawing too much attention to our curious crew.

After finding a Motel 6 with free wi-fi and a room big enough to accommodate three, we settled in. Patty said she needed a shower before heading over to Kingdom City, so, with a little time to kill, Hendricks and I both logged on to the Internet. Paying little attention to the kid, I was checking out the news and a few sports scores when the techie suddenly let out a whoop, "WHOA! Check this out, Mr. Blood-Jet!"

Irritated at the interruption, I snapped at the kid, "Yo, Ted, drop the Blood-Jet... Okay? Just call me Frank."

"Yeah, okay... sure... sorry... But you need to see this, Frank... Come over here." Hendricks gestured toward his open laptop, obviously excited about something. I looked at the screen expecting to see some dumbass cat video or crap like TEN TOP REASONS TO EAT CONCRETE! but at first glance, I was stumped. All I could see was a bunch of empty rooms, a dozen or more static images, each remaining on the screen for several seconds before dissolving to the next, then repeating the pattern. Puzzled, I looked closer and as I watched, I noticed a middle-aged man anxiously pacing one of the rooms. Dressed head to toe in camo, he was smoking a cigarette in a long holder stuck between his teeth. The man appeared to be talking, but no one else was in the room.

Dumbfounded, I looked at Ted Hendricks, the computer whiz, and asked, "Is that..."

"...Crawford Beasley!" He said, answering my question before I could finish it.

"But how..."

"We're watching a live feed from the PAGWAG surveillance system. Remembering the security scheme used by Beasley at the tea warehouses, I assumed he would have something much more elaborate at the compound and guessed that a hidden link accessing the system could probably be found within the PAGWAG website. It was a lot easier than I expected. For a paranoid, millionaire gun nut, his tech chops are pretty weak. The idiot uses 'PAGWAG' as his password. A ten-year-old kid could..."

"Wait... Are you saying that we have access to the security system in Crawford Beasley's compound... whenever we want it?"

"That's pretty much it... well, we have to have Internet access, of course."

My mind was completely fucking blown! We now possessed intimate access to the sanctum sanctorum of a madman... access I never dreamed possible. As we watched the series of rooms flash by, I found myself sucked deeper and deeper into the lunatic's psycho psyche. Many of the rooms were obvious and not especially interesting: a garage containing Beasley's beloved Hummer, a kitchen, bedrooms, laundry room, etc., but some were much more compelling. One space, containing dozens of photographs, seemed to be dedicated to an older woman that I could only assume was Beasley's mother. The dominant feature of the room was a large romanticized portrait adorned with an ornate gilded frame and accompanied by what appeared to be several dried funeral sprays, implying that the older woman was dead.

Another of the more striking spaces was one I could only describe as Beasley's armory. Containing what appeared to be a collection of antique firearms and various weapons, it also housed his vast assortment of functioning firearms: pistols, hunting rifles and automatic weapons, as well as a limited selection of small artillery, such as bazookas, mortars and grenade launchers. When and if the apocalypse came, Crawford Beasley was prepared to hold it at bay for quite a while.

But the scene that kept grabbing my attention was the one containing Crawford himself—the madman's control room. On one side of the space was a large map of the United States with a conspicuous route drawn from Kingdom City to an area not far from Los Angeles. The rest of the room was occupied by wall-mounted monitors accessing Beasley's computers, along with the security system we were currently watching. But the madman's silent, nonstop monologue was easily the most compelling feature of the room. I had to hear what he was saying.

"Ted, is there any way you can stop the picture and turn up the volume of the room where Beasley is? I want to hear what he's saying."

"Yeah... I should be able to do that. Wait just a second." In no time the kid brought a small control panel onto the screen, allowing him to freeze the image on the wacko's control room. Then, as he accessed a slider at the bottom of the panel, Crawford Beasley's maniacal voice entered the small room:

"But I do understand why people believe in God... there are so many random occurrences in life, existing without justification, antecedents or reason, that we are compelled to classify this happenstance FOR THE SIMPLE SAKE OF SANITY! For me it was my ultimate moment of liberation, my release from the bonds of hamster hell... IT WAS WINNING THE LOTTERY! And, were I of a less uncommon mind, I would undoubtedly have labeled this occurrence as... THE MAGNIFICENT MOMENT!... THE BLESSED BOON!... THE GREAT GOODIE!... HA! But there was one more stroke of luck... Divine Intervention, some might say, enabling my unwed status when the Magnificent Moment arrived... consequently, IT'S ALL MINE! Free from the clutches of bimbo babes, the ones that demonized my days, sucked my soul and drained my dick, I was free to pursue PURITY, GRACE AND GUNS! PRAISE THE LORD! HA!"

At that point Beasley suddenly stopped, turned toward the door and left the room.

Patty had joined us as Ted and I watched Beasley's rant about the benefits of winning the lottery. "WOW! That guy is really bonkers!" Out of the mouths of babes... sober and grounded, there was no denying the young woman's words. Crawford Beasley was a certifiable nut.

For Patty and me, this was our initial encounter with the quasi-military madman. The guy was obviously off his rocker, but I live in L.A.—I see wackos every day. Regardless, I was not prepared for the sight of Ted Hendricks' blood visibly draining from his face. Completely unnerved by the presence of the man whose grating and gloating voice gloried over the death of his friend Willy, the kid's entire body was shaking.

Patty was the first to react, reaching over and grabbing the techie's hand. "Ted, are you okay?"

Squeezing her hand, he stammered, "It... it's okay... I'll be all right... it... it's just the sound of his voice takes me right back to the explosion... and Willy's death... poor ol' Willy... " The kid stopped, staring at nothing, haunted by memories still too fresh to process.

Understanding the depth of Hendricks' connection to his dead friend, I said, "Hey! This is going to be hard for you... I get it. We have a map showing the location of Beasley's compound. If you want to check out now and go home, it's okay... we understand." Still holding the techie's hand, Patty nodded her head in approval.

"No... no... I'll go on with you guys... At least as far as the warehouses and the compound. If it gets too heavy, maybe I'll leave, but thinking about Willy makes me want to get this guy... BAD!" Passionate and determined, Hendricks then paused and looked at Patty, their eyes locking for an uncomfortably long moment.

Uncomfortable for me, at least. "Okay, guys, where are we headed first?"

Snapping back to the task at hand, the techie looked up, removed his hand from Patty's grip and paused, obviously considering something. "But... well, something just occurred to me... what exactly are we after? I mean, we have access to Beasley's security system... you saw the way he is. It's easy enough for me to record these crazy rants. Can't we use them as evidence against him?"

"That's a great idea, Ted... yeah, do it. But there's nothing illegal about making crazy statements. You know, free speech and all that. What we need is proof... especially evidence of the bomb he made intending to kill you and Willy. We have to connect Beasley to the gold Cadillac, to bomb-making supplies, to the recording he played just before the explosion... get it? This is the type of proof that will stand up in a court of law and put this guy away. And your recordings would be great support, but we have to have the hard evidence to back it up."

"Yeah, okay, I get it. I'll start recording him." Lost in thought, the techie paused for a moment, then continued, "Okay, this is about the time that Beasley eats lunch at a café in Kingdom City so he's probably headed that way now. Let's grab something to eat and drive over there."

An hour later, the three of us were in Patty's Jeep headed toward Kingdom City. His nerves under control, Ted Hendricks was still leery of the uber-unpredictable Beasley: "He usually has lunch at the same place every day before supervising the delivery of tea bricks. After that he'll probably return to the compound. Hopefully he'll still be at the restaurant, but look... we definitely don't want to follow him to the warehouses. The guy's not an idiot. He spotted Willy and me pretty quick."

DrIving along, I found myself lost in thought as Ted and Patty continued their courtship, chatting about nothing in particular. It was easy enough to say we needed hard evidence, but getting it was something else. If the techie's description of the stronghold was true, it would be easier to get out of Fort Knox with a boxcar full of gold bars. Uncertain, I decided to interrupt the lovebirds. "Uh, hey guys... I know I said we needed real proof to put the cops on to Beasley, but, well... I don't have a clue about how we're getting into that compound. I mean, from the way Ted described the place, it would be easier to break into the fucking White House. You guys have any ideas?"

Apparently, the problem had not occurred to them so we all sat in silence for the next few minutes. Finally, hoping to stimulate something, I spoke up again, "Okay, we don't have two tanks and a battalion of troops, so we're not gonna bust our way in there. Right?" Nothing but silence until we suddenly passed a sign announcing the corporate limits of Kingdom City. "Hey! Thanks for all the input, guys..." Frustrated, I shook my head. "Okay, maybe we'll have an idea when we get to the compound."

Entering the tiny hamlet, the first thing we saw was Crawford Beasley's Hummer parked around the corner from Nell's, a small café that fed the hungry hordes of Kingdom City. Instantly alert, Hendricks' lanky frame began to wilt. Ducking the best he could, the techie barked, "FUCK! That's Beasley's car! Just drive on past, Patty! We don't want him to see us!"

"Hey Ted! Chill out, dude! The guy doesn't know Patty or me and certainly won't recognize her car. Just pull around the corner and stop by that feed store and I'll check things out. Okay?"

"Yeah, sure...." Pulling into a parking spot, Patty cut the engine then glanced over at the ever diminishing Ted Hendricks. "Are you okay, Ted?" Looking up from an obviously uncomfortable position, the kid nodded, jerking his head around and searching the street at the same time.

Nearing the café, I arrived just as Crawford Beasley exited onto the sidewalk—and there he was in all his glory, fully plumed in warrior drag, cigarette holder tightly clenched between his teeth and .45 automatic at his side. Barely avoiding a collision, I stopped as Beasley turned, seemingly staring into my soul. With a hand gripping the butt of his .45, the madman eyed my bandaged nose for a long, uneasy moment, then, dismissing me as a threat, he nodded awkwardly, entered the Hummer and drove away. As the preposterous car turned a corner and disappeared, I instantly understood Ted Hendricks' apprehension. The guy was incredibly fucking creepy.

Luckily one of the few business establishments in Kingdom City was Al's Package Goods. Whipping into Al's, I nabbed a pint of Jack Daniel's and headed back to the car. I would need it.

After rejoining Patty and Ted, we decided to drive by the warehouses and, as expected, the stretch Hummer was parked outside next to a semi being unloaded by the driver. With Beasley nowhere in sight, Hendricks still scrunched his lanky frame onto the floor as Patty sped by the two buildings. The creep had obviously made a home for himself under the kid's skin.

Apprehensive, the techie unfolded his legs and, returning to the shotgun seat, remarked, "Okay... now you know where the tea warehouses are... Let's go to the compound."

Patty drove us to the stronghold under Ted's direction, after which the content screener showed us the spot where he and Willy observed the wacko entering and exiting. If anything, Hendricks had not been nearly explicit enough in describing the structure protecting the heavily fortified space. The outermost barrier was a chain link fence that must have been ten feet tall and topped by an additional two feet of razor wire. Beyond the fence was a twenty-foot no-man's-land covered with broken glass and crisscrossed by lasers designed to detect any movement within the area. Beyond that, an eight-foot concrete wall displayed a series of gun slots allowing protected counterattack against potential invaders. Obviously no one would be entering—or leaving—Crawford Beasley's stronghold without his knowledge and approval. But equally curious was the relatively modest appearance of the building located within these all but impenetrable defenses. Having observed an ample array of interior rooms via the compound's security system, I could only assume that the majority of the structure was underground. The madman had built a veritable fortress for himself, obviously designed and constructed to keep interlopers like me and and my bush league cohorts out. This was a problem—and one with no obvious solution.

As we watched, the Hummer returned, easily navigating the gamut of security protecting the compound. Within moments the huge vehicle had disappeared behind the second gate, leaving me to ponder the seeming conundrum of breaking into an apparently impregnable fortress. "We've gotta find a way in there, guys, but it beats me. The wacko seems to have the place locked up tight. Any ideas?"

Hendricks was the first to speak, "Well, I saw this movie once where a couple of guys pretended to be telephone repairmen and got into a bank like that."

At least it was an idea but, duh… I just shook my head. "Sorry, but no way, José. I saw that movie, too. Those guys had plenty of money and weeks to plan the caper. Try again." Silence blanketed the car for several moments.

Finally speaking up, Patty ventured a thought, "Ted, did you see him getting deliveries? Could we sneak in in the back of a UPS or FedEx truck?"

"Yeah, Willy and I saw him get a couple of shipments, but Beasley would come out and meet the driver between the two gates and take the package. The truck never actually entered the compound."

More silence. I kept thinking about the Hummer and its effortless passage through a pair of all but impassable gates. "You know, I keep seeing Beasley's giant SUV gliding through those gates. If we just had some way of, like, breaking into his car and hiding…"

At that point, Ted Hendricks piped up again. "Well, we wouldn't actually have to break into his car."

Frustrated, I barked at the kid again. "What the fuck are you taking about, Ted? I mean, the asshole is not exactly going to leave the car wide open and invite us in, is he?" Shaking my head, I pulled out the bottle of Jack and took a slug.

"No… I expect not… but I do have a set of keys."

"WHAT!?! Are you kidding me? Are you saying you have the keys to Crawford Beasley's Hummer? You're joking, right?

Reaching into his pocket, the kid pulled out a set of car keys. Casually holding them up he said, "Well, it was actually Willy's idea. He insisted that we keep the keys in case something went wrong. He said Beasley would have an extra set… and he was right. I'm not exactly sure why I kept them but…"

"KID! Way to go!" As I patted Hendricks on the back, Patty threw her arms around him and planted a big smacker on his lips.

It looked like we had our ticket through the gates of hell.

Later that night we were back at our motel. Patty and I sat watching some horrible crime shit on TV while Ted Hendricks, nearby on headphones, was recording Crawford Beasley ranting on his surveillance system. As the nut case stalked the compound, reciting a seemingly endless series of soliloquies concerning the evils of the world and the need to protect its most precious resource, pure, clear and clean water, the techie shook his head in amazement.

"Hey, Ted... How's it going. What kind of stuff are you getting?"

"Well, the guy is unbelievable... I mean, he never shuts up for one thing, and he's completely unbalanced, but some of the stuff he says can be compelling... kind of... or maybe I'm getting brainwashed... here, check this out."

As Patty and I gathered around the techie's computer, we watched as Crawford Beasley stood in the center of his armory cleaning the barrel of an AK-47 and speaking to the air:

"God... GOD! What a concept! Now if God was a Gun, I'd believe. If God was a Gun, I'd receive the Holy Sacrament of Gunpowder and Lead every day. If God was a Gun, I'd weave truth from lies with bullets and cries for mercy. Don't give me the Blood of Christ as a cheap facsimile of suffering—give me instead the Crimson Rivulets of my enemies, freely flowing from the Holy Holes piercing their misguided and dying flesh. If God was a Gun, Might would be Right and Power would fill the empty hours wait-

ing for Redemption, Truth and Righteous Targets!"

As Ted paused the recording, we all looked at each other in slightly stunned amazement. Yeah, the guy was a kook, but down in there somewhere, beneath the bluster and contempt, was the soul of a poet, pathetically buried in bullshit. "Play some more of this, Ted..." Shaking my head in shock, I continued, "Yeah, he's nuts all right, but..."

With my words trailing off, Hendricks began another recording:

"CEE-LEB CITY... The Land of Lost Angels... LAND OF LOST LOSERS, if you ask me. I have to admit the idea of defiling all that exquisite, pure water agonizes the essence of my being. Doubtless, L.A., home to the LORDS OF ARROGANCE, is the only target capable of abating the pain I feel in enacting such blasphemy, but GODDAMMIT, IT MUST BE DONE! No one wanted to kill innocent infants in Nagasaki, but WAR DICTATES EVIL NECESSITIES! The arrogant liberals speak of the 'One Percent' as if being rich is such a DESPICABLE ACT! But, as I see it, many of the affluent, like me, are committed to enhancing the benefits of our culture. It's the vile and loathsome celebrity class, built on values of testosterone and pretty, that constitutes the TRUE EVIL of society. Once the ENTIRE L.A. BASIN is cursed with BLACK TEETH like mine, the celebrity class will be begging to TAKE IT UP THE BUTT, bent over and whining, while also certifying and guaranteeing the need of pure, clean and pristine water, along with a well-armed and disciplined militia to protect it. It's not that complicated."

As the techie paused the recording again, we looked at each other in stunned silence, one thought dominating our unspoken conversation: how weird can this shit possibly get?

The next morning we were having breakfast at a small café in Mexico... okay, I know it sounds weird, but don't blame me... I just live here and take notes... Anyway, we were chowing down on grits and scrambled eggs, trying to come up with a plan for breaching Beasley's Hummer.

"Okay, there are only two places where we're sure to have access to the Hummer, at the café where he eats lunch and at the warehouses... but both are fairly exposed. Ted, does he always park in that same spot around the corner from Nell's café?"

"I think so... I figured he parks there so the Hummer doesn't stick out into the street and maybe get hit."

I thought about it for a minute and said, "Okay... I opt for the café, but we need some kind of distraction. Something to keep the fucker occupied while we get in the car. Patty, I think that means you..."

His protective instincts aroused, Hendricks immediately reacted. "No way, Frank! I don't want Patty in here with that nut! He's got a gun and..."

"But... wait, Frank... listen..."

"NO! ABSOLUTELY NO WAY!"

The cute young female, my designated diversion, had listened quietly up to that point, but she immediately spoke up, "Shut up, Ted... I want to hear what Frank has to say."

"But... but..."

"Quiet, Ted! I make my own decisions... Okay? Go ahead, Frank. What are you thinking?"

"Well, I keep remembering the way you put the whammy on ol' Duane... I'm not saying you need to sashay into Nell's wearing a negligee, but..." I paused, knowing I was headed into delicate territory.

"But what, Frank... I'm listening."

"Well, okay..." I paused for a moment, took a breath and continued. "It... It's about your father..."

"My dad? What's he got to do with this? I don't get it, Frank."

"Okay... okay... let me explain... your dad has Gulf War Syndrome... right? And Beasley, in his Desert Storm drag, is obviously obsessed with the military... maybe he's a vet... who knows? But if you could go in there and somehow connect with the fucker about your dad, I'm willing to bet he would shit in his pants making nice. Meanwhile, Ted and I could get into the Hummer and have everything all set for you to join us after ditching the wacko. We shouldn't need more than five minutes... Ten at the most. What do you think?"

Still feeling protective of his young companion, Ted Hendricks wasn't buying the plan. "It's too dangerous, Frank. The guy is nutso... there's no telling what he might..."

I looked at Patty, recognizing that steely look in her eyes. Without hesitation, she said, "It's okay, Ted... I can do it... unless you have a better plan."

"Well..."

This was it, big time or bust, so I jumped back in. "Well, what? Look, Ted, if Patty's okay with this, then we have to do it... Hey! I know you've got the hots for the kid, but..." I paused. It was the first time anyone had openly acknowledged the obvious chemistry between them, but what the fuck! It was time to get real here... sort of...

Shocked, they looked at each other in a knowing way, both uncertain as to what to say. Finally, Patty spoke, "He's right, Ted..." Realizing the underlying truth of her statement, the cute chick paused, blushing slightly, then continued, "I mean about Beasley and getting into his car. I can do it. It's okay." From the look on his face, Hendricks still wasn't convinced, but at least Patty shut him up.

"Okay, that's settled then. I'll pay the bill and we'll head over to Kingdom City." Getting up, I walked toward the cashier, but as I reached for my wallet, something outside grabbed my attention. Passing Patty's Jeep parked on the street, a black-and-white Missouri Highway Patrol car came to a sudden halt. It was Duane and we were in trouble... big trouble. Hurriedly paying the check, I watched as the trooper, in full John Wayne swagger, exited the cruiser and approached the Jeep, simultaneously scanning up and down the street.

Rushing back to the table, I blurted out the news, "IT'S DUANE! He's right outside and he spotted Patty's car. QUICK... out the back... HURRY!" Awkwardly forcing our way through the tiny kitchen, we found ourselves in an alley walking back to the motel. With no other choice we decided to dump Patty's car and continue in the Honda.

The day was not getting off to a good start.

Quickly gathering our stuff, we checked out of the motel and crowded ourselves into Ted's small car. By this time we knew Duane had a definite make on the Honda, so, trusting the ever alert Ted Hendricks, we escaped the small town, and headed in the direction of Kingdom City.

Shocked that the hyper-aggressive cop had actually located us in Mexico, I turned to Patty and remarked, "So what the fuck is Duane doing here anyway? Isn't he way out of his territory?"

Giving me a worried look, my young companion responded, "He can be pretty tenacious, Frank... and if I know Duane, this has become personal with him by now. And... well, I don't think he likes you very much."

Great! So now I had to contend with Bulldog Duane AND Bonkers Beasley. I patted my pockets in search of Black Jack.

Continuing, Patty said, "Duane's probably spent the last two days driving through every small town in Northern Missouri searching for us. He won't give up either."

Comforted by that thought, we quickly covered the short distance from Mexico to Kingdom City. Avoiding the overly zealous trooper madly crisscrossing the state in search of my balls, we pulled up at Nell's slightly early for lunch. Parking the Honda in an inconspicuous spot, we sat, quietly awaiting the madman's arrival while pondering the random arrangements of fate.

It didn't take long. Also apparently on an early schedule, Beasley pulled the Hummer into its customary spot, stepped out, straightened his jacket, and entered the café. Meanwhile, Patty, having changed into a skirt and blouse back at the motel, was ready for action. After escorting her to the front of the café, I watched to make sure everything was okay, but the chick was a natural. Casually walking past Beasley, she paused, turned, checked him out and nodded approvingly. It took a moment for the presence of another human to penetrate the multilayered defenses insulating Crawford Beasley from the rest of the world, but once his radar zeroed in on the mondo cute Patty, the wacko was hooked. Watching the kid play the big fish would have been fun, but we had business to take care of. Returning to Ted in the Honda, I gave him a solid thumbs-up and we hurried over to the Hummer; as the techie pulled out the keys, we approached the rear door of the giant SUV. Sure, anything could happen after we breached the madman's lair, but getting in was looking like a piece of cake... until...

Nervously scanning the immediate area, I waited as Hendricks fidgeted, inserting first one key into the lock then, failing, he tried another, then the first one again—no luck. Panicked, Hendricks looked up, his eyes wide with terror. "IT WON'T WORK! THE FUCKER MUST HAVE CHANGED THE LOCKS!"

FUCK! There was nothing to do but bail. Motioning for Hendricks to return to the Honda, I went back to the café, hoping to catch Patty's eye while calmly flashing the old get-the-fuck-out-of-there-pronto sign. But, executing the coquette role all the way, the young woman's attention was focused on Crawford Beasley, seemingly hanging on every word. Freaking out, I had no idea what to do next when suddenly, I saw something familiar laying on the table next to Beasley's hand. It was a set of keys, almost identical to the ones used by Ted Hendricks in our failed attempt to breach the Hummer.

This was it! Make or break! Do or die! Suck tit or eat shit! Retrieving my trusty bottle of Jack Daniels, I took two mondo slugs and staggered into the café.

"Patty! Patty! Where did you go, Honeybunch? Your daddy needs you, Patty... Come to Poppa!" Lurching across the room with my arms spread, I watched the wide-eyed young woman, the wheels of her mind spinning furiously, gamely struggling to figure out what the fuck I was up to. Deliberately slurring my words, I pressed on, "Patty... my darling daughter... who's your friend, honeypot? Huuuuuhhh?" Weaving back and forth, I plopped a hand on Patty's shoulder, attempting to control my erratic movements.

Playing along, Patty turned to her table companion and said, "Uh... Mr. Beasley, I'd like to introduce you to my... father... like I said earlier, Daddy fought with our forces in Iraq during the Gulf War and..." Pausing dramatically, the kid actually reached up and wiped away a tear, before continuing, "...sadly, he was exposed to sarin gas during the war and..." Pausing again, my bogus offspring looked up, her eyes swelling with pathos. "Daddy often still feels the effects... and he's, uh, having a bad day... isn't that right, Daddy?"

Revealing no recognition from our earlier encounter, Beasley's soulless façade, obscured behind dark glasses, momentarily cracked, as the madman gingerly reached out, attempting to add support to my hapless and unstable stance. Sensing his momentary vulnerability, I collapsed, sprawling my floundering carcass across the table and sliding into his lap, causing both of us, as well as the entire contents of the table to crash, spreading itself across the floor of the tiny café.

Immediately bouncing back to his feet, Beasley roared, "YOU OAF! YOU CLUMSY FUCKING CLOD!" Looking down at his coffee-stained camo jacket, the quasi-military lunatic was livid. Not missing a beat, Patty grabbed the table and returned it to an upright position as I flopped around the floor, nabbing Beasley's car keys in the process.

Maintaining our game of confounding the kook, Patty pleaded, "He didn't mean it, Mister... really he didn't... Daddy's just having a bad day. Here, let me help you." Brushing french fries and bits of bacon and tomato from Beasley's soiled Desert Storm attire, while I pathetically struggled to regain my footing, the earnest young decoy continued, "I'm so sorry, Mister... I'll take Daddy out and get him settled down... I'm so sorry..." Helping me back up, she said, "C'mon, Daddy... we've ruined this poor man's lunch... c'mon, we have to leave now."

At that point, the two of us slowly made our way out of the café as the dumbfounded Crawford Beasley stood glaring, completely uncertain as to what he had just witnessed. As soon as Patty and I were safely outside, the obviously excited female immediately threw her arms around me, land-

ing a huge wet smacker on my lips at the same time. Startled, I stammered, "Uh, thanks, Patty... but we gotta hurry... we have to get into that Hummer and you have to return the wacko's keys before he realizes what's up."

"Sure, Frank... I get it."

Hurriedly we rushed back to the Honda where the freaked-out Ted Hendricks, oozing anxiety like a lost lamb, nervously waited. "WHAT HAPPENED? I THOUGHT WE WERE BAILING... WHAT TOOK YOU SO FUCKING LONG, PATTY! ARE YOU OKAY?"

"Change of plans, kid... LOOK! I got the keys, but we have to hurry before Beasley gets wise."

"But, wait... What's going on?"

"COME ON! I'll explain later." Frantic, we raced the short distance between the Honda and the SUV. Quickly unlocking the rear of the big car, Ted and I scrambled in as Patty hurried back to return the keys while making more apologies for her doddering dad; within seconds, the plucky blonde rejoined us in the rear of the Hummer. Searching the roomy rear cabin, we discovered several large storage compartments beneath the seats and scrambled in, sliding the doors closed behind us.

It was going to be a wild ride.

Fifteen minutes later, Crawford Beasley entered the Hummer. Separated as we were, the weight of the madman's combat boots clomping around the large vehicle produced three distinct pockets of anxiety, isolated in the dark and each marooned in its own mind. After a relatively short ride, we felt the SUV turn in to the compound, pause as it passed through the two gates, then glide into the garage. Concealed beneath the seats, we remained hidden for fifteen or twenty minutes before cautiously crawling out and convening in the rear of the giant car. Momentarily safe inside the Hummer, we clearly had to leave soon, but avoiding Beasley's security system wouldn't be so simple. Undaunted, the ever diligent Ted Hendricks, techie supreme, had a plan.

Having spent several hours inspecting the compound's surveillance setup, the kid was fairly certain he could substitute a static frame grab for the active camera feed in each room. Since the field of each camera would never change, a careful observer could possibly detect the ruse, but since Crawford Beasley was the only occupant, changes would be fairly subtle and confined to the room he was in—as long as that was the case, we should be okay.

Meanwhile, with Patty and me looking over his shoulder, the kid logged on to the system. As expected, with the exception of the control room where the loony Beasley was ordering supplies on Amazon, the rest of the building was completely quiet until, without warning, an alarm bell suddenly sounded, alerting the compound of a visitor. Watching, as several cameras focused on the heavily secured outer gate, we were shocked to see a familiar black-and-white cruiser parked at the entry. Who else... Duane! Stunned, we listened in fascination to the conversation between our two primary and wildly contrasting antagonists.

Responding to the alarm, Beasley barked, "What can I do for you, officer?"

"To whom am I speaking, sir?"

"Crawford Beasley, officer. I am the Executive Director of PAGWAG. How may I be of assistance?"

"Mr. Beasley, I am pursuing three suspects involved in an incident of domestic terrorism. A map pinpointing this location was found in one of the suspect's vehicles and I would like to ask you a few questions. May I come in?"

A long and increasingly uncomfortable silence followed, expanding the tension between the two men. After patiently waiting for several moments, the trooper spoke again, "Mr. Beasley?" More time passed and still no response. His irritation beginning to show, Duane repeated his request, this time more forcefully, "MISTER BEASLEY... MAY I PLEASE COME IN? I'D LIKE TO ASK YOU SOME QUESTIONS!"

Showing no emotion, the compound's occupant responded, "I'm sorry, but I'm busy right now officer. Can we do this another time?"

"This is strictly a routine matter, Mr. Beasley. You are not under suspicion and have no obligation to allow entry or answer questions. If you prefer I can return later with a backup squad and a search warrant. At that time you will no longer have any choice. Is that what you prefer, Mr. Beasley?"

Another awkward silence ensued before a metallic clicking sound was heard and the gate slowly swung open. As we followed his progress on a series of surveillance cameras, Duane returned to his cruiser and eased through first one and then another security gate before finally stopping in front of the compound's main entrance. Despite the heavy security measures used to safeguard the enclave, the madman's house, a typical low-slung suburban home, was warm and inviting. Standing on the landing, the state trooper paused for a moment until the front door opened and a smiling Crawford Beasley greeted him at the threshold.

Gesturing toward the interior of the building, the quasi-military maniac spoke, his voice calm and seemingly pleasant, "Step this way, officer. I apologize for the delay... this is our pledge season... a demanding time of the year for PAGWAG." After passing through a dark hallway, the pair emerged into a large and seemingly little-used living room.

Hyper-vigilant, Duane paused for a moment, scanning

the interior of the nondescript building, then spoke, "So what exactly is PAGWAG, Mr. Beasley?"

"I'm pleased that you're interested... Officer...?"

"Duggan... Sergeant Duggan. You were telling me about your organization, Mr. Beasley."

"Yes, of course, Officer... PAGWAG is an alliance of patriotic Americans. Brave men and women dedicated to the preservation of clear, clean and pristine water, as well as the unflinching defense of our glorious rights under the Second Amendment. A man like you must surely agree with those principles... am I correct, Officer?"

Satisfied with his inspection of the room, Duane returned his focus to Crawford Beasley, slowly absorbing the older man's foppish façade. After lowering his gaze from the madman's beret to his cigarette holder, ascot, camo uniform, beret, and immaculately shined combat boots, the trooper frowned slightly, returning his stare to Beasley's shaded and hidden eyes.

As both men stood, two feet apart, their eyes solidly fixed on each other, another sustained silence invaded the conversational space, slowly building tension until the older man finally spoke, "So what's this all about, Officer?"

Patient and methodical, Duane returned to his original inquiry, "We have evidence of an incident involving domestic terrorism, Mr. Beasley. It appears that a car bomb was exploded in a remote area of southern Missouri; in addition, we have reason to believe this bomb was possibly part of an assassination plot aimed at the President. Ironically, it seems that the stupidity and ineptitude of the terrorists is the primary reason the plot failed."

Wincing slightly at the words "stupidity" and "ineptitude," Beasley remained calm, and after a brief pause, he said, "Excuse me, Officer, I think I'll have a cup of coffee." Turning, the madman continued and walked toward the kitchen, "Can I get you some?... please, have a seat."

"No, thank you... I prefer to stand."

Taking his time, the older man poured himself a cup of coffee, then spoke again. "It's interesting that you should mention that, Officer Duggan... Someone recently attempted to break into the PAGWAG compound. They failed to get past my security system, of course, but I did manage to take their picture... would you like to see it?" At that point, Beasley opened a drawer and pulled out a piece of paper containing an indistinct black-and-white image.

"Yes... that could be quite helpful, Mr. Beasley... I appreciate your cooperation."

As the grim-faced fanatic approached the lawman's outstretched arm, the paper suddenly slipped from his grasp, slowly floating toward the lawman's feet. Instinctively reaching down, Duane never saw Beasley's .45 as the crazed lunatic fired his pistol eighteen inches from the trooper's right temple.

Mesmerized in the rear of the Hummer, Patty, Ted and I saw the shot on the techie's computer while also feeling the deep resonance of gunfire as it echoed throughout the compound. Without thinking, the young blonde screamed, "DUANE! NO!" and immediately broke down sobbing as Hendricks and I stared at each other, abandoned by sanity in a sick, sordid and monstrously malignant moment.

Moments later, with Patty's chest heaving and tears streaming down her cheeks, Ted Hendricks was the first to speak: "Patty, get it together... we have to go." Pointing at his computer, the kid continued, "I'm sorry, but Duane's dead... and we have to get out of here." As we watched, the madman retrieved a large sheet of plastic then struggled to roll the trooper's hulking corpse onto it. "We have to find a place to hide... Beasley's gonna be dealing with Duane's body for a while... I'm gonna hack the fucker's surveillance system, then we have to get out of this car."

After masking our intrusion from Beasley's surveillance system, Ted nodded and I quietly opened the rear door of the Hummer as we stepped out into the cool air of the garage. We noted the various rooms of Beasley's compound during the kids' earlier hack, but the overall layout of the structure was a blank; all we knew was that the madman was somewhere else, a living room-like space, while we were in the garage. Examining the large open area revealed two roll-up doors, one at either end of the big room; apparently the limited maneuverability of the Hummer was such that it entered through one door and exited through the other. The only additional way out of the garage was a single door leading into the main part of the compound. Using care, we turned the handle and inched it open, immediately finding ourselves staring into an empty hallway. Easing down the corridor, we cautiously continued to another door leading to a second hallway, which appeared to be circular, arching away from us in opposite directions and containing a series of doors leading into various unknown rooms within the compound.

Puzzled by the strange setting, we looked at each other in confusion. Beasley's house, as observed from the outside, was an ordinary wood-framed suburban type, but the structure we were in was made of concrete, appearing more similar to a bunker than a ranch-style home. Since the number of rooms observed on the security system had never quite jibed with the modest nature of the house, Beasley's compound was somehow much more elaborate than it appeared. Barring a detour into the Twilight Zone, there was one obvious answer: confirming my earlier hunch, we had to be underground.

Turning to look at my younger companions, I whispered, "We must be under the house... nothing else makes any sense... and it figures that a nut like Beasley would create a concrete fortress under his home. This is where he plans to wait out the apocalypse."

Nervously looking around, Hendricks responded, "So where is the fucker now?"

"He has to be upstairs. The room where he shot Duane was on the ground floor... he'll be busy cleaning up for a while so we should be safe long enough to find a hiding spot, but we have to hurry."

Moving quickly, we checked out all the various spaces, including a bedroom, kitchen, generator and battery room, an armory, laundry, exercise room, another bedroom apparently dedicated to his mother, lots of storage and a large central control room. Overall the lower level of the compound was much larger than the house above; wasting no time, we soon had a solid feel for the layout—and a plan.

Of all the different rooms, the one obviously dedicated to the memory of Beasley's mother was easily the most compelling. Containing a bed, a bathroom and a closet full of clothes in addition to her large framed portrait and several dried funeral sprays, it appeared that the room was originally intended for the older woman's occupation, but she died either before or shortly after moving in. Adjacent to the mother's room was the largest of the storage areas, primarily consisting of shelves loaded with food and water—Beasley's stockpile for surviving Armageddon. By moving spare bedding from a closet in the dead woman's room into the rear of the storage space, we were able to build a small nest that was unlikely to be discovered. Hiding within the storage space also gave us easy access to food as well as a nearby bathroom in the rear of Mom's bedroom. All we had to do was wait a few hours until the lunatic made his daily trip into Kingdom City for lunch and to the tea warehouses; at that point we would have several hours to search for the evidence we needed. Later we would leave in the rear of the madman's Hummer, exactly the same way we came in. Settling down in our little hideaway, I was beginning to think this crazy plan might actually work.

Meanwhile, the passionate connection between my young companions had continued to heat up. Hanging out in our cozy little hideaway at the rear of the storage space, their hands were like small animals, touching and rubbing, as they amplified and absorbed the tension flowing freely between them. It was as if the witnessing of Duane's violent death had triggered some curious counterintuitive reaction in the trooper's ex-girlfriend, and instead of grieving, she was compelled to replace whatever animal outlet Duane had provided—with Ted Hendricks as the all too eager recipient. Needless to say, all this touchy-feely crap was not going down so great with me, but they did maintain some consideration, stopping somewhere short of a full-on dogs-in-heat rut, whamming away like lust-plagued lizards right beside me... but it was obviously just a matter of time. Meanwhile, employing skills slightly short of genius, I had managed to score not one, not two or three, but five more pints of Jack Daniels shortly before we entered the back of the Hummer and so, fully fortified, I soothed my bruised soul to the tune of Romeo and Juliet panting like twin tornados in hell.

After waking up the following morning, we scavenged breakfast from Beasley's emergency stockpile, and while the idea of canned tuna, peanut butter, dried apricots and crackers had little appeal... Hey! It wasn't so bad. But we knew Beasley would be leaving for Kingdom City soon and needed a plan for best utilizing our time.

Not part of the burgeoning bliss, I spoke up, "Patty, Ted, as soon as Beasley leaves, I think we should split up. We can cover a lot more territory if each of us searches a different room. I think we're okay down here for now but we have to find the evidence we need and get out. The guy may be a murderous creep, but he's not an idiot." Viewing more than ten seconds apart akin to a vacation in Vladivostok, the lovers reluctantly agreed.

But Beasley didn't leave. The circular layout of the lower level of the madman's compound placed us on the opposite side of the building from where the Hummer normally exited, meaning we could hear the big car as it entered but not when it left; but, around 10 a.m., we curiously noted the sound of a car entering the garage. Puzzled, Ted hacked back into the surveillance system to check it out, and as we watched the image slowly circulating from one camera to another, we soon found ourselves viewing the garage, and there it was: Duane's highway patrol car sitting next to the Hummer.

Mesmerized, we watched as Beasley, dressed in coveralls, drove a forklift carrying Duane's plastic-covered body into the garage. Pausing in front of a large workstation, he reached over and twisted an unassuming piece of hardware attached to the rear of the work space, causing the entire unit to slide sideways, revealing an unseen chamber behind. In disbelief, I uttered in a loud whisper, "A panic room! Of course, the fucker would have a hidden safe room."

Working quickly, Beasley drove the forklift into the safe room, unloaded the body then returned, leaving the doorway open. At that point he crossed the space to another workstation where he picked up a pair of heavy gloves, some goggles and an acetylene torch. Dragging the tools back across the room, he promptly put on the safety gear and fired up the torch. Dumbfounded and glued to the screen, we watched as the madman methodically began the tedious process of carving the patrol car up into hundreds of small pieces.

At that point Ted excused himself and went to the bathroom, leaving me and Patty alone for the first time in several days. As we sat wrapped in blankets in our strange little cocoon hidden behind a dozen or more racks of shelving, I reflected on the look of stunned disbelief I'd seen on Patty's face as we watched Beasley wrangle Duane's corpse into the safe room. While her body had certainly reacted in kind to Ted's affection and desire, she hadn't spoken more than a dozen words since we witnessed the gruesome sight of Duane's execution.

"I can't say Duane was one of my favorite people, but no one deserves to go like that. I guess you guys must have been pretty close, Patty."

Lost in thought, the aggrieved young woman looked up, taking several painful moments to gather her thoughts before speaking and when she did, her words were slow and deliberate. "Duane... he... he was my first boyfriend... the first serious boyfriend I ever had..." As she paused, I could feel the weight of Patty's grief, an emotional holocaust hidden in the heat of a frenzied lust fest. Grief is a weird thing, not that I'm exactly an expert, but it seems that it's a lot like love... maybe it's the same thing, just twisted around in a different direction. And similar to the way that love can connect and morph into other related emotions—kindness, dependence, lust, anger—grief often pulls the same trick. It's like people getting pissed off at each other during a funeral or a wake, and this was the deal with Patty, her grief mutating into sexual desire. After all, the kid had lost her mom, her brother and, in reality, her entire life up to that point—and all within the last week. No wonder she seemed so eager to escape into the warm and fuzzy glow of Ted Hendricks' embrace.

Speaking with obvious difficulty, she continued, "He... Duane... he wanted to have children with me, Frank. That means a lot to a woman... any woman... okay, I guess I was over him, but... but to see him gunned down like... like a dog..." At that point she completely broke down, collapsing into my arms... guarded, I told myself it was just the father figure thing again and nothing more, but Ted's sudden reappearance, wide-eyed and flustered, didn't make things any easier. Not knowing what to do, the kid grabbed his computer, moved across the room and plopped down on the floor, as I, equally uncomfortable, continued consoling his lover.

Okay! It was weird.

So much for part one of the plan. Beasley obviously wasn't going anywhere, consequently the idea of trying to search the compound outside of our little safe spot was nuts... Okay, just being there was fucking nuts, but still...

It took the madman about eight to ten hours of steady work to completely dismember and dismantle the patrol car, and, using the forklift for the engine block and larger parts, he gradually moved the fragmented vehicle into the panic room next to Duane's body. Later, after completing his work, Beasley disappeared somewhere in the interior of the compound. Mildly concerned about what the nutcase was up to, Hendricks checked into the security system after an hour or so and BINGO! Wackarama... The nuttiness never stops.

The series of images from the various security cameras placed around the compound switched from one to another as usual, until the picture reached the dining room in the house upstairs. In the dim light, little was visible except Crawford Beasley, illuminated by the candles of a small birthday cake, and the large portrait of his mother that he had retrieved from the bedroom downstairs. Also on the table was a small, ancient 45 rpm record player. Immediately drawn into this odd and compelling scene, we locked the surveillance system onto this camera and turned up the sound as the madman recited yet another bizarre monologue, but the tone of his speech, soft, tender and caring, was remarkably different. Speaking directly to the portrait, the madman's voice was little more than a whisper.

"...as you well know. Mumsy, another aspect of the human folly known as religion that I actually do embrace is the deification of MOTHER. Mary, Mother Earth, the Ultimate Source, YOU... these concepts both haunt and rejuvenate, as my thoughts daily rejoice in the memory of your dearly departed goodness and grace. You were the light... A beacon... A shining force of virtue and honor... giving me so much more than I deserved. So often I'm tortured by the specter of your final days... The pain permeating every pore of your being... The agonizing attempts to smile and touch the soul of your beloved Crawbaby one last time. It pains me to say it but my solitary fear in life is that my memories of you, dear Mumsy... the thoughts I cherish and hold so precious, will someday fade, like the scarlet sunsets of summer. Yes, the cruelty of life and the frailty of men cannot be overstated, but I WILL NOT LET IT HAPPEN, MUMSY! NEVER! NO! NOT EVER! I love you... like the sun loves the inky blackness of space... like the robin loves the lively newness of spring... like the fragrance of the flower loves the nose that gives it meaning."

With that, the surprisingly warm and sentimental but obviously insane Crawford Beasley switched on the record player, lifted the arm and placed the needle onto the disc. As the sound entered the room, the scratchiness of the well-worn record pushed the fragile voice into the background but the message, after decades of use, was still clear.

(To the tune of "You Are My Sunshine")
"You are my Crawbaby, my only Crawbaby
You make me happy when skies are gray
You'll never know dear how much I love you
Please don't take my Crawbaby away.
　"It's Mumsy dear... It's Mumsy and this is your sixth birthday. You're a big boy now... My little Crawbaby is practically all grown up... And you've never had a single cavity... Not one... I'm so proud of my big boy. Oh, I know you've hated brushing so often and you certainly have no fondness for tea... I know that, too... But see how it's paid off... Oh yes, boys do need a father and I know how you've missed your daddy, but the military life, with all its fussy rules... Well, it just wasn't for me... I do hope you understand... I do... And I love you oh so much... My little Crawbaby. Happy Birthday, son."

　The following morning Patty, Ted and I were just finishing breakfast when another alarm suddenly sounded. The warning signal, identical to the one that announced Duane's arrival, instantly charged the space with apprehension. Switching on his laptop, Ted cracked into the security system just as Crawford Beasley was responding, but this time, instead of a single officer in a highway patrol car, it was two SUVs containing a tac squad—at least a dozen men.

　Again, Beasley's response was slow and deliberate. "How can I help you, gentlemen?"

　Standing at the outermost gate, the officer in charge barked into the intercom, "Please state your name and position, sir."

　Continuing to take his time, the madman responded, "I

am Crawford Beasley, officer... Director of PAGWAG and the owner of this estate. Is there a problem?"

"Yes, there is a problem, Mr. Beasley. A state trooper is missing and the PAGWAG compound was his last reported location. We would like to come in and ask you a few questions. Do we have your permission to enter the premises, Mr. Beasley?"

"Of course... of course... I'm happy to do anything I can to help, gentlemen."

Echoing Duane's entrance, a short delay was followed by the metallic sound of the gate opening. As the two vehicles passed through the portal, a pair of officers wearing body armor and wielding automatic weapons jumped out, positioning themselves by the outer opening. After proceeding through the second gate, the large vehicles stopped immediately outside the entrance to the house. As a smiling Crawford Beasley stepped out and greeted the men, two more tac squad members took positions on either side of the door.

His eyes concealed by sinister black glasses, Beasley looked around, sizing up the situation. "I'm flattered that PAGWAG has been deemed worthy of such attention, officers. The situation you are pursuing is obviously quite serious."

Showing little regard for Beasley in his faux military drag, the cop stepped to within a foot of the madman's face and stated flatly, "As I said, Mr. Beasley, a fine officer is missing. We take that quite seriously. May we come in?"

Nervous despite his outward calm, Beasley nodded, "As well you should, officers.... as well you should. Of course you can come in... right this way, gentlemen." Attempting to cover his uneasiness with polite chatter, the madman continued as he escorted the police squad into his living room. "My father was in the military... sadly, he died in the service when I was young... I volunteered, of course, but was declined due to, uh, health reasons... but I'm happy to do anything I can to help the protectors of America's freedom... anything I can..."

Upon reaching the living room, the tac squad, on full alert, stationed itself around the perimeter of the room as the group's leader turned and faced Crawford Beasley. "We are doing everything possible to find our missing officer, Mr. Beasley. Since this was his last reported location, I'm sure you understand the necessity of thoroughly searching the premises. Do we have your permission to search the compound, Mr. Beasley?"

As soon as the presence of the tac squad was announced, a small knot of panic instantly roiled the pit of my stomach. By the time the words "search the premises" were uttered, the knot had swelled to the size of a basketball lodged at the base of my throat. Looking at my companions in abject fear, I pleaded, "THEY'RE... THEY'RE SEARCHING THE BUILDING! THEY'LL FIND US! WHAT CAN WE DO?"

As I reached for my pint of Jack Daniels, Ted stood up and barked, "We don't have any choice. It's Beasley's safe room or the tac squad... QUICK! We have to make it look like no one's been here... PATTY! Help me gather up this bedding so we can take it with us. HURRY! The cops will be here any minute!"

Looking like she'd just eaten a rat, Patty froze. "Patty! C'mon... We have to hurry!"

Stammering, she spit out, "The... the safe room? But... but... Duane... Duane is in there..." Her face was the unappetizing color of concrete.

"I'm sorry, Patty, but we don't have any choice. The tac squad means jail for all of us... HURRY! PLEASE!" Terrified, I grabbed the small bag of clothes containing my three remaining pints of bourbon, as Hendricks pushed Patty out into the circular hallway connecting the rooms in the lower compound. We hurried down the passage leading into the garage as the sound of men entering the circular hallway echoed behind us. A barking voice issuing orders to search all the rooms, followed by loud footsteps spreading through the compound, heightened our panic as we burst into the garage, stumbling and lurching our way toward the entrance to the safe room. Shaking, Ted reached across the work stand where, facing him, were a dozen or more screwdrivers, wrenches, ratchets, a hammer and more. Desperately grabbing every tool and implement on the rack, Ted finally twisted a small hand chisel, causing the work bench to slide sideways and reveal Crawford Beasley's secure panic room. Staggering into the space, the techie activated the switch securing the room as we tumbled on the floor, the door closing behind us. Frantic, we listened as the sound of footsteps and loud voices abruptly filled the space on the other side of the door.

Crowded into the small opening near the entrance, we sat frozen in silence, terrified of making a sound as Duane's equally silent and unseeing eyes stared up at us through the musty plastic shroud enclosing his body.

Six, seven, eight hours went by as we sat in fear until the muffled sound of the Hummer starting and leaving the garage penetrated the walls of the safe room. We had no idea where Beasley was going. The muted sounds of footsteps moving through the building had faded but, by this time, it was too late for the madman to rendezvous with his daily delivery of tea bricks. Regardless, we were alone in the compound with no idea when the quasi-military nutcase would return. Maintaining a guarded posture, Hendricks triggered the door mechanism, opening the safe room to the garage again. Tired and hungry, we cautiously re-entered the empty space and slowly made our way back to our tiny hidden area in the rear of the storage room.

Another hour passed, then two, until, as we raided Beasley's food stockpile, the throbbing sound of the Hummer's engine announced the madman's return. Meanwhile, the makeout madness of Ted and Patty was on full display. Magnified by an intimate connection to the white-hot passion of my pals and compounded by two days of hiding in a hole like a crippled cockroach, my angst was nearing outer orbit. Black Jack was never a better buddy.

Declaring a nature call, Ted excused himself. More than a little sloshed, I decided it was time to confront Patty over her rapidly mushrooming involvement with Ted Hendricks as compared to her once eager interest in me. Overly self-conscious and awkward, I blurted it out, "Uh, Patty... I mean, like, okay, sure, I respect that you are a free agent and all, but... well, you know, I thought me and you kinda had a thing going and now it seems like you and the techie nerd are like, lip-locked forever... I mean, what gives?"

With her face quickly turning the tint of a medium rare ribeye, Patty paused. Gathering her thoughts, her eyes, circular pockets of pain oozing liquid sorrow, finally met mine.

"I'm sorry, Frank... I really am... it's just..."

"It's just what, Patty?" Needing all my courage to continue, I mouthed a mondo slug of bourbon and said, "Okay... I know it's been tough for you lately... with your mom... and Tommy Joe... and now Duane... and I guess I haven't been much help... but... but... what about me? I mean... I'm not a brick over here, you know..." And with that, my own well of emotion turned to tears suddenly leaking around the corners of my eyes.

"I am sorry, Frank, I am, but... but..." Something was caught in the kid's throat, something that throbbed and ached, desperately fighting the idea of coming out into the air where it could be seen, tasted, touched. Finally, after another prolonged and painful pause, she coughed it up, "It's your drinking, Frank... it's the alcohol... I told you how much you reminded me of my father... I guess... I guess I didn't realize how true it was... how true it is. My dad is an alcoholic, Frank... and I just couldn't go back there again... I'm sorry, but I couldn't do it."

So there it was. Patty's lust-infused dive into the arms of Ted Hendricks wasn't just about escaping the loss of her family or Duane or her entire dumbfuck life, it was also about me. She was running from me. And there was nothing I could do about it... except take another drink. Knowing that Ted would soon return, and with him the desperation fueling their frantic souls—frenzied fingers grasping, rubbing, clawing, embracing... it was too much. I had to leave.

Grabbing my bottle of Jack, I staggered out into the hallway, too drunk to grasp my own stupidity, as the sound of Crawford Beasley's grating voice, broadcasting yet another inane monologue, was approaching from somewhere around the bend of the brightly lit hallway.

"*GOOD! GOOD! GOOD! I want to do GOOD! I NEED TO DO GOOD!*"

Panicking again, I rushed ahead, plunging through the nearest door with the madman's voice still echoing along the corridor behind me.

"Is there a more confusing concept in the English language? And is it any coincidence that the word *GOOD* is so similar to *GOD*, another monumental mass of confusion and lies!"

I was in the lunatic's downstairs living room. The space was dominated by a large television; in front of the tube was a tray containing a hot TV dinner. Hurrying to the rear of the space, I paused by the back door until I realized that Beasley was also coming in. Aware of my presence or not, the fucker was following me! Panicked, I hurried into the adjoining room.

"The Romans... The Romans were undoubtedly doing GOOD when they crucified Christ. Of course, the irony of this GOOD is how it enabled the creation of Christianity, the decadent force behind religious persecution and the slaughter of native people for hundreds of years."

The next room over was the kitchen, also brightly illuminated, where Beasley had just finished making his dinner. Fearful that he might return, I crawled beneath a table covered by a cloth hanging down a few feet below its surface. Cowering on the floor in the shadows below, I listened as the madman droned on.

"HEY! Liberals were doing GOOD as they pilloried poor Joe McCarthy, the valiant scourge of postwar communism, and the Indians were no doubt doing GOOD as they massacred George Armstrong Custer and his men at Little Bighorn, who were undoubtedly doing GOOD by attempting genocide on the Cheyenne."

Casually entering the room, Beasley took something from the refrigerator then returned to his living room, his monologue loud, unceasing and monotonous.

"Will I be doing GOOD by fouling billions of gallons of wholesome, unadulterated water? It's human to doubt, but TRUE GOODNESS begets faith and confidence. My goals are pure and my resolve remains unshaken!"

Finally shutting up, the madman changed channels, listening to a weather report noting a new storm front moving into the area and dumping inches of snow on northern

Missouri. After a few minutes of relative calm, I assumed the madman was settling down, and used the moment to exit the kitchen, returning to the circular hallway. Hurrying back to the storage space where I left Patty, I re-entered only to discover that she and Ted were finally DOING IT! Moaning like crazy, the pair was going at it like two beavers in a dried-up ditch. Unable to take it, I bolted back into the hallway, ducked into Beasley's mother's room, crawled under the bed and passed out. It was a rough day.

The next morning I was awakened by a sound that was by now both gnawingly familiar and friendly as a chainsaw. As I lay on the floor beneath the bed of Crawford Beasley's dead mother, the madman clomped into the room, exhorting as always. This time the monologue concerned his father but, not unlike the birthday soliloquy to his mother, the tone was different, evolving from brash to gentle over the course of sixty seconds.

"Oh Mumsy, Mumsy... So often I come in here to speak to you, but is it not true that where goes The Mother has also tread The Father... The Warrior... The Vindicator... The Force of Fury and Fire... My greatest shortcoming, one I rue moment by moment, is my failure to follow in your fearless footsteps. Is there a greater calling than military life... the worthy quest of sanctuary, safety and security for one's family, friends and fellow countrymen? If perhaps your pursuit of perfection in me, your only son, was at times overly zealous, your spirited discipline echoing my failure to rise to and embrace your standards. Fate, the serendipitous gap between life and death, sadly called too soon, Dad, long before your guidance fully formed the man you desired... but I persevere, sir...in sadness for the sacred profession I cannot pursue, I do persevere... please forgive the imperfections I cannot overcome. I love you, Dad."

Totally unprepared for the madman's emotion, I realized that Crawford Beasley was weeping, his chest softly heaving as he maintained a reverent silence for what felt like an eternity before finally slipping out of the room and quietly closing the door behind him. Laying on the floor, my head throbbing, I too was overcome by conflicting thoughts, feelings and emotions, engendered by this overly complex and dangerous man, the most disturbing of which was disappointment—the lunatic was not allowing me to solely see him as the demonic force of pure evil I so desired.

I mean, what the fuck?

I waited almost an hour before crawling out from under the bed. It was around 11:30 a.m. and my hangover was no less potent than it was when I first woke up. According to Ted, Beasley normally left for Kingdom City around 11:00 so I figured it was safe to venture back out into the rest of the compound. Patty and Ted would undoubtedly be awake and wondering what the fuck had happened to me but first I had to make sure the asshole was gone. Sneaking back to the hallway leading to the garage, I then followed it into the space normally occupied by the big SUV. It was empty.

Reassured, I returned to the storage area where Patty and Ted greeted me with a combination of relief and anger. Sheepish, my one-time lover hugged me, while Hendricks first hesitated, then barked, "Where the fuck have you been, Frank? Shit, we thought maybe the asshole got you, too. C'mon man, you can't leave us hanging like that. What gives?"

Releasing her embrace, Patty slowly backed away while giving me a look reflecting both guilt and complicity, as she burrowed back into Ted's welcoming shoulder. "Look guys… I'm sorry, okay? I had a little too much to drink and kind of needed a break… a little time to myself… I mean, you guys are pretty intense… you know what I mean?" Blushing like a rose in a room full of ferrets, the embarrassed blonde looked away.

Unaware of the unspoken communication between Patty and me, the techie softened, "Okay, I get it, but you gotta be careful, Frank… and lay off the booze… we… Patty and me… we'd hate to see something happen to you…" At that point Patty's look of remorse, peeking back at me from the womb-like safety of Ted's embrace, said mondo more than the tech screener's words.

Releasing a sigh of resignation, I moved on, "Yeah, yeah, I get it… you guys think I'm hot shit… you groove to the tune of my awesomeness… shit like that… and I dig you, too. But right now my head feels like a bloated cantaloupe and I'm starving, so where's the sardines and Spam?"

A half-hour later my inner id was nearing the neighborhood of subhuman—all things considered, a major triumph. We figured we had a good two hours before Beasley returned and earlier resolved to split our search three ways, with Ted looking through the psycho's workshop and Patty checking the big storage area, while I examined the control room. We needed something that would connect Crawford Beasley to the Escalade, the bomb and the curious crater near Clinton,

Missouri. But before starting the search, I grabbed another pint of Jack Daniels from my small overnight bag and gulped a mondo slug—you know, hair of the dog and all that.

Thus buttressed and ready for action, I entered the large central room containing the madman's computers, communication system and surveillance setup. Other than a quick peek, none of us had actually spent any time in the nerve center of Beasley's stronghold. Well designed and laid out, the facility housed an impressive display of audacity, organization and technology. Two areas of the room were immediately striking. The first was a large round table set in the dead center of the space; rising from the middle was a six-foot spire, the design of which awkwardly fell somewhere between a miniature Eiffel Tower and a dinky oil derrick. In keeping with Beasley's favorite motif, the wooden spire was painted in camo and flaunted a neon revolving PAGWAG logo at the top. The other area featured an array of six large monitors mounted on the west wall of the room, three of which displayed computer data, while two constantly broadcasted images from the compound's surveillance system, systematically alternating from one camera to another. The sixth screen was tuned to a local news broadcast currently airing severe weather warnings regarding the potent storm system entering the area; a large semicircular steel desk sat in front of the cluster of monitors. Completing the room was a long curved sofa set against another wall, an elevator entrance, a closet, a large map displaying the route of Beasley's fluoride pollution plan, several filing cabinets, and a small undetermined structure across the room.

After entering, I took a couple of slugs of bourbon and placed the bottle of Jack Daniels on the round table. Scanning the space for anything that could potentially be used as evidence against the insane Crawford Beasley, the first thing I noticed was a stack of papers on one side of the steel desk facing the monitors. Crossing the room, I grabbed the docs, my mind racing as I quickly shuffled through them. BINGO! THIS WAS IT! A schematic for making a bomb, receipts for C-4 plastic explosive and blasting caps, unfiled registration docs for the Escalade. I couldn't believe it! It was almost like the fucker had laid everything I needed right out on the table, nice and neat, waiting for me. Apparently Beasley's fanatic sense of order and arrogant belief in the sanctity of his stronghold allowed him to leave shit like this lying around.

Excited, I stuffed all the papers into a large envelope and walked back toward the round table in the center of the space; as I reached it, my eyes focused on the bland enclosure stationed across the room. Distracted, I absentmindedly reached for the pint of Jack, knocking it over and shattering the bottle with a loud crash as it hit the concrete floor. At that moment the purpose of the unexplained structure made itself crystal-clear—it was a doghouse and I HAD JUST WOKEN THE FUCKER UP! Immediately bounding upon me was one hundred and fifty pounds of savage, snarling Rottweiler in its full and unbridled fury. Scrambling for the top of the table, I almost made it before the beast clamped its teeth onto my ankle, dragging me down to the floor. Panicked, I kicked wildly and connected, my other foot slamming solidly into the dog's nose and stunning it just long enough to scurry up onto the table where, by hugging the PAGWAG tower, I remained just out of the nasty bastard's reach.

With the Rottweiler's savage growl filling the room, I stood on the table desperately clutching the flimsy spire and took a deep breath. Scanning the room in disbelief, my mind was screaming at me. The fucker had a dog! THE FUCKER HAD A DOG! We had been in Beasley's compound for three days, had watched countless hours of surveillance video, AND DIDN'T HAVE A FUCKING CLUE! How was that possible?

Lost in my own bewildered brain, I suddenly noted an

especially loud and menacing howl, and turned just in time to see Fido charge again; running at full speed, the beast was attempting to mount the table. As he leaped, mouth open wide and saliva glistening on his teeth, I flinched, abruptly causing my flimsy support to collapse, dumping me back down onto the floor and into the jaws of hell. This time the beast immediately clamped on to my calf. Desperate, I unbuttoned my pants, shoving them down over the dog's head, then hammered him with both fists, but I could've been whacking concrete. The fucker had me in a death grip and the pain, the mother-of-God searing sharpness, pushed me to the verge of blacking out. With my arms outstretched, blindly groping, frantic to find anything to defend myself, my hand suddenly seized on something hard and sharp—it was the neck of the broken bottle of Jack Daniels. Lashing out, I jabbed, stabbed and slashed... again and again and again until the beast, bleeding like a headless hog, finally released its grip, staggered across the floor and collapsed. In agony, I picked up my bloody pants, tore off a strip of cloth and looped it around my thigh, furiously trying to stop the bleeding.

Shaking and wracked with pain, I crawled over to the large semicircular desk, somehow managing to pull myself into an upright position. Standing there, gasping for breath, my eyes were suddenly drawn to one of the surveillance monitors displaying a familiar large camo-colored vehicle pulling into the garage—BEASLEY WAS BACK! The storm must have forced the fucker to return earlier than expected. Terrified and naked from the waist down, I frantically scanned the space; spotting a closet across the room, I hobbled over, opened the door and collapsed on the floor.

Moments later, a door opened and Crawford Beasley strode into the room. The quasi-militant froze, stunned, as he surveyed the scene of carnage before quickly zeroing in on the static corpse of the Rottweiler. Obviously moved, he bent over, affectionately stroking the dog's lifeless corpse, and spoke, his voice soft and tender, "Chester... Chester, who did this to you?" Moved but aware of the warmth still radiating from the dog's body, the madman's moment of grief was brief. Acutely aware that the killer might still be in the building, he immediately focused his attention on the two screens monitoring the compound's surveillance system. Up to this point, Beasley had remained unaware of Ted Hendricks' device for deceiving his security setup, but as he watched the series of cameras scan the various rooms of the building, the absence of an updated image of the control room, the area he currently shared with the dead Rottweiler, became obvious. Freezing the picture on the compound's nerve center, instead of a scene cluttered with the aftermath of chaos, he saw a clean and pristine space, exactly as it was when the techie created the frame grab three days earlier. Bringing the system's control panel up on the screen, Beasley immediately triggered a reset, restoring the system to its initial settings. Satisfied for the moment, he watched as the series of images resumed, scanning one empty room after another until it finally reached his mother's bedroom, where, in all their naked glory, Patty and Ted were fucking like two rats on a sinking ship.

Outraged, Beasley screamed, "NO! NOT IN MUMSY'S BED!"

With no hesitation, the madman unholstered his pistol, cocking it as he bolted through the door. Sitting in the dark, my mind raced ahead, wanting, needing, pleading for a way to warn my friends of their impending, looming and booming death. I didn't have to wait long. Moments after the lunatic left, a roar of eight shots, the entire clip of the fully loaded .45, hideously thundered throughout the compound.

Unable to believe the series of events erupting around me, I sat in stunned silence. I told myself there was nothing I could have done to save Patty and Ted... nothing... and, as I repeated that hopeless mantra over and over, I also said that maybe... just maybe, I could still save myself... but I had to act... I had to move... limping, crawling, dragging myself... whatever it took, to get out of that closet and hide. The compound was big. With any luck, it could take the asshole hours, maybe days to find me. All I had to do was make my way back to the Hummer, hide inside again and wait for Beasley to take me out of there. It could work. It had to.

The safest place to hide was the large storage room where Ted, Patty and I had taken cover for three days; but, aware that his stronghold had been breached, Beasley's guard was up. I had to be careful.

Miraculously, the tourniquet had worked and my leg was no longer bleeding. Examining my wound as I left the closet and re-entered the control room, I realized my ankle was possibly broken but, hobbling slowly, it somehow bore my weight. The nasty gash in my lower leg undoubtedly needed stitches, but the pain, while still substantial, had subsided. Moving as fast as I could, I grabbed the envelope of documents, then unplugged the control room computer, knocking out the compound's surveillance system. That way I could move through the building undetected—at least until Beasley restored the system. Guessing which entrance the madman would likely use re-entering the control room, I then cautiously exited on the opposite side. Shaking as I stood in the hallway, I waited until I heard the sound of two doors opening and closing, as my antagonist left his mother's room and returned to the compound's hub.

Knowing that I had a few minutes while Beasley investigated the messy aftermath of my confrontation with Chester, the dead Rottwéiler, I quietly limped back to the storage space, instantly collapsing on the pile of bedding I had recently shared with Patty and Ted. Sobbing, as I watched my tears collecting into tiny pools on the concrete floor, I struggled to regain control of my emotions. As my thoughts locked in on the specter of Crawford Beasley emptying his pistol into the writhing bodies of my companions, my sorrow was slowly replaced by outrage. At that point I had what I needed to put the fucker away, but I could only do it by somehow escaping the madman's hellish black hole.

Exhausted, hungry and still in pain, I decided to eat and rest then wait a few hours before attempting to conceal myself in the rear of the Hummer again. I assumed the surveillance system was back up but my hiding place in the storage area was well concealed. Regardless, I remained tense and edgy until finally, around 4 a.m., I decided to go for the Hummer.

Assuming the compound's security cams were online, my hope was that by this time, Beasley would be fast asleep, consequently I wouldn't be seen limping through the hallway and into the back of the big SUV; also, after the execution of

Patty and Ted, it was possible that the madman thought the threat was over. As far as he knew, they were the ones that offed the dumbfuck Rottweiler.

Opening the door and stepping out, the first thing I noted was an absence of light in the circular corridor. Patty, Ted and I never left the safety of our little womb at night, so maybe this was a normal power-saving device, but feebly limping into gloomy darkness only inflated my already looming feeling of dread. Amping my apprehension even more was a series of lasers, beaming across the open corridor, another security device designed to detect intruders. The pinpoint rays of light, a few inches above the ground, crossed the hallway at intervals of about three feet. By painstakingly stepping over each beam, I slowly moved a few feet down the passageway until a subtle and curious sound grabbed my attention. It was a faint whooshing, almost like an electric fan, emanating from somewhere near the ceiling of the dark corridor. Confused, I froze, listening as the sound continued, and as it did, I suddenly noticed the presence of something else: a moist ephemeral presence appearing, then vanishing, leaving a wet and slightly slippery spot near the bridge of my nose. Then I felt another, lightly caressing my fingers, as more landed on my head, my shoulder, my arm, until, raising my right hand, one settled upon it with the lightness of a tiny cloud, but this one, instead of disappearing, remained for a few moments, allowing me to raise it to eye level and, squinting into the darkness, the sense of recognition was immediate: it was a bubble! A soap bubble, and in the same instant, I realized the hallway had somehow become engulfed in airy, aimless blobs... hundreds, thousands, maybe millions appearing, floating and popping on every surface within the dark, connecting corridor. Unnerved, I attempted to resume my tricky passage down the hallway, but as soon as I took another step, I instantly grokked my dilemma.

The floor, suddenly shrouded in the oily residue of bursting bubbles, was like an ice rink slathered and lathered with K-Y Jelly, a slick and slimy nightmare that quickly had me sprawled on my back, writhing in pain and watching as my supine body broke the beams of several lasers, triggering yet another soon-to-be-suffered security device.

Laying in the darkness of the hallway, I couldn't actually see the apparatus, obviously designed to disable an unknowing intruder, but based on the results, it wasn't hard to figure out. A series of muted whizzing sounds was quickly accompanied by several sharp, stabbing pains in my side, shoulder, and thigh. Grabbing at the small darts penetrating deeply into my flesh only increased the pain radiating from my broken ankle. Unlike anything I had ever endured, the agony was all-consuming, rising from my ankle and abruptly swallowing my misery into a sucking, screaming and endlessly sinking pit. I was burnt toast.

The first thing I noticed when I finally woke up was a series of parallel stripes crossing a bright area enclosing my prostrate body. Attempting to clear my beyond-the-valley-of-mondo-murky head, I noticed that the stripes were actually shadows and, by forcing my throbbing brain to function, I came to the realization that the shadows represented a lack of brightness caused by objects blocking the passage of light from its source to the surface on which the shadows appeared. Consequently, I assumed, there had to be a series of parallel objects between myself and a light source. Simple deduction... and by scrutinizing the surrounding area, I quickly discovered several evenly spaced, equivalent objects—bars... steel bars, crossing an opening that separated me from the brightly lit area on the other side. Working really hard, I slid over to the barrier and peeked through, recognizing Crawford Beasley's control room just beyond the bars. I was in the doghouse... the space last occupied by Chester, the once deadly but currently deceased Rottweiler.

Occupying the room on the other side of the obstacle was Beasley himself. It was early morning and the madman, still dressed in camo robe and pajamas, was fondling his .45, the same one he used to kill Patty, Ted and Duane. As I began to stir in my canine-scented cell, he spoke: "Is that you, Franky... finally awake in there, are you? How's the memory, there, Franky? Huh? The Midazolam in those darts makes some people go bonkers, Franky... can't even remember their goddam name... do you know who you are, Franky? DO YOU KNOW WHO I AM? Cat got your tongue... OR MAYBE THE DOG! I was VERY UNHAPPY after you killed Chester, Franky... he was my pal... my pal... how do you like it in there, Franky... do you like living in Chester's doghouse?"

Okay, I was groggy as hell... apparently from the drug Beasley used in the tranquilizer darts that whacked me in the hallway, but I knew who I was and I sure as shit knew who he was. All right, I was locked in a doghouse... the fucker had me, but I didn't have to just sit back and take his abuse... pausing a moment, I looked around... the space was roughly six by six... it was dark and the only thing between me and the concrete floor was a filthy, mud-caked blanket... and it smelled like a dog... What the fuck! Maybe I did have to take the asshole's abuse. "Okay, yeah, I killed the fucker but he was chewing my goddam leg off... and how do you know my name... Crawbaby?"

"DON'T CALL ME THAT! ONLY MY MOTHER WAS ALLOWED TO CALL ME CRAWBABY! It sounds disgusting and profane coming from you... Franky." The madman paused for a moment then reached over and picked up something laying on his desk. It was my wallet. Smirking, he looked toward me and continued, "It looks to me like Chester was doing his job... right, Franky?... good old Chester... did he rip your pants off? Good dog... and there it was in the back pocket of your blood-soaked pants... all the information I needed... California driver's license... credit cards... Social Security card... and a membership card from the Southern California Writer's Association? It seems you're a writer... correct?... is that right, Franky boy... you're a writer..."

Yeah, a writer locked in a doghouse being toyed with by a maniac. My normal bubbly sense of optimism was starting to fade. "Yeah... So what?"

"Well, the 'so what?' is that's the only reason you're still alive, Frank. The world needs to hear what I have to say... and you're gonna tell it... do you understand, MR. ELL-AY WRITER?"

I paused to reflect on this unexpected turn of events. Apparently, the only reason the madman hadn't already offed me like Duane, Patty, and Ted was because he wanted me to document his life story or his philosophy or his favorite jokes or something. What a weird fucking world. It was like some of strange reverse Scheherazade. The only way I was going to stay alive was by listening to this crazy fucker rant hour after hour... day by day... forever?... in a doghouse? This was not life. It was hell—I had to be dead.

"So often... oh so often there simply is no justice in life. HA! My words give this trivial truth the weight of sagacity but every child who has had his ice cream usurped and slurped by brigands learns this lesson at an early age. I was only four years old when they started calling me Beastley... BEASTLEY!... mocking my teeth... I still hear their vicious little voices, 'BLACK TEETH! BLACK TEETH! BLACK AS COAL! BLACK TEETH! BLACK AS SATAN'S SOUL!' Hell... They weren't even black... just dark brown! Cruel! Cruel! Life can be so CRUEL!... Did you get all of that, Franky?"

Infused with his personal philosophy and words of wisdom, the madman Crawford Beasley was telling me his life story as I dutifully archived it for posterity. "Yeah, yeah, just give me a second to clean it up... Okay, what now?" We had been at it for over an hour. I had had way more than my fill of the fucker's bullshit... but he was just warming up.

"All right... This next one is about the monumental joke known as marriage... Are you married, Franky?"

"Huh? Well, no, not anymore... I mean I was, but..."

"BUT? BUT? Of course you say 'BUT... BUT...' because it's nothing BUT a big joke!! Here is the plain and simple truth... Legalize brothels! LEGALIZE BROTHELS! Of course that's the answer! How many hollow marriages and superfluous children enter the world every day in the name of a nonexistent deity, when the ultimate intention is, of course—SEX! SEX! Yes, as a species we do have to reproduce... yes, we do need more children, but DO WE HAVE TO HAVE HORDES AND HORDES OF THEM? UNWASHED... UNEDUCATED... AND UNLOVED... All worshiping a vast cornucopia of absent almighties—JUST TO GET A LITTLE PUSSY! LEGALIZE BROTHELS! Sex should be a public utility like water and gas. IT'S SO FUCKING SIMPLE!..."

"But what about love? I mean, marriage wasn't so great for me, but don't you believe in..."

"'Love'... LOVE? I've been married three times, Franky, and I loved them all...WHEN I WAS HORNY! Love? I loved my dear Mumsy but... but..." Staring into space, Beasley was lost in the dark whirlpools of his own self-sustaining fantasies. Enthralled with the power of having an audience for his insane ranting, the madman was compelled to continue, expounding and elaborating. How long could this continue? I feared finding out.

"Yes, I loved my dear Mumsy, but... but..." Pausing again, the madman wiped away a tear before continuing, "I can't say how much it pains me to reveal the degree to which my own beloved mother succumbed to the heinous and insidious plot of FLUORIDE! Convinced of the healthful benefits of that cancer, Mumsy demanded that I brush my teeth TWELVE TIMES A DAY with fluoride toothpaste. She also insisted that I consume an additional twelve servings of tea, the result being THIS!" Grimacing, Beasley paused, pointing at his cola-colored teeth, then resumed his tirade. "But the truly extraordinary outcome of this treachery was how remarkably inept the Communists were in capitalizing on their success! Regardless, the determination to pollute our water and numb the minds of our children STILL EXISTS! Hence the need for PAGWAG. With diligence as our watchword, the glorious irony of our movement is how, by blackening the teeth of the so-called celebrity class, PAGWAG will successfully turn the conspirators' plot against them! WHO SAYS THERE IS NO JUSTICE IN LIFE?"

"But can't you see... you're a criminal... a murderer... you have hundreds of millions of dollars... you could have worked within the system... sponsored candidates with a clean water agenda... but PAGWAG... PAGWAG is crazy!"

Oops. As the madman's glare suddenly narrowed and focused on me, the thought occurred that maybe I'd gone a little too far. Cringing as he charged across the room, Beasley abruptly stopped and bent over, thrusting the .45 into the doghouse. With his face pressed against the bars, the asshole screamed at me like a burning baby. "WHAT? WHAT DID YOU SAY? BECOME PART OF THE SYSTEM? A SYSTEM

BASED ON CORRUPTION, HYPOCRISY AND LIES! MINGLE WITH A MINDLESS MASS OF SHEEP? LED BY EQUALLY MINDLESS SLOGANS, DELIBERATELY DESIGNED TO CONFUSE, MISLEAD AND DECEIVE? TO FULFILL NO OTHER PURPOSE THAN ENSURING THAT THE POWERFUL RETAIN CONTROL OF THEIR MEANINGLESS, SHEEPSHIT-FILLED LIVES? IS THAT WHAT YOU THINK I SHOULD DO, FRANK? IS IT?" By this time the veins on Crawford Beasley's forehead pulsated like swollen squid, bulging about the perimeter of his beet-hued face. "NO! I SAY NO! AND I HUMBLY BEG AND BESEECH ANYONE THAT SEEKS TO SALVE A SULLEN SOUL! STEP OUT OF THE SHADOWS, SHEEP! BUY GUNS, DRINK PURE WATER AND FROLIC IN THE SUN! LIFE IS GOOD WHEN FREEDOM SINGS!" Composing himself, Beasley pulled the gun back and plopped himself down on a chair just outside the doghouse, a self-satisfied smile tweaking the corners of his mouth. "Did you get that, Frank... That was a good one."

Okay, that was it... doghouse or no doghouse... gun or no gun, I couldn't take any more of the fucker's smug, sanctimonious and bogus bullshit. He was fucking nuts and his plan was pure insanity... and it was time he heard it. "Yeah, *CRAWBABY*, that was a good one... Almost as good as your looney-tunes plan to pollute L.A.'s water supply. What a fucking joke!"

Caught off guard, the madman leaned forward in his chair. "Huh? What... what do you mean?"

"I mean you are nuts, wacko, bonkers... do you have any idea how many celebrities actually live in L.A.? LIKE ZERO, YOU STUPID MORON! Yeah, okay, they occasionally come to L.A.—FOR WORK!... but when they do, do you think they drink TAP WATER, BB BRAIN? FUCK NO, THEY DRINK BOTTLED WATER! Evian, Arrowhead, Crystal Geyser, Perrier, San Pellegrino... yeah, I can just see Julia Roberts or George

245

Clooney walking up to a faucet, filling a glass and THEN DRINKING IT? IN YOUR DREAMS, FUCKFACE! Hey! Tell me, bozo… exactly how much money have you blown on this dumb fucking plan that can't possibly affect anyone except a few thousand poor Mexicans… WHAT A FUCKING JOKE!"

The ensuing silence enveloping the room was breathtaking… as in the air being suddenly replaced with a vacuum, vile, venomous and evil, and as the silence swelled, consuming the space like a tiger shark sucking baby seals, I wormed my butt into the back of the doghouse… okay, I asked for it…

His face the color of a putrefying pomegranate, Crawford Beasley exploded out of his chair, thrusting the gun back between the bars as he screamed, "LIAR! LIAR! IT'S NOT TRUE… IT'S NOT… IT CAN'T BE!" And with that, he aimed the gun at my head and pulled the trigger… and nothing happened… jerking it back, he cocked the .45 and fired again… nothing… again… and again, until the madman finally realized that he had forgotten to reload the clip after killing Patty and Ted. Furious, he turned and bolted from the control room headed for the gun belt he left in his bedroom, leaving me alone sitting on the floor of Chester's doghouse staring at Ted Hendricks' laptop.

For some reason the fucker had given me both laptops, mine and the kid's. I can only assume he didn't know which was which, and with me locked in the doggy hoosegow, he probably didn't care, but now, in total panic, my mind screamed into the void created by the madman's feverish exit. Hendricks had used his laptop to gain access to the compound's security system and now I had it. I knew I didn't have much time. As I watched the lunatic rushing toward his bedroom on the control room's surveillance system, I opened the techie's laptop, immediately spotting an alias labeled "PAGWAG_Security_Remote_Access." Clicking on the icon got me into the system, then thirty seconds later I was looking at a screen labeled "Intruder Deterrents."

Glancing up at the surveillance monitor again, I watched as Beasley re-entered the hallway, loaded .45 in hand, but just as the madman reached for the handle opening the door to the control room, I found and clicked on a pane labeled "All Doors Locked." Hearing the deadbolts sliding into place, Beasley grabbed the door handle, but it was no use—he was trapped in the hallway. Confused, he reached for his cell phone enabling remote access to the system, but I was ahead of him, immediately triggering the panes labeled "Bubble Defense," "Laser Sensors," and "Tranquilizer Activation."

A look of horror gripped the madman's face as the first bubble popped on the end of his nose, then another, and another. As he twitched and jerked, swatting and flailing his arms, the glistening blobs bore down on him relentlessly, like a swarm of bees digesting a bear. And as I watched, the corporal form of Crawford Beasley began to fade, buried beneath a teeming mass of eager, undulating bubbles. In panic he attempted to flee, pirouetting down the hallway like a futile pile of pimples, popping and erupting in pain. Two seconds later the first dart struck. Slathered as he was, the exact point of contact was vague, but the madman's scream was sharp and clear. Twisting away from the impact, he slipped on the slick floor, toppling over as the discharge of three more darts struck his body with a dull thudding sound. Waving his arms, the wretched mound of misery made one final move, pathetically rising to his knees before the drug hit him and he collapsed, leaving an odd and undetermined lump lost inside a swirling sea of bubbles.